"My lord Warleigh, I am not prepared to receive you at this time."

"Not prepared to receive me? You can not have forgotten that we share this chamber."

"I have not forgotten. You may come back after my maid has prepared your bed."

Simon scowled, then shook his head. "Nay, 'twill not serve. This is my chamber and you are my wife. It is not improper for me to be alone with you." He stepped before her, perusing her slowly. "To do anything I wish with you."

She sucked in a deep breath, as a rush of something dark and unknown raced through her. Desperately she fought for control at her reaction to him.

"I would not say that you may do as you wish with me, my lord. Wed though we may be, it is not a real marriage."

"Do I detect a note of disappointment, Isabelle?"

Praise for Catherine Archer's previous works

Summer's Bride
"A delightful read!"
—Romance Reviews Today

Winter's Bride
"…a pleasurable medieval romance with conventional characters and a tried-and-true plot."
—*Romantic Times Magazine*

Fire Song
"This finely crafted medieval romance…
(is) a tale to savor."
—*Romantic Times Magazine*

Lord Sin
"…deftly done and sure to please."
—*Romantic Times Magazine*

DRAGON'S DOWER
CATHERINE ARCHER

HARLEQUIN®

TORONTO • NEW YORK • LONDON
AMSTERDAM • PARIS • SYDNEY • HAMBURG
STOCKHOLM • ATHENS • TOKYO • MILAN • MADRID
PRAGUE • WARSAW • BUDAPEST • AUCKLAND

ISBN 0-373-29193-0

DRAGON'S DOWER

This edition published by arrangement with Harlequin Books S.A.

® and TM are trademarks of the publisher. Trademarks indicated with
® are registered in the United States Patent and Trademark Office, the
Canadian Trade Marks Office and in other countries.

Visit us at www.eHarlequin.com

Printed in U.S.A.

Available from Harlequin Historicals and
CATHERINE ARCHER

**Velvet series
*Seasons' Brides
†The Brotherhood of the Dragon

Please address questions and book requests to:
Harlequin Reader Service
U.S.: 3010 Walden Ave., P.O. Box 1325, Buffalo, NY 14269
Canadian: P.O. Box 609, Fort Erie, Ont. L2A 5X3

To my sisters-in-law, Edie, Iris, Lillian and Bev,
for their continued interest and support
of my writing for all these years. Thank you.

Prologue

England, 1188

The three boys sat facing one another. The flames of the fire they had lit at the center of their circle burned no hotter than the anger in their eyes.

Simon, who was the oldest by three months, took up his knife and held it over the flames. "I, Simon Warleigh, swear my allegiance and friendship to you, my brothers in arms, for the rest of my life."

He drew the blade across his palm, barely flinching as it left a long shallow cut that began to bleed immediately. He passed the blade to Jarrod on his right.

The dark boy took the blade, held it over the flames and said, "I, Jarrod Maxwell, swear my allegiance and friendship to you, my brothers in arms, for the rest of my life." He made no sign as the knife slit his flesh, passing it to his right.

Christian was the youngest by nearly a year. His brown hair was glossy with golden streaks in the firelight. He took the blade. He looked to his companions, then held the knife over the flames as they had done. His voice was as firm with conviction as theirs had been. "I, Christian Greatham, swear my allegiance and friendship to you, my brothers in arms, for the rest of my life."

He flicked his tongue out to wet his lower lip, then dragged the knife over his palm with a frown of concentration. He looked up at the other two.

All three stood in unison and they held their dripping palms out over the flames.

Simon spoke with a maturity far beyond his thirteen years. "Brothers we are, bound by the blood we shed and by our love for each other and the man who brought us together. May we never forget The Dragon and the wrong done him."

"The Dragon," intoned the other two boys.

Jarrod reached out to clasp Christian's wrist. Christian did the same to Simon, who closed his own palm around Jarrod's wrist.

Simon called out to the star-studded sky overhead. "Does it take our whole lives, my lord, we will see the man who wronged you punished." The pain and sadness in his voice was echoed in the others' faces.

They stood like that, bound by their love for one another and for the man who had acted as foster father, mentor and teacher to the three of them. The man whom they had been forced to testify against.

Jarrod spoke in a harsh voice. "We should have lied."

Christian shook his head, his blue eyes dark with misery. "He would not have had us do such a thing, even to save him."

Simon nodded. "Aye."

Their foster father had had no idea what would come

when he'd told them to tell the truth. Yet Simon knew that none of them would ever rid themselves of the guilt of having given testimony that would incriminate him.

Though Simon had loved his own father deeply neither he nor anyone else who had ever known Wallace Kelsey, known by friends and foe alike as The Dragon, could deny the impact of his character and genuine care for all who came into contact with him. That was, no one but The Dragon's own brother, Gerard Kelsey.

It was he who, due to his treachery, now bore the title of Earl of Kelsey. It was he who sat in the place of honor in the great hall at Dragonwick.

At that moment Jarrod spoke up, "I have something that I wish to give each of you before we leave here." He went to his horse and took a velvet bag from his belongings.

He came back to the fire and removed three objects, holding them out to the light. Simon saw that they were brooches, each containing a circle and within the circle was a magnificent dragon, its wings unfurled.

Jarrod held one out to Simon, then to Christian. "These will keep us from forgetting each other or him."

Simon's voice was as husky as his friend's as he pinned the brooch to his cape. "I will never forget."

"Nor I," said Christian as he pinned his own into place.

Swallowing hard, Jarrod did the same. Then, with no further words between them, the three mounted and headed back to the keep, which after the events of the previous day no longer felt like home. It was the day when their innocence had died, the day The Dragon's brother had attacked the keep and killed him.

Chapter One

England, 1201

"There is one way, my lord, for you to keep your head." King John's keenly assessing gaze held him.

Simon Warleigh, Lord of Avington stiffened where he stood before the king. King John leaned forward, his elbows on the table before him, as Simon spoke with a tone of calm that surprised him no less than it did the king. "And that would be?"

John Lackland was so called because his father Henry had made no great provision for him as he had his brothers. He had ruled with an iron hand since inheriting from his brother, Richard Lionheart, after his death in 1199. The king smiled thinly, reaching down to run a slender hand over the head of the sleek-coated hound that sat beside his heavily carved chair. "Take Kelsey's daughter to wife."

Simon sucked in a breath of shock. He was aware of the quick glances of the two guards who stood back from the king's chair, though neither man made any other outward sign that they were taking note of the proceedings. The guards were the small stone chamber's only other occupants, but their presence was hardly necessary. Even if Simon was foolish enough to try to escape this private audience he could never hope to make it through the castle without being apprehended.

But that was not the greatest of his problems at the moment. "Why would I take my accuser's daughter to my very bosom?" As soon as he said the words Simon realized he must go carefully. Though he was not guilty of plotting against the king John clearly believed that he was. The king's harsh dealings with his nobles had certainly caused much unrest and gave him good reason to suspect insurrection amongst his subjects. Were Simon not so occupied with his own conflict with Kelsey, he might indeed have fallen in with those who had asked him to join their efforts to rein in this king. But he had little time to afford such activities.

The king shrugged, his shoulders narrow despite the heavy red velvet tunic he wore. "Because as I have just informed you, it is the only way to keep that head of yours attached to the shoulders the women at court seem to make so much of."

Simon ignored the jibe. He had no care for the foolish tongues of women who had nothing of import to occupy them.

Simon had Avington to see to first and foremost. He had come back from the Holy Land to learn of the inheritance that had fallen to him with both a sense of responsibility and a deep sorrow. He would never have expected the death of both his father, who he learned had been dead these many months, and his elder brother only weeks prior to his return to England. Yet he'd had no time to grieve their loss, for he had immediately become embroiled in this conflict with the Earl of Kelsey. It galled him so to call the usurper by that name, the title that had graced his former foster father.

It was near beyond comprehension that the king would now make Kelsey Simon's father-by-marriage. He shook his dark head, trying to fathom some way out of this untenable situation. Never for a moment had he, Jarrod or Christian foreseen such a complication to their budding plans to bring Kelsey to ruin. He spoke almost absently. "It makes no sense. Why would you ask this of me? What possible gain could there be from it?"

King John watched him for a moment, stroking his long narrow cheek. "In spite of your long absence from England you can not be ignorant of your father's, and after him your brother's, influence with the other nobles. Do I execute you I risk their enmity. Do I marry you to a man as loyal to me as Kelsey, the very man who alerted me to your perfidy, I prevent you from continuing to plot against me. And mark me well, Kelsey will prevent that."

Simon spoke carefully, knowing that this man had the power to take Avington from him if he chose to do so. "Perhaps Kelsey will not have me for his daughter." Kelsey knew very well that it had been himself Simon was referring to as the target in the intercepted letter that had been used as evidence against him.

"He will do as I say, even to the point of taking you into his home. His loyalty to me is unquestioned."

"You mean for me to abide at Dragonwick?"

"You could not believe I would allow you to go home to Avington where you would be able to make whatever mischief you might conceive of. You will abide at Dragonwick and Kelsey will serve as guarantor of your conduct until such time as I am assured of your loyalty.''

''By controlling my every movement.'' Simon could not quite keep the bitterness from his voice, for it was even worse than he could have imagined.

The king regarded him coldly. ''Aye.''

Resentment rolled through him at the very thought of being in the bastard's control. ''And if I refuse?''

John smiled again. ''In spite of any ire that might be garnered amongst the nobles by your death I would see it done in order to assure that you cause me no difficulty.''

Simon took a deep breath, knowing he had to try this one last time to convince the king of the truth. ''I repeat, Sire, that I have done naught against you.''

The king raised dark brows and looked down at the letter before him. The letter that outlined much of Simon's wish to destroy Kelsey, without actually naming the man. The letter had been on its way to Christian at Bransbury when it had been intercepted by Kelsey's man, who had the messenger killed. Although he regretted the death of that good man, Simon knew that it had likely been the one thing to save Christian and Jarrod. If Kelsey had had an opportunity to question the messenger, he might very well have divulged his destination.

Simon said, ''I have told you, Your Majesty, that letter has been taken out of turn. The man I spoke of was not you, but Kelsey himself.''

The king shook his head. ''And as I have told *you,* my lord Warleigh, there would be no reason for Kelsey to lie to me in this. He says that he does know for a fact that it is me you plot against and not him because you approached him in that vein. Indeed, why would he lie if he knew that it was he who was the target of your machinations? Surely a loyal man such as he would simply seek my protection.''

Simon knew why. Kelsey had thought that by making it appear that Simon was plotting against the crown he would rid himself of an enemy with little effort on his part. Yet Simon knew it was pointless to reiterate this fact. John, knowing that many of the nobles were discontented with him, was ready to believe the worst.

The king seemed angered anew! ''Well, Warleigh, what say you? Take Kelsey's daughter, or...?'' He arched dark brows high.

Simon reached up and ran a hand over the dragon brooch that held his heavy woolen cloak over his shoulder. He spoke deliberately. ''I must think on this.''

John nodded sharply. ''You have until morning.'' The king's gaze raked him. ''Kelsey's daughter has been summoned. 'Tis her or the axe.''

Simon raised his own dark brows, outraged at what was revealed by the king's words. It was clear that Kelsey had agreed before Simon was even informed. ''I begin to see that this marriage is a bid by Kelsey to gain my lands....''

John stopped him with a raised hand. ''Your accusation is ridiculous, for my lord Kelsey was not eager for this union. Yet *he*—'' the king's scathing gaze raked Simon ''—is loyal to me and will do as his sovereign desires. Even had I been inclined to heed your accusations against the earl, this new charge against him would convince me of your lack of honesty. You will say no more against him.''

Simon felt a stab of self-directed anger at his rashness in speaking without thinking. Of course Kelsey had not engineered the marriage. As Simon's nearest neighbor and favorite of the king he would have some hope of gaining the lands without such a drastic step, or at least holding them if the king wanted them for himself.

Simon could see no choice but to agree to this marriage. He took a deep calming breath. "I understand."

The two guards started toward him. He stopped them with a raised hand, his dark eyes proud as he looked to the king. "Their escort will not be necessary. I can find my own way back to the village."

John eyed him, then shrugged when Simon's gaze did not waver. "Very well. See that you do not leave the town and be warned, if you do, I have the power to take Avington. You would also forfeit your life, for my patience would be at an end and my offer of leniency revoked."

Again Simon bowed, making no reply, though he would not have called what had been offered to him here leniency. Not marriage to Kelsey's daughter.

The king then gestured toward the door. "Leave me."

Simon swung around and strode from the chamber. He must indeed think on this matter, though what could come of thinking he did not know.

He went directly to the stables, heedless of the chill autumn breeze that cut through his light cloak. His very life was at stake here—and more importantly, Avington. With his father and brother dead he finally had an inkling of why his father had always put Avington first, even before his own well-being. 'Twas a great responsibility to care for not only the heritage of his family, but the lives of so many who depended upon him as their lord.

He now realized how mad he had been to embark upon this feud with Kelsey. Yet upon returning from the Holy Land, all his old outrage against the earl had been awakened when he learned that upon his brother's death the earl had sought to gain control of Avington. The longtime steward had told Simon enough of the earl's machinations to make his blood boil, including the fact that Kelsey had tried to gain access to the keep with his men a week before Simon returned home. The steward had only been able to put him off by declaring that he had no right to grant anyone permission to enter with his lord dead and the new lord not yet returned. That he would be happy to do so if the earl was to come with edict from the king.

Simon's arrival at Avington had clearly only just prevented the earl's obtaining that edict.

Newly come from the Holy Land with him, both Jarrod and Christian had been eager in their insistence on joining his quest to see Kelsey pay for his wrongdoings. When Simon had stated that this was his fight and that he would not have them risk their own skins, they had reminded him quite forcefully that Kelsey had wronged them as well. They had been mere boys when he murdered The Dragon and took his lands. Now they were men, hardened by hardship and battle. They would not have Simon cheat them of this chance to strike back at one who had done such wrong.

These thoughts reminded him that the only two men he fully trusted on earth awaited word of what had occurred in the king's chambers. They appeared within hours of each other at the inn where he had been allowed to stay when he arrived at court two days before. Neither had admitted how they knew what was going on, but Simon suspected that it had been the steward who had sent them news of his summons to court. That good man had cautioned against retribution toward Kelsey, who he knew was an intimate of the king.

Simon had failed to heed that advice.

To his detriment. For he had not foreseen how devious Kelsey would prove.

Kelsey had already been at court with his stolen letter when Simon arrived. Nothing Simon had said in his own defense had been heeded and he would not have been allowed any other witnesses even if he had been inclined to let his friends stand for him.

Kelsey could not know their identities or they would have been accused, as well. Simon would keep it that way.

He pressed his horse to a faster speed.

So preoccupied was he that Simon was nearly upon the wagon blocking the center of the road before it gained his attention. Casting a puzzled gaze over the wagon he immediately realized that one of the rear wheels was lying beside it in the road. Several men, most of them garbed in mail and obviously soldiers, were working to raise it in order to get the wheel back on. Horses of decent breed, as well as a glossy black mare of exceptional quality, were tied to a tree just off to the right.

Two women, one in a long hooded cape of good wool and another in a hooded cape of heavy burgundy velvet stood looking on. A noblewoman and her entourage, he assessed quickly. Most likely they were on their way to court.

In spite of all that was going wrong in his own life, Simon found himself stopping. He greeted the two women. "Is there aught I might do to help you?"

The taller of the two, the one in the velvet cape raised her head....

Dear heaven, he thought as his eyes met hers, which were almond shaped and the most unusual color he had ever seen, for they were the exact shade of newly budded lilacs. Her alabaster skin molded features of perfect and pleasing symmetry like those he had seen on statues while travelling through Italy, the nose straight, the cheekbones high. Her lips were such a luscious wild berry hue that he wondered if she had been biting them. The dark ebony hair that rimmed the inside of her hood seemed to come afire with subtle streaks of deep red in the morning light.

She was beautiful, undeniably, incredibly, mesmerizingly beautiful.

It took Simon a moment to realize that those perfect lips were moving, answering the question he had forgotten he'd asked. Her voice, having a slight huskiness for a woman, was soft and evenly modulated, and it stirred his senses as greatly as her beauty. "I do not know what it might be, sir." She did not fully meet his gaze for more than a brief moment as she gestured to the men who had not ceased in their efforts to raise the wagon. "There are hands enough to see it done."

A firm rejection of his offer, but perhaps just what a gently bred young woman should tell a strange man.

Still he lingered, finding himself asking inanely, "Do you go on to court?"

She kept her gaze cast down and he noted the way her lashes lay very thick and dark over her ivory cheeks. "My lord, I do appreciate your concern but we really require no aid. And my father would not have me converse with a man unknown to me, lest there be some pressing need for it."

Simon was not at all surprised. The man who counted

himself this damsel's father must certainly have a care with her.

Truth be told he was somewhat of a blackguard to linger about here staring like an untried lad. He might soon find himself wed, and though it was not of his choosing, his circumstances made his attentions to the young woman less than honorable.

Simon bowed, his tone softer than it might have been had he not felt somewhat doubtful of his own reasons for continuing to tarry. "Pray forgive me, my lady. I did not mean to cause you such discomfort by gawking as so many others must."

She looked up at him then, seeming to really see him for the first time, her uncertain gaze moving over his face. He smiled reassuringly, feeling a deep desire to put her at her ease.

Her lashes fluttered down, then up as she cast him a shy look. For a moment her gaze seemed almost wishful.

One of the men spoke up. "Is there a difficulty, my lady?"

Immediately that expression of cool dismissal fell into place. "Nay, Sir Brian. This man was only asking if he might be of help. I have told him he may go on his way."

Simon looked to the man, who met his gaze with disapproval. He had no right to the resentment he felt. The fellow was only doing his duty.

Yet Simon could not resist one more look at those haunting eyes, which now seemed to hold no expression at all. He felt unexplainably disappointed.

He bowed again and prodded his horse onward. Christian and Jarrod awaited him.

Yet he found himself looking back to see that the

young woman was watching him. Then his horse took him around a bend in the road and she was gone.

Feeling oddly bereft Simon gave himself a mental shake. He had no time to allow himself to entertain romantic notions toward a young woman with whom he had exchanged no more than a handful of words at the side of the road.

No matter that she was the most beautiful woman he had ever seen. Marriage to his enemy's daughter would mean that he would no longer be a free man, in spite of the fact that the very notion was abhorrent to him.

Jarrod and Christian swung about as he approached them where they sat at a narrow wooden table in a window alcove within the dim interior of the inn. The low-beamed chamber's other occupants paid more heed to their cups than to each other, which was one of the reasons for choosing this location. Both his friends' expressions were grave.

As always, Jarrod spoke first, his black eyes piercing in their intensity. "What said the king?"

The question brought a new rush of shock and disbelief over what John had proposed. Yet Simon's tone was amazingly matter-of-fact. "His majesty has proposed a solution in the form of a wedding."

Christian shook his gold-streaked brown head in confusion. "A wedding?"

"Aye, between myself and Kelsey's whelp."

"What say you?" Jarrod rose from the well-worn bench, his hand going to the hilt of his sword.

Simon sat wearily on the other bench beside Christian, telling him, "Desist, my friend. Anger will gain us naught." He felt Christian's strong and comforting hand upon his shoulder. It was ever thus, Jarrod needing to be soothed, and Christian soothing. He knew these two men as well as he did himself. They were his brothers in all but flesh. Now that his true brother, Arthur was dead, his only brothers. He accepted each as he was, the aspects of his personality being all that Simon would ask for.

Jarrod sank back down, speaking more evenly, though there was still a gleam of outrage in those black eyes. "Pray tell us what you are talking about."

Simon took a long drink from one of the two half-filled cups on the table before replying. "King John informs me that unless I agree to wed the daughter of the very man we have sworn vengeance upon, I will lose my head."

Again Jarrod reached for his sword, though this time it was clearly a symbolic gesture for his other hand went to the brooch at his broad shoulder. His tone was filled with outrage. "You can not agree to such a demand. And if resistance means your death, then we go with you."

Simon answered him calmly. "And what would our deaths solve? For that is what the outcome would be. The three of us can not hope to triumph against the crown. It would in no way cause Kelsey to suffer the consequences of his despicable acts."

Even the more levelheaded Christian sounded angry and horrified. "But to pledge yourself to Kelsey's daughter?"

Simon took a deep breath and another drink of the cool ale. "I know. 'Tis an untenable thought."

Christian said. "What precisely did the king say? Perhaps you have not understood him aright and there is another way...."

Simon halted him with a raised hand. "I understood

all too well for he put it baldly enough. 'Tis the axe or Kelsey's get.''

"But why? What purpose does it serve?"

"Because, my friends, he wants me where he can be sure that I am being watched and by one whose loyalty to him is unquestioned." Simon gave a rueful laugh. "The king informed me that he does not really wish to kill me lest he must. He feels that my death will bring about a certain amount of dissent amongst the nobles and he would avoid that if he is able. It is really a question of what will bring him the least amount of inconvenience."

The scowl on Jarrod's face was as black as his hair. "We should have stayed in Jerusalem. Life there was hard but the enemy was better known, more easily identified."

Simon shook his dark head. "I had to return to Avington when I got word that Arthur was gravely ill."

Christian spoke up. "Aye, and my own father is getting on as well and has been ill of late. His death would leave no one but my sister, Aislynn, to look after the lands. You are free to do as you will, Jarrod, we are not. Your brother will see to Kewstoke."

Simon watched for the familiar darkness that hovered in the back of Jarrod's black gaze whenever he thought of his family, for it was only his place as bastard that precluded his inheriting the lands and titles his younger brother now held. Jarrod turned away as he said, "King John is correct in one thing at least. There would be an outcry against him at your death."

Into the weighty silence that fell Christian said, "You must agree to this marriage."

Simon nodded. "As I had realized."

Jarrod looked at them as if they had surely lost their

minds, once again standing up from his place on the bench across from them. "What say you? Have you both gone mad?"

Casting a quick glance about the crowded chamber, Simon motioned for him to sit down. "Pray remember yourself, my friend. The king allowed me to go where I would, but there is no reason to believe he would not have me followed. You must have a care lest we be overheard."

"But you can not marry Kelsey's daughter."

Christian shook his head. "What real choice has he, Jarrod? John is king. Even if Simon were to escape to the continent, he would not be free. He would know that he had forfeited his lands, left them to the mercy of whatever toady the crown finds favor with at the moment. As things stand, that could very well be Kelsey, lest the king be wise enough to see that granting any man more power than the earl already wields would be a mistake. Simon can not abandon Avington no matter that he must marry the daughter of the very devil himself."

"But to marry himself to that family? What know you of her? I recall her but little, other than that our foster father seemed to dote on her as he did his own Rosalind whenever she was visiting."

Simon was not unaware of the regret in Jarrod's voice as he spoke Rosalind's name, nor that the sad expression in Christian's gaze matched his own. None of them could forget the sight of her crumpled body beneath that sheet.

He took a deep breath and forced himself back to the matter before him. He vaguely recalled Isabelle Kelsey from visits to Dragonwick with her father. He had seen little of her, though, as he and his friends had preferred to make themselves scarce when their foster father's brother was about. He had a vague recollection of a solemn child with overlarge eyes and dark hair that had been arranged carefully at all times.

Simon shook his head. "I know nothing of her, but that she is the get of my enemy. Yet what matter if I did? I must fall in with King John's wishes. I can only assume that he has already informed Kelsey of his intent in this because the girl has been sent for and will, I assume, be awaiting me on the morrow."

"That was presumptuous." Jarrod frowned.

Christian added, "The king must have been planning this all along. Listening to the evidence was a mere formality."

"Aye, the letter condemned me from the beginning. It takes more than a day to travel here from Dragon-wick. If the girl is to be here by morning…" Simon took a deep breath. "Christian has indeed come to the crux of it. Even if I could escape the king's 'justice' I could not abandon my responsibilities."

"But marriage?"

Simon leaned closer to them, pitching his voice so it could not possibly be overheard. "The king has offered only two alternatives of which I have told you, and marriage, though only slightly more so, is the most palatable of the two. Yet haps the marriage might not be such a drastic step. Haps there is a way to leave my options open."

Christian leaned toward him, his blue eyes intent with new interest. "And what way might that be?"

Simon shrugged. "If the marriage is not consummated, an annulment might be obtained at some point in the future."

Now Jarrod smiled coldly. "You mean at some point when we lay siege to Dragonwick and win her."

Christian shook his head fiercely. "Nay, there is no hope of that now. Not with Simon already under punishment from the king. We could never convince him that our cause had been just."

Simon nodded, his regret tingeing his voice. "Aye, it is too late to hope to win Dragonwick from the knave. What I must think on is getting free of his control." He turned to Christian. "Your father was friend to mine."

Christian nodded. "Of a certainty."

"Then perhaps, for the sake of the lands he held so dear he would do me a service."

Christian sat up straighter. "What have you in mind?"

"My father was friend to many. If your father was to write those who might be willing to come to my aid and enough of them did so, John might be forced to free me."

Christian nodded. "Of course. John would be forced to release you if enough pressure was brought to bear. I am certain there will be no difficulty in finding those who are willing. Kelsey has made many enemies."

Jarrod scowled. "I will not offer to approach my brother. He would not be likely to even grant me entrance to Kewstoke."

Again Simon heard his pain, and knew he had no answer for it, but his own love. He faced him. "I would ask a different, but equally dear, boon of you, my friend. Could you make your way to Avington and watch over it in my absence?"

Jarrod bowed. "Of a certainty." He then raised a tight fist. "Kelsey can not be allowed to roam free, to escape retribution for all he has done, including this new evil. He must meet his reward.''

"And he will," Christian added. "Eventually we will find a way to get to Kelsey in spite of King John's support."

Simon shrugged, fighting his own frustration. "But for the moment I will be in no position to see it done, trapped as I will be beneath his very thumb."

"But we shall not be." Jarrod narrowed his black eyes.

"Nay, we shall not," seconded Christian.

Simon cast them both a quelling glance. "You must do nothing to put your own lives in jeopardy. Kelsey has proven himself a more slippery eel than any of us has foreseen."

Jarrod nodded. "When I strike it will be with care and none shall have reason to believe you involved. He will ride around a bond in the and...."

"Pray give this notion of garnering support amongst the nobles a chance. Haps Kelsey would find himself on the receiving end of the king's wrath if enough information was brought to light." Simon did not imagine that Jarrod could act against Kelsey without being found out.

With obvious reluctance, Jarrod nodded, as did Christian.

Feeling only somewhat relieved, Simon raked a hand through his heavy dark hair, addressing Jarrod, "You will go to Avington until I am able to get further word to you?"

Jarrod nodded. "Aye."

Christian sighed. "I will go to my father. In the event I am needed, Jarrod will send word on to me at Greatham."

Again Jarrod nodded his midnight-dark head.

"You have my thanks," Simon told them earnestly. "I will tell my men that they are to accompany you, Jarrod. There is no need for them to come to Dragonwick. Does Kelsey mean me harm, they will not be able to prevent him."

Christian frowned, his expression direct. "You will watch your back?"

Simon reached for the cup and took a long drink. "I will, for I have no doubts that I must do so if I am to come out of this alive. For we have seen how far Kelsey is willing to go for what he wants." His free hand covered the dragon on his shoulder.

Jarrod and Christian did the same. "Aye, after murdering his own brother to gain an earldom, your death would not trouble him in the least."

Chapter Two

Quietly, Isabelle waited in the crowded and poorly appointed chamber she was sharing with several other ladies of the court. She had seated herself on a narrow backless chair some distance from where the other women chattered whilst pretending to attend to their sewing.

She did not know why her father had summoned her here to Windsor, nor had she wanted to come. She had only been to court on one other occasion with her father, who seemed to like court life little better than she. He preferred to be on his own lands where he was the law.

Nay, she had not wished to come. The first time she had been to court, she had been gawked at and disdained by the other ladies, though she could not understand why they would behave so cruelly to a girl of no more than fourteen years. This visit had proved no different. If only she could return home to Dragonwick. But what choice had she in it? Her father was master of her fate as he had reminded her more times than she could ever begin to count in the twenty years of her existence.

She was infinitely aware of the fact that to anyone,

including her father, viewing her from the outside she would appear completely unmoved. Yet her mind rolled with questions and fear of what he might be about.

Why had he sent for her? When he had left for court he had seemed agitated about some matter. Yet he had shared nothing with her.

It had crossed Isabelle's mind that there might be a possible suitor involved. But her father had not told her to make herself amenable as he had each time he had dangled her before a hopeful at Dragonwick. And there had been more than a few. Possible alliance to an earl drew those who would further their own positions. Thus far none of the men had offered enough on their own part. The Earl of Kelsey would not give up his pawn, for keeping her unwed had made allies of those men who still sought to win her.

She had not even seen her father except at dinner the previous evening. He had done no more than cast a sweeping glance over her, saying that she was looking well enough and that she was to garb herself carefully. She had not wasted breath in asking him to tell her what he was about in bidding her to come to court. He would say nothing until he was prepared to do so. No amount of coaxing had ever changed that, as she'd learned from early childhood.

Again Isabelle wondered why her father had her summoned here. Dared she even hope? Surely he would choose the weakest, most malleable of men, the kind who fawned and cowered before him. And when he did, Isabelle herself might hope to exert some influence over such a man. Marriage would bring the possibility of freedom from the tight fist of her father's control.

Unfortunately until that event occurred Isabelle must

play the part of dutiful and obedient daughter. It was a part she had learned to play very well.

To cover her extreme agitation she focused her attention on her clothing, her jewels and her hair. She ran her hand over the deep-blue velvet of her skirt, concentrating on the roughness of the silver embroidery beneath her fingers. She knew that the silver slippers she wore and the sheer veil with its silver circlet were the perfect complement for the gown with its tight bodice and low square neck.

Unbidden, thoughts of the stranger who had stopped to ask if she required assistance the previous day came into her head. He had indeed been very handsome with his well-formed masculine features, dark hair and warm brown eyes. Those dark-lashed eyes had also looked on her with appreciation as he raked his thick straight hair back from a high, intelligent forehead.

Unlike other times when she had been viewed thusly, his appreciation had made something shift inside her, something feminine and vulnerable. For the stranger had been seeing her—Isabelle—and with gentle eyes. He had not known that she was the only offspring of the Earl of Kelsey.

Though many men had professed to find her attractive they knew her father had no other heir to his earldom but her. They sought power, as her father had done in attaining his earldom—from betraying his own brother. That man had been her uncle, the one other warriors had called The Dragon because of his skill and fierceness in battle, and because of his fierce sense of honor, duty and love. It was to her uncle that she owed thanks for the vast dower her suitors sought.

Isabelle's heart ached afresh at the thought of the loss of him. For though she had been a small child when he died she had loved her uncle Wallace like no other human being. He had been kind and gentle and all that was good in the world and thus became the prey of one who would do what he must to gain power and position.

Her father. She hated her father more for that than for all his many cruelties to her. But he was all she had. Her mother had died when she was very small and the only thing she knew of her folk was that they lived in Normandy. Once, not long after her mother's death, a woman had visited, saying she was Isabelle's aunt, but her father had sent her away and she had never returned.

All Isabelle could do to try to make things right was to think of the dower that would someday be hers as her father's only heir. In memory of The Dragon she would teach her child to be like his great uncle Wallace had been.

The knock that sounded at the door did not surprise her, nor did the presence of her father's man, Sir Fredrick, standing there when one of the other women opened it. Father had sent word this morn that she was to be at the ready for his summons.

Without haste Isabelle stood, again smoothing her hand over the skirt of her kirtle.

She kept her head high beneath the gazes of the women of the court. She was grateful when the door closed behind her and she no longer had to endure their hurtful speculation.

Sir Fredrick paid her little heed other than to clear the hallway for her passage. She did not need to be told that his efforts were more in aid of hurrying to reach her father than any concern for her. He had been with her father for as long as she had memory and made his complete loyalty to the earl known at all times. Though Isabelle was amazed that her cold and distant father could have inspired such devotion in any man, she had come to accept it.

They moved on to a more sumptuously appointed portion of the castle, finally arriving at a door, which the knight opened without knocking. Still trying to remain impassive, Isabelle moved ahead of him when he stepped aside and motioned her forward.

What she saw on the other side of the door was a surprise to test the skills of self-possession that she had spent her lifetime perfecting.

The long narrow chamber bore four occupants. At the far end of the chamber, her father, King John and another man stood with their backs to her. With them was a priest.

Her gaze went to her father, even as she felt the eyes of the king come to rest upon her face. There was something familiar about the third man, who still stood with his back toward her, his wide shoulders encased in dark-green velvet. There was something about the thick, straight dark hair that brushed the velvet of his collar.

Her questioning gaze went back to her father. He cast an approving glance over her, assessing her to determine if she was properly representing him, as he always did, but not seeing *her*. He nodded and said, "Very well, then. Isabelle has arrived. We may begin."

Isabelle met the king's sharp gaze for a brief moment as she asked, "Begin what, Father?" She was pleased at the cool unconcern of her tone. It betrayed none of the agitation that made her heart pound painfully in her chest. Peripherally she became aware that the other man had finally turned around.

Isabelle's gaze moved to his face. Her heart stopped, then thumped to life again as she saw, saints above, that it was the very man she had met upon the road the previous day. The very man who had been so much in her thoughts in spite of her wishes to the contrary.

If the shock on his handsome face was any indication, he was as surprised to see her here as she was him.

What indeed was he doing here in this chamber with her father, the king and a clergyman? Forcing herself to speak evenly, she asked again, "Begin what, Father?"

There was a long heavy silence. "Haven't you even told her?" It was the stranger's deep voice. His brown eyes met hers. In them she saw resentment.

Odd. Odder still was her reaction to his expression. The ripples of annoyance and unwanted regret that rolled through her made it difficult to retain her pose of calm. She was not sorry when he turned to glare at her father.

Her father scowled. "What I tell my daughter is none of your concern."

"It is if she is to be my bride."

"Bride." The word was nothing more than a whisper of outgoing breath. She had hope, but... It was so sudden.

Her shock was lost to the others as her father replied, coldly, "You have me there, Warleigh. But recall as you consider yourself master to my daughter that I am master to you."

The man who, if she was hearing aright, was to be her husband, answered with equal lack of warmth. "'Tis only through dastardly doing that it be so. Had you not falsely accused me—"

Her father blustered. "Dastardly? I'll have you keep your accusations to—"

King John halted them with upraised hands. "No more." He cast her father a warning glance. "You assured me that you could see to this matter. Keep this man in check.''

Her father bowed. "That I will, Sire.''

"And you, my lord, you will recall that it is only by my mercy that you have been granted this opportunity to live. You will create no trouble for your father-by-marriage. Is that clear, Warleigh?''

Warleigh. In all these years she had not forgotten the names of the three fosterlings who had given evidence against her uncle. Shock rolled through her anew. Not only was she to marry one of the ones who had done her such ill, the marriage had clearly been foisted on the angry and resentful Warleigh as a punishment.

Never had she expected love, or even affection. But she had not thought to be given in such a state of resentment, had even hoped the man she wed might be malleable to her own wishes. Warleigh's outraged pride told of a strong and commanding will. Heaven help her, it would take every ounce of her self-control to see this through without breaking.

But that was precisely what she must do.

Never could she let anyone see how devastated this turn of events had left her. Especially not the man who, for a brief moment yesterday, had made her think about what it would be like to be young and free, to be looked on with favor by a handsome young man.

From his place beside the priest, Simon watched Isabelle's impassive and beautiful face.

So this woman, the one he had met along the road the previous day, was Isabelle, daughter to the Earl of Kelsey. He would never have guessed that she was the one he had been ordered to wed, and had he done so not even a beauty as great as hers could have moved him.

His gaze raked her face. His faint recollections of the child he had seen a few times so many years ago would never have prepared him for the woman she had become.

He had much clearer memories of her younger cousin, the scarlet-haired Rosalind, who had died the day Gerard Kelsey attacked the keep. The very thought angered him anew.

Simon's lips thinned as he focused on the woman before him again. There was no hint of reaction to her father's declaration that she was to be married in those astonishing lilac eyes, nor was there any rise of color in the porcelain cheeks. Those perfectly formed pink lips did not thin, nor did they purse. Her slender white hands with their long delicate fingers rested lightly on the skirt of her lavish gown. Her dark head was held at a proud but relaxed angle, further betraying her lack of concern.

How could she possibly listen to the exchange that had just taken place without reacting in some way? Yet she had.

He now realized that she was beautiful indeed, but it was more in the way of a marble statue he had seen in Rome. Unbearably lovely but lacking the animation that would fully impassion a man.

She started toward them, her slender hips drawing his gaze as she moved forward with sensuous grace. In spite of his revelations his body reacted to her grace and beauty with a will of its own. Meanwhile his mind continued to view her lack of emotion with displeasure. He told himself 'twas unnatural for a young woman to be so cold. Even the most obedient of daughters might have hoped to hear of her marriage before the moment was upon her.

Alas, he reminded himself, he could not expect more from the earl's daughter. Simon was infinitely conscious of the pale perfection of her face as she came to a halt beside him. And, heaven help him, her slender but enticing form. The gold belt about her slim hips drew his wayward gaze but when he forced it upward he was equally captivated by her long, narrow waist and high, proud breasts made all the more enticing by the deep blue of her gown, which clung lovingly to each curve.

Determinedly he pulled his gaze to his own hard fingers, which had curled into a fist at his side. He forced himself to recall his plan to remain apart from his wife. It was his only hope of being free of her and thus her father.

Unfortunately he had not at the time of making that decision realized that the very woman who had so occupied his thoughts since he left her at the side of the road yesterday was the one he must deny himself.

King John interrupted his tormented thoughts. "Shall we have it done, then? I do have other matters to attend."

Kelsey spoke before Simon could. "Of course, my lord. It would greatly trouble my sleep to think that I had brought you any undue inconvenience."

Simon felt his lips twist in derision. The man was a toad. As he had always been.

He must keep this in mind. Raised by one such as the earl the girl could not be but less than honorable of character. The longing he had thought he had seen in her eyes yesterday was nothing more than the wishful thinking of a man who had found himself in the company of a very lovely woman. A man who had just been told he must marry in order to save his head. He could not afford himself the luxury of allowing one such as she to become the lady of Avington.

No matter how beautiful she might be.

An indeterminable time later Simon left the chamber where the marriage had taken place, pausing in the hall outside as he realized that he had nowhere to go. There was no sign of his bride, who had exited just moments before him with no more hint of emotion than she had displayed on entering, hardly a word having been exchanged between them, nothing save their replies to the priest's intonations.

Simon heaved a silent sigh, aware of the angry and watchful eyes of the man who stood as if guarding the door. He had been the same man to bring Isabelle to the chamber, which told Simon that he was Kelsey's man even if his resentful blue gaze had not. He must guard himself even now with Kelsey still inside with the king, who had informed him that he was to await them in the hall. As parting words King John had again made it very clear that Simon would be accompanying his wife and her father to Dragonwick this very day. And that he would be remaining there indefinitely.

Dragonwick.

The very thought brought back so many memories. It had been his home for two years as squire to The Dragon. He had spent many a happy day there riding, sword playing, exploring the lands with Jarrod and Christian. Not that Wallace Kelsey had been an easy mentor. He had expected much from those under him, including Simon and Jarrod and Christian.

It had been a good life until The Dragon was accused of supporting those who plotted against King Henry.

Through it all, The Dragon had declared his innocence
and support of the king. He had been accused of meeting in secret with two of Henry's son, Richard's, most
loyal allies. It had been to this that Simon, Jarrod and
Christian had been forced to testify.

It had not gone well and The Dragon had decided he
would not give up his lands without resistance. He was
determined to stand by his principles. Never had Simon
or his friends imagined what would happen next. Somehow they had believed that their foster father would
triumph. No one had suspected that his brother Gerard
would convince the king to provide him a force to lead
against him.

They had not realized how very desperate King
Henry was to rid himself of Wallace Kelsey when it
appeared he had allied himself against the crown. Simon
had not participated in the fighting the day The
Dragon's brother attacked the keep. Under protest he,
Jarrod and Christian had been locked away in a shed to
keep them out of the battle.

They had only been released in time to see the bodies
of The Dragon and his three-year-old daughter, Rosalind, who had been brought down to lie beside her father
in the bailey. Gerard Kelsey had loudly declared his
regret that his niece was dead, claimed that she had
inadvertently fallen from the top of the inner stairs trying to get to her father, who had been fighting in the
hall.

Simon had been sickened by the blackguard's false
regret and the sight of that tiny crumpled body, glad the
nurse had wrapped the child in linens to cover her broken form from the eyes of her enemies. These many
years later he remembered the sweetness of the carrot-
haired child who had followed them about the castle

grounds and he felt his chest tighten. He'd wished that he could give vent to the tears that threatened even now.

Aye, Dragonwick would be filled with memories and not all of them good ones.

Surely, he would eventually find a way to extricate himself from this odious situation. King John had much to occupy him with his nobles' anger and resentment against the crown, not to mention his own recent divorce and remarriage. John could not afford to divert his attention to a favorite such as Kelsey for very long.

From behind Simon came Kelsey's voice. "We will be leaving court within the hour."

Simon stiffened, as he faced him. "I must only retrieve my belongings from the inn where I have been staying."

Kelsey scowled. "Do not attempt to escape, my lord. I take the charge to keep you under my eyes most seriously."

Simon shrugged, casting a glance over to the dark knight with the resentful blue eyes, who had moved to stand at the earl's right. "Send a guard, if you will. It will only delay me. I have no wish to try to escape you. I hold my own lands too dear to risk them over such foolishness."

The older man's expression remained disapproving, but he nodded. "Very well then, but know I shall send them after you if you do not return and the king will hear of it."

"You will have nothing to report." Simon could not quite hide the disgust in his tone, nor could he keep it from his eyes. Quickly he turned and left the man who was now his father-by-marriage. For the moment.

As he rode to the inn Simon realized that perhaps this circumstance could be used for good purpose. Perhaps he could discover something that would aid them in their quest to see Gerard Kelsey robbed of all he had stolen.

Isabelle moved quickly to her waiting mare. She was earlier than her father had commanded but she was eager to leave this place of intrigue and unhappiness.

The task of being ever on her guard, of never showing a hint of emotion was just too difficult to maintain. At least at Dragonwick she had those moments when she was alone in her chamber to let go of her rigid self-control.

Surreptitiously, her gaze swept the mounted men. There was no sign of her new husband.

Husband. The word seemed strange. The ceremony had been accomplished so quickly and with so little fanfare that it seemed completely unreal. At no point had the baron so much as touched her. Then her father had dismissed her, informing her that she was to make ready for the return to Dragonwick within the hour.

Even as she told herself she had no real interest in Simon Warleigh, he came galloping through the castle gate. She could not help noting that he rode his enormous chestnut stallion as if he were one with it. His straight thick hair was drawn back by the wind of his passage, leaving those well sculpted, masculine features bared to her lingering gaze. He looked handsome, strong and untamed.

Her heart thudded in her chest.

Quickly she busied herself with getting fully settled in the saddle. Isabelle was determined to set her attention on the ride ahead. She loved riding, lest it involved hunting. She cast a quick glance at her father.

Her father called out, "Where is my horse?" An ex-

pression of impatience had replaced the one that had
told her he had been congratulating himself on his ability to control everything and everyone around him.

For a moment, watching him, she could almost feel
sympathy toward her newly wedded husband. That
emotion was quickly dismissed as her gaze went to
Warleigh's face. There was no mistaking the pride and
arrogance she saw there, the confidence. Again she was
reminded that her hope of eventually gaining the ear of
a pliant husband would never come to pass. The man
was nothing more than her father's prisoner and yet he
retained this prideful stance.

She could not help wondering from whence his self-
confidence came. She had always admired strength.

It was a quality she knew her father lacked, for all
his ability to control others. If he had not wrought such
misery and pain by his actions she would have felt pity
for him. She felt her lips twist wryly. God help her, she
did pity him still. Yet she could not allow herself to
display it in any way for he would simply use it against
her. As he had always used the weakness of others
against them.

That she was his own daughter had no bearing on his
behavior. He had no loyalty greater than that toward his
own power and greed.

Isabelle found her gaze going back to her husband.
He seemed to have no fear of facing her father. Yet that
was no good to her, for he clearly felt nothing but resentment toward her for her part in his imprisonment.

Then the sound of pounding hooves drew her gaze
back to the gate as two more riders came galloping into
the bailey. One was quite young, perhaps thirteen or
fourteen years of age, with a thatch of unruly blond hair
and strong features that were too large for his face. The

other was an older man, wide shouldered, gray haired and steady of regard, his bearing and accoutrements marking him a knight. They rode directly to Simon Warleigh and halted.

The knight spoke to Simon Warleigh, "My lord, we are at your disposal."

Warleigh scowled, his wide brow creasing. "I appreciate your sense of duty, Sir Edmund, but I do not require your service at the moment, else I would not have informed you that you were to return to Avington."

The knight raised his head high as he held his overlord's gaze. "Aye, my lord. But there were others who agreed that it would be best if we were to accompany you."

Isabelle watched as her husband took a deep breath before replying. "I say again, I do not require your attendance." His gaze flicked to the young rider, who, from the look of him must be a squire. "You must take Wylie home to Avington."

The older man frowned, "But, my lord—"

Her father's voice interrupted. "This will not serve." He made a sweeping motion. "You may not accompany us."

They ignored him, continuing to look to their overlord with genuine concern, even love. Isabelle was amazed by loyalty that seemed to have no basis in fear.

The boy, whom Warleigh had called Wylie, cried, "My lord, we can not go off and leave you to…" His angry gaze raked the assembled company.

His patience obviously at an end, Isabelle's father motioned to his men. "Remove them from the bailey." Two of them moved forward to take hold of the reins of the man and boy who voiced such concern for their master.

The lad resisted, making his horse dance away from the reaching hands.

Simon Warleigh again told his men, "Go in peace. Have no concern for me. I will be well."

Her father laughed coldly. "Nicely said, Warleigh, but you really have no say in this. Take them."

Seeing the way her father was enjoying this display of power Isabelle felt an unexpected sense of rebellion. She had no connection to Simon Warleigh, no reason to set aside her accustomed mask of disregard. Yet it was her own voice that said, "Pray let them come, Father. You are most equal to the task of keeping them at heel."

Her father seemed surprised that she would concern herself with such a matter. But he nodded thoughtfully. "Aye, you advise me well, daughter." His superior gaze then swept the men. "I would not wish for them to think I fear their ability to free their master from my guardianship."

Simon Warleigh, her husband, cast her a glance that was at first surprised and then puzzled. But his puzzlement was quickly masked behind an unreadable expression.

Again she noted that Warleigh's men had made no visible reaction to her and her father's conversation. Their attention was all for Simon, who said, "You may accompany me but you—" he looked to the boy "—will remember yourself and do nothing but what you are instructed to do, lest I send you home."

The boy nodded.

Her father said, "You must first consult me before giving any order, even that of sending your men away from Dragonwick. I must answer to the king for your actions."

Simon eyed him closely. "As you will, my lord. I will certainly consult you before giving such orders. My instructing my squire against foolhardy behavior should certainly come under close scrutiny."

Isabelle had to restrain a smile at the look of shocked displeasure in her father's face. Once more she was surprised at her reaction to the man's open defiance of her father. It was admirable, but completely mad. Gerard Kelsey always succeeded in getting what he wanted.

Had he not succeeded in seeing Simon Warleigh placed beneath his very thumb? Not that she doubted her husband deserved it. From what she had heard in the king's chamber it appeared he had been caught plotting against the crown.

Whatever madness had prodded her to interfere between him and her father was now overcome. She had no interest in Warleigh. Her hope of attaining some influence with her husband was dead. Her hope to have a son whom she could love was not.

She chose not to dwell on accomplishing that deed. Somehow she would find the courage when the time came. Any hardship could be faced in order to see her goal of having a son realized.

But when would it happen? When would she and...

No one had even so much as alluded to the coming night.

Almost of its own accord her gaze went to her husband's undeniably handsome face. What would it be like—to be taken into his arms, to feel his body against hers? She felt a strange rush of warmth that shocked her.

As if he sensed her attention, Simon Warleigh's gaze met hers. His was assessing, raking the sheer silver veil, which was pinned atop her carefully arranged hair, and her face. It then passed over the length of her blue gown, which was visible through the opening of the scarlet cloak she wore. Isabelle knew the gown was overfine for a journey, but she had been so eager to leave that she had refused when her maid Helwys had suggested changing it.

His gaze did not in any way lead her to believe that he was interested in...

In point of fact, nothing he had done or said during that painfully tense marriage ceremony or afterward had made her think he had even considered the wedding night, let alone wished for it to happen. Isabelle tore her gaze away from his coolly assessing one as her father called out again, "My horse."

At last his squire, Karl, came leading the wildly straining black stallion from the stable. The lad was disheveled as he tried to hold the horse steady and his uncertain gaze fixed itself on her father's face.

Isabelle felt her whole body tense at the cold anger she saw there. He strode to the lad, reaching out for the reins with one hand, while back of the other snaked out to connect with Karl's cheek.

The squire sprawled in the dust of the courtyard, his hand going to his cheek. There was utter stillness as her father mounted without a glance in the lad's direction. Into the achingly heavy silence Simon cried, "Are you mad?"

Her father swung to face him. "You dare not question me concerning my treatment of my own folk, Warleigh. Lest you care to go back and tell King John that his will for you is not to your liking?"

Seeing the familiar icy fire in her father's gaze, Isabelle knew how near they were to being taught one of his lessons. Not even Simon could stop him no matter how confident he might be. Desperately Isabelle cried out in a hoarse tone as her eyes met her husband's, "You have no power here. Pray leave be." She knew he would see the pleading in her gaze, but cared not. She would spare Karl, nay all of them, the harsh reality of her father's enmity.

Her face flaming with emotions that she could not quite identify, Isabelle was filled with relief as her father flicked her an approving glance and gave the order to ride out. Guiding her horse out onto the road that would take them south to Dragonwick gave her something to do besides think about what would come next between her and Simon Warleigh.

Chapter Three

Kelsey ordered the men to stop and make camp before dark had fallen.

Simon did not question this. He was too occupied in considering the motivations of the woman he had married. And perhaps his own motives as well. For a brief moment, when she had faced him after her despicable father had knocked his squire to the ground for the crime of having difficulty with the horse, he had thought he'd seen fear and pleading in her gaze. It had been that which made him subside, that and his certainty that King John would only uphold the knave's right to mistreat his folk if he so desired.

Yet as he had ridden on ahead of his captor, Simon had thought about the actual words she had spoken. Though he'd thought he sensed a hint of contempt along with those other more gentle emotions, Isabelle had surely meant nothing but to remind him her father held power here.

She had paid him not even cursory attention since leaving Windsor. She rode at the center of the entourage, looking neither right nor left, speaking to no one, obviously completely lost in her own concerns.

Her father's acceptance of her words as confidence in his power seemed somewhat dull-witted and self-serving at the same time. Simon had sensed a sarcasm in her he would never have expected. Why would she address her father with contempt, however carefully veiled, on Simon's account when she seemed disinterested in anything but herself?

Though Simon wished he could deny it he had been quite preoccupied with her. Each time he glanced up ahead of him he was reminded anew of her beauty. She was enough to take a man's breath away with the sunlight glinting on hair that, though black, held a hint of dark flame in those glossy tresses. It framed a profile so delicately lovely that it drew his gaze again and again.

Only once had she glanced back for the briefest of moments. Those amazing lavender eyes had slid over him, her expression seeming strangely uncertain for a moment before her lids cast downward. But when he had watched her even more intently to attempt to understand this, he had realized he must have been mistaken. There was no hint of any emotion in those eyes as they skimmed over whatever passed before them.

Aye, lovely she was, breathtakingly so, but there was indeed a coldness to that beauty. He would not forget who and what Isabelle was. Even as he felt drawn to her, he suspected that any man who allowed himself to fall victim to her loveliness might have cause to rue such a weakness.

Deliberately Simon averted his gaze from both Isabelle and her patronizing father as they dismounted and began the evening's preparations. He fixed his attention on several of Kelsey's men as they erected two tents.

He looked away only as Isabelle and her woman entered the smaller of the two tents. Gerard Kelsey beckoned one of his men to his side and motioned to Simon with a sharply voiced command to prevent him from leaving. He then disappeared into the other tent with the watchful knight who never left his side, leaving Simon both relieved and irritated.

Neither his wife, nor her father had said so much as a word to him. What, then were his sleeping arrangements to be on his wedding night?

Simon shrugged even as he tried to deny that there was a certain stirring deep in his body at the very thought. In spite of all that he had told himself of her, he was less than certain as to his reactions should she be waiting for him.

Simon drew himself up. Better to bed down around the fire with the men than to go into the darkness of that tent with Isabelle. He was not concerned about sleeping out under the stars. He had done so many times, under countless skies from here to the Holy Land and back.

Yet what could he say, if he might be expected to share that tent with her?

How could he refuse? Simon did not wish to arouse suspicion as to his true intentions concerning the marriage. King John had made his feelings clear. He would not take any defiance lightly. There was no doubt in Simon's mind that Kelsey would be more than pleased to inform the king that he was not being obeyed.

Frustrated with his thoughts, Simon turned to his own men, who stood nearby. ''Wylie, groom our horses and ready our bedrolls for night.''

Wylie scowled and looked about at the other men, who were occupied with their own duties. It was clear that he felt uneasy at the notion of mixing with Kelsey's men, but Simon was confident that no harm would come to the squire with Sir Edmund nearby. He cast the knight a meaningful glance over the squire's head.

Sir Edmund nodded almost imperceptibly. "Come along lad, we've work to do."

Wylie moved to obey. Simon knew it would do well for him to see to his accustomed duties. They must all attempt to find some ease with the situation. But having given over these tasks to his men, he had naught to occupy himself.

Simon swung around and strode to the edge of camp. He was surprised to feel a restraining hand upon his arm.

He swung around to meet the determined gaze of the same man whom Kelsey had ordered to watch him. "My lord has bid me keep you here."

Simon shook off that hand. He could hear the strain in his own voice, the barely leashed anger. "I tire of proclaiming my honor at every turn. I will not try to escape, but neither will I beg permission to leave this camp for a few moments, no matter what your lord orders."

The man frowned, looking toward Kelsey's tent.

Simon rolled his eyes. "I am going for a swim. If you value your hand you will take it from me."

The man looked at him for a long moment, then stepped back. "I have simply been told to do my duty."

Simon nodded. "Aye, and you may say that you have done your best to do so." With that he turned and stalked away. He had no wish to cause the man difficulty. He was, as he said, only doing as he had been instructed. But neither would Simon submit to Kelsey's desire to see him completely subjugated. He had indeed been forced to proclaim his honor far too many times in the past two days.

And all in aid of a man who would not know what honor was did it rear up and bite him on his bony backside.

Isabelle chafed inside the small confines of her tent, ever conscious of the watchful and worried gaze of Helwys. She decided to occupy herself and the maid by rearranging her hair. But Helwys's expression did not ease throughout this familiar activity and she finally broached the subject of the coming night. "Will he come to you, my lady?"

Isabelle was forced to inform her maid of the dismal truth with as much self-possession as she could muster. "I have no idea what is to happen." It was true that her father had called a halt to their journey rather early in the evening but he had given no indication of why.

"Oh, my dear lady."

Though Isabelle did love the older woman it was sometimes difficult to deal with her worry and sympathy. It was oftimes displayed when Isabelle could least afford any sign of weakness, any hint of self-pity. Such was the case now. She must retain her equilibrium. "My father will inform me of what he wishes for me to do when he wishes it. And not a moment before, as you well know."

Helwys put her plump hands to her bosom. "'Tis unnatural, his treatment of you."

Isabelle hushed her with a raised hand. "Do not say so." She looked about them. "These walls are very poor protection indeed to guard against my father's many ears and eyes. Were he to think you against him he would send you away...or..." Her voice broke as she recalled the beating Helwys had once received at her father's command, and all because she had dared question one of Isabelle's lessons. He did not feel that forcing five-year-old Isabelle to sit at table each evening for a fortnight without eating as a punishment for spilling her cup was cruel. She took a deep breath. "We can not risk angering him." Though that had not been the last beating Helwys had suffered by his order there had been none in recent years and Isabelle would keep it so.

The older woman sent Isabelle a glance that told of just how much she understood. They two had been together since Isabelle was a child, but like everything else that had ever meant anything to her, Isabelle hid her love for the serving woman lest her father, who viewed such emotions as weakness, find some way to use it against her.

Weakness was not tolerated.

Even though Helwys desisted, the sadness and worry did not leave her brown gaze. Feeling as if she would surely explode with the tension of staying calm in the face of her maid's anxiety Isabelle took up her scarlet cloak, saying, "I am going for a walk before it grows dark."

Helwys frowned. "But, my lady…"

She took a quick breath through her nose, speaking with barely leashed strain. "If I do not do something, I shall go quite mad."

The wide-eyed maid said no more in the face of this unaccustomed outburst and Isabelle slipped from the tent. She was afforded a measure of privacy as she hurried into the cover of the tall green pine and yew, as well as the rapidly turning ash and willow that grew close to the nearby stream.

Leaving the sounds of the camp behind, Isabelle took a deep breath, rubbing her hand over the base of her neck. Her cheeks felt hot and flushed. With a sigh she made her way to where the brush was thicker at the edge of the stream, moving forward carefully in order to make certain that the ground was firm beneath her.

It seemed soft and dense with moss but not unsafe. Isabelle knelt down and reached out to dip her hand in the cool water, meaning to bring it up to her heated cheeks.

In the very act of bending over, the sound of a splash came to her. Looking toward the noise, she stopped still. There, in the water just a bit farther downstream was a man. He was standing with his bare back to her in the shallows on the opposite bank as he splashed water over his upper body and over his thick, straight dark hair.

Isabelle jerked back, her hand going to her mouth as she realized that the man was Simon Warleigh. Her husband. The man who had already caused her so much unrest this day.

She knew that she should go away before he saw her. She could not imagine how she would ever live with his knowing that she had seen him this way. But another part of her, one that would not be denied, argued that he would never realize she was here.

And after all, was he not her own husband? It was not unusual that she would wonder about him, wonder about the body that must eventually be joined with hers if a child was to be made. She told herself that seeing him thus would surely help prepare her for the act that must come.

Isabelle had no wish to appear frightened or unsure of herself if he should come to her. And the more prepared she was, the more likely that she would be able to hide any anxiety she might feel from her husband.

Thus having convinced herself, she carefully leaned back out from behind the brush. Her gaze moved over those wide golden shoulders, down his back to his narrow waist and lean hips. When Warleigh raised his arms to scrub at his dark hair she saw the hardness of the muscles as they flexed in his forearms, his shoulders and down his back.

Isabelle frowned thoughtfully. She had not expected him to be so muscular. Simon was a slender man, as her father was, but from what she could see it was obvious that his body was far harder, more masculine.

He was strangely appealing, she realized as a faint tingle of awareness came to her belly. Her gaze grew wide. Now where had that thought come from?

However strong and attractive he might be, Warleigh did not appeal to her. If they came together it would be in the interest of producing a child. Nothing more.

Nonetheless she watched as he dove into the deeper portion of the river, then emerged far closer to her hiding spot than she would have expected. Again Isabelle ducked back behind the brush, while being careful to keep him in sight between the branches. She held her breath as Simon stood, his body glistening in the low-slanting, evening sunlight, his dark hair slicked back from his broad brow.

Her heart thumped in her chest, for he looked like some pagan god of old, risen from the very waters in which he stood. Again came that strange, pleasurable tingling. Quickly Isabelle called herself to task. Such fanciful thoughts were completely foreign to her.

Since early childhood Isabelle had been taught to control her feelings. No unwanted physical sensations or girlish daydreams had ever arisen in a mind that was completely fixed on doing what was expected of her and thus preventing any lessons. But now, with one glimpse of this man, she was entertaining notions that were quite unacceptable to her.

She drew herself up, pulling back as she closed her eyes. It would not serve, however fascinating the man might appear in the glory of his nakedness.

A flash of scarlet amongst the green drew Simon's eyes. He stopped in the act of reaching for a handful of sand to rub in his wet hair, his gaze searching the bushes along that stretch of river.

Nothing.

Yet he had not imagined what he had seen. And the red was too vivid to be created by a trick of light on water.

Perhaps he told himself, it had been one of Kelsey's men, sent to watch and make sure he did not try to escape. Yet he did not recall seeing any of the men wearing such a bright color. Then a vivid image of Isabelle entered his mind. She had been dressed in a scarlet cloak this day.

Shock jolted through him.

Why would Isabelle have come here to spy upon him? He could not credit that her father would send her to do so. Surely even Gerard Kelsey had more sensibility toward his own daughter.

Even more unbelievable was the notion that she might have come for her own purposes. The cold beauty had shown no sign of vague curiosity as far as he was concerned. The very thought of her having an interest in him made his body tighten although his will bade it do otherwise.

Isabelle Kelsey seemed to have little care for him.

Yet somehow he knew it had been her. An image of her looking back at him the first time he had seen her flashed through his mind. It made no sense in light of her behavior this day. Other than her defense of his keeping his men with him.

He dressed himself, then quickly made his way to the spot where he had seen the flash of scarlet. In the soft moss near the edge of the water he saw the imprint of two small shoes. It had to be a woman. Even the squires would have bigger feet. The only other woman on the journey besides Isabelle was the maid and she had been garbed in dark colors.

Far from clarifying anything, this further evidence that it had indeed been his wife left him even more at a loss. Again he wondered what possible reason she could have for such behavior.

Thoughtfully Simon made his way back to camp. Scanning the camp, he saw that Isabelle was not amongst those who had gathered around the fire in the growing gloom.

Disappointment made his lips tighten as he moved to sit on a log beside Sir Edmund just a bit apart from the others. Simon greeted him quietly. "All has gone well?"

The knight shrugged, "Well enough, my lord. It seems we will be tolerated for the most part." Simon knew the knight would not complain lest things were particularly unpleasant. He had been one of his brother's oldest knights and was much recommended by the steward at Avington.

"Wylie?" he asked, for he was not as certain of the squire's behavior.

"Down by the stream watering the horses. I told him to have extra care with them."

Simon nodded. "Well done." Sir Edmund understood the importance of keeping the squire busy. He raked a hand through his hair, which was drying quickly in the heat of the fire. As he dropped his hand to his side, he caught a flash of red from the corner of his eye.

Isabelle. He swung around to look at her where she stood beside her tent.

That cool lavender gaze slid over him, away, then came back. For a brief moment their eyes locked before she turned away, her face as impassive as ever. Yet he was not blind to the deep rose coloring in her cheekbones.

Again he raked his hair straight back from his forehead. That flush seemed a sign of agitation for the cool beauty. Did it mean that beneath that icy demeanor there beat a passionate heart? Did she perhaps find him more appealing than she wished him to know? Was that why she had been at the stream?

His next thought, that he wished for this to be so, appalled Simon so completely he knew he must find something else to occupy his mind.

His gaze came to rest on Kelsey who now stood before his tent. The dark knight hovered, as ever, just behind him. The earl surveyed the activity of the camp with a disapproving expression. Seeing the degree of efficiency with which the men worked preparing for the coming night Simon was surprised. He knew his own men, many of them trained in haste by the necessity of the battlefield, could not have done better.

Noting Simon's attention, Gerard Kelsey came toward him, his shadow following. "Well, Warleigh, I hope you are not finding our duty over you too chafing.'' His tone said that his true hope was far different from that contained in his words.

Simon shrugged. ''I am content, my lord. For the moment.'' It did not seem that the knight who had attempted to detain him before he went to bathe had mentioned the matter of their confrontation. Simon felt no need to do so.

He watched as Kelsey smiled at him. '''Twould be best if you stayed content, my lord. I will not tolerate any disregard of the king's wishes.''

Simon bowed. ''Rest easy, sir. I have no wish to trouble the king.'' He did not add that he had no such feelings as far as Kelsey himself was concerned.

''Very good.''

Then Kelsey was distracted by something behind Simon and shouted out, ''Have you not been reprimanded enough this day? Have a care with that animal do you value your hide.''

Simon swung around to see the young lad who had been violently punished at Windsor, holding the reins of the magnificent black stallion once again. It pranced and fought at the bit, its hooves flashing at everything that came close to foot. Now it was clear the horse's agitation was clearly caused by poor temperament, rather than improper handling, and that the stallion had been chosen for appearance rather than anything else. The lad had been harshly and unjustly punished.

He failed at keeping the disdain for his host from his voice as he said, '''Tis a beautiful horse.''

Kelsey raked him with an equally disdainful glance. ''I would have no less in anything I possess.'' He cast an oddly unreadable glance toward Isabelle's tent.

Simon could not help realizing that he was speaking

of Isabelle. He found himself asking, ''Including your daughter?''

The older man raised gray brows high in challenge. ''Including my daughter.''

How could the man speak of his own child so dispassionately, as if she were no more to him than any other possession and before his man, even though he be a knight? The thought was strangely disturbing and he found himself watching Kelsey's face for any hint of fatherly affection. He saw none, only conceit.

He felt a tug of sympathy. Perhaps here was a clue to the veiled sarcasm he had heard in her voice when she spoke to her father before leaving Windsor.

Simon gave himself a mental shake. Isabelle would not welcome his pity. She seemed to be more than content with her lot in spite of her apparent sarcasm toward her father. He would do well to expend his energies in thinking how he would get out of this situation, away from this man, while still retaining his lands.

He was distracted from these thoughts by the sudden angry babble of his squire's voice. Simon sighed, wondering what could have set the lad off this time. Had he known that his journey to court would end in his being in the custody of his most hated enemy, he would never have taken Wylie to Windsor. He had taken him to service under his longtime squire, Martin, who had served him in the Holy Land, because Martin would soon be receiving his spurs and Simon had been impressed with Wylie, who was the son of one of the other knights at Avington. He had noted a quickness of intellect in the lad that he had thought to hone with discipline and training.

Unfortunately the boy was also somewhat impulsive. Simon knew that the lad's admiration and gratitude to-

ward him was great. All of this complicated things and
did not bode well for his hope that Wylie would be able
to control himself enough to stay out of trouble until an
opportunity to return to Avington presented itself.

Quickly Simon moved to where Wylie was standing
with his arms folded over his chest in the midst of the
other men who had quickly gathered at the edge of the
camp where the horses were tied. Rage radiated from
his squire in waves. "What goes on here?" Simon demanded.

Wylie turned from his angry contemplation of one of
the other men, another boy really, Simon realized as he
took a closer look at the object of Wylie's displeasure.

His squire exploded. "He says I may not bring our
blankets close to the fire, my lord. He says that the best
places are for Kelsey's own men."

Simon sighed. "I am sure no insult was meant. Of
course, as his lord's squire he would be most concerned
with making sure that his lord's men be given their just
due of honor. We are newly come and would not usurp
anyone's position. I am sure there will be comforts
aplenty for all at Dragonwick."

Wylie scowled at the other squire, who smiled slyly.

Simon felt a rush of irritation with Kelsey's squire
himself. At the same time he knew it was unrealistic to
expect more from Kelsey's retainers. A good example
must be set in order to receive honorable behavior from
underlings.

Kelsey interrupted his thoughts with a gruffly voiced
order. "You must keep your men under control."

Simon knew a tug of resentment, even though he had
been thinking much the same thing. He kept it well
hidden. "Of course, my lord." He looked to his squire.
"There will be no more problems, will there, Wylie?"

The lad bowed, keeping his head down.

Kelsey seemed to be somewhat mollified by Simon's lack of resistance to his position of power. But he continued to keep his nose raised to a haughty angle. "I mean to finish attending some matters in my tent. Sir Fredrick, you are to see that there are no more disturbances."

The shadow nodded, his narrowed eyes sliding over Simon. He slipped a caressing hand to the hilt of his sword as he leaned close to whisper in his master's ear. The earl shook his head sharply as he whispered, "Not now, my friend. We must remember John's wishes."

The knight's disappointment was obvious and it took no great amount of imagination to guess at the subject of their exchange. Simon realized he must watch his back with this one, though it seemed he would heed his master as far as an open attack was concerned. There was no doubt in Simon's mind that he had naught to thank for his continued good health but Kelsey's determination to hold him for the crown. From that whispered phrase it seemed he would not be averse to changing his mind.

Sir Fredrick continued to study Simon as he took up a rigid stance outside the ring of the fire. Simon dismissed him, focusing on the arrogant earl as he strode away with no concern whatsoever for the fact that the exchange might have been overheard. His back rigid, Simon balled his hands into fists at his sides. He would very much like to change the straight angle of that autocratic nose. He forced his hands to open, for he must remember Avington, and the folk who lived there, were what mattered here not some self-indulgent sense of injured dignity.

If they did mean him ill, they would not find him so very easy to kill.

Through his anger, he heard Wylie whisper, "'Tis a disgrace, my lord, you being held by that blackguard."

Deliberately, Simon made a greater effort to gain mastery over his feelings. He was certain no one could have heard the exchange but himself, and he would keep it to himself. He put a soothing hand on the squire's shoulder, a warning hand. "Pray hold your tongue, lad. I am not pleased by events but neither am I uneasy in my mind. All will right itself soon enough."

The boy raised hopeful eyes to his face. "You are too easy with them, my lord. We should fight our way through this as Martin has told me you were forced to many times in the Holy Land."

Simon leaned closer, his tone admonishing. "Heed me, boy. What happens here is not the same. There we fought the enemy. Here, the king himself has ordered that I be put under Kelsey's rule. We would be committing not only a foolish act, but a suicidal one in defying Kelsey and through him the king." He held that light-blue gaze. "Dost understand me, Wylie? 'Twould be treason. You must keep your head till I devise a way to make the king see that I have no desire to plot against him." Which was a true enough statement. He did sympathize with the other nobles but he had no intention beyond that at this moment.

It was Kelsey he wished to see brought low. Yet that anticipated outcome must wait. Hate him though Simon did, he would not risk Avington.

Simon was not completely reassured when the boy said, "Aye, my lord," for his lips were set in a stubborn line as his resentful gaze flicked over the earl's men, lingering longest on the prideful countenance of the squire who had so offended him.

That grudgingly muttered acquiescence was all he would get and would have to do, in these circumstances. Simon need simply keep ahead of the willful boy.

Kelsey must be lulled into believing he posed no threat no matter how difficult that feat might prove, no matter how hotly his anger and resentment burned inside him. Simon only hoped that he would begin to ease his vigilant eyes ere long. He did not wish to resort to accepting Jarrod's wild notion of laying in wait for the earl and killing him even though the situation had become dire enough to warrant casting chivalry aside. Not whilst he was the one most likely to be suspect.

If they could only garner the support of the other nobles to petition for his release he might still find a way out.

He must find a way.

And he must do this in the midst of trying to understand his own unwanted awareness of his enemy's daughter. He could not afford himself the self-indulgence of giving in to his attraction for her, not if he meant to be free of her and her supercilious and reprehensible sire.

Chapter Four

Isabelle lingered far from the camp for as long as she dared to avoid meeting Simon. When she returned night had nearly fallen.

She made every effort to avoid looking for her husband amongst the men. Yet she found him near the blaze of the fire, his dark hair dry, his powerful body hidden by the fine garments he wore. That did not prevent a vision of how he had appeared in the stream from coming into her mind. Simon did not seem to notice her at all, let alone her discomfiture. She could not but be grateful though she knew theirs must be the oddest marriage ever entered into, even amongst arranged marriages. A deep flush heated her face and neck.

She ducked into her tent. The relief on Helwys's face made her chest tighten with guilt. She opened her lips to apologize when a commotion from without made Helwys look at her with an unvoiced question that mirrored her own.

Isabelle, not wishing to come face-to-face with Simon, said, ''Will you go to see what has occurred?''

The maid nodded and hurried out, clearly curious.

Isabelle continued to hear the deep rumble of men's

voices and a slightly higher one that was still distinctly male, but it was impossible to make out the words any of them spoke. Not until Helwys scurried back into the tent was she able to learn what had occurred.

The maid raised clear brown eyes to hers. "It was Lord Warleigh's squire, my lady. He took issue with your father's squire telling him that he could not put their blankets beside the fire."

Isabelle moved to sit on the pile of furs that made up her bed. "Oh."

The maid's approving tone brought her gaze back to her. "Your husband acquitted himself most fairly, my lady. He smoothed all over by saying that my lord Kelsey's men must have first choice as he had no wish to displace any man. He seems bent on trying to make peace betwixt the men. His manner in the incident was naught as your—" Helwys blanched and Isabelle knew she been about to refer to her father in a derogatory manner. She continued carefully, "Your lord husband behaved in a way that was quite admirable. 'Tis a good sign, for I do hope he will be kind to you."

Isabelle was troubled by Helwys's approval of Simon Warleigh. She had no wish to look for nobility in him. She had never known anything but disappointment in any man other than her uncle Wallace. Thinking of him made her recall that no matter how compelling the sight of Warleigh's body might be, he had been one of those to condemn her uncle.

Quickly she interjected, "Haps my husband is simply weak." Isabelle knew this was not true even as the words left her mouth.

Helwys frowned at her. "I would not say so, my lady. He speaks most confidently."

Isabelle did not wish to discuss this, or to think about

Simon, or the sight of his strong body. Yet this conversation had made her do just that.

A male voice intruded on her thoughts, "My lady."

Isabelle would know that voice anywhere. She moved to the door of the tent and looked out. "Sir Fredrick."

The knight did not face her as he said, "My lord Kelsey would speak with you in his tent."

Isabelle nodded. "You may tell him I shall attend him in a moment."

He bowed even as she ducked back inside. She looked to Helwys, who had begun to wring her hands. "I am going to speak with my father."

Both of them knew the likely purpose of this summons.

The maid said nothing to this but continued to wring her hands as Isabelle left. At the door of her father's tent, she faltered, her mouth opening but no sound issuing forth. She wanted nothing so much than to run away.

There was no telling what she might have done had Sir Fredrick, whom she had not noted hovering nearby, not spoken for her. "The lady Isabelle has come, my lord."

Her sire answered from within, "You may enter, Isabelle." There was no emotion in his voice from which to gage his intent.

Taking a deep breath Isabelle forced herself to don the mask of cool indifference that served her so well when dealing with her father. She entered the tent with squared shoulders and a deliberately unconcerned expression.

Candles lit the dim interior and she saw that her father was seated on a low stool. He was sipping sparingly from a silver cup, which he lowered as his gaze came to rest on her. Isabelle was rocked by a sense of loneliness in those eyes such as she had never imagined, but it was so fleeting that she told herself it could not have been anything but a trick of the flickering light. For when she looked more closely his eyes were, as she was accustomed to seeing them, without expression.

"Isabelle."

She refrained from sighing and the effort to retain her equilibrium was made doubly difficult by that fleeting impression, no matter how false. "You sent for me, Father?"

He smiled, though there was no warmth in that smile. "I would have you prepare yourself for Warleigh."

Even though she had known this could be the case, shock rolled through her. She had just met the man this very morn and his resentment of the marriage was more than clear. Her tone was hoarse with surprise and uncertainty as she said, "You mean for me to bed with him?"

Her father watched her closely now. "Would you have me say that I do not, daughter?"

A chill rolled over her at his tone and assessing expression. She had made a terrible mistake in betraying so much. Self-preservation required an immediate recovery of her accustomed pose of indifference. When she was twelve her father had seen her turn away from the sight of him slitting the throat of a deer during hunting. He had forced her to watch each and every time thereafter, telling her she must not shy away from anything, must be strong enough within herself to let nothing disturb her. He must have no reason to feel she had not learned this lesson.

She faced him squarely, her voice betraying none of her inner turmoil. "I am only tired from traveling, Father. I have no preference in the matter of Warleigh. I would prepare myself if that is *your* desire.''

His gaze raked her. ''You truly are without feeling, aren't you, Isabelle? Though I did have to think on how you would best be trained you have taken to my guidance well.'' For a moment there was something strange and unreadable in that gaze as there had been so many times over the course of her life. Then he said, ''I am gladdened to see this. It means you would never allow emotion, love, nor hate to make you act rashly. I have seen to it that you will not allow passion for anyone or anything drive you.''

She nodded, holding the hurt engendered by his assessment to her tightly, keeping her gaze level. She knew that, to him, this was indeed a compliment. ''I would do what pleases you, Father.''

He smiled that cool little smile which told her he was indeed happy with her in his way. ''Then I will tell you what pleases me in this.''

She waited, her insides twisting with anxiety but giving no hint of it.

Her father smiled again. ''Methinks it would serve me very well for you to bed Warleigh. You, being the dutiful daughter that you are, Isabelle, will please me by getting yourself with a son. In the event that Warleigh was to meet with an untimely end his holdings would fall to the lad, who would do quite well under my capable tutelage. And your dower, which was not discussed as a term of this marriage, also remains in my hands. Indeed this union with Warleigh could prove quite profitable.''

Isabelle was able to hide her disgust with only the greatest of determination. Her father would not raise her son in his image. He would not do as he had attempted to do to her, trying to wipe out all emotion. For though he had succeeded in teaching her to hide her feelings, he had not destroyed them. Isabelle was still capable of loving and she intended to shower all the love she had buried inside her on her own son. She would be the one to teach him what was right and wrong, that true strength lay in not being afraid to love. He would be like the Dragon.

She thought she had managed to keep her reaction to his pronouncement hidden as she always had, until her father said, "What is it I see in those pretty eyes, Isabelle?" There was no mistaking the surprise in his tone. "Reassure me that is not rebellion."

Quickly she pulled herself up short, the accustomed mask falling firmly into place as she met his eyes without wavering. "Nay, why would you think such a thing? What would I rebel against?"

"You are not concerned about the possibility of your husband meeting an early end? It simply may prove necessary in the event that the king ever allows him to return to Avington. Now that I have pointed out his plotting against the crown to King John, I will be his target. It is only wise to secure the succession of the lands as soon as possible at any rate. Even if it does not prove necessary for me to act against him, a man who is the enemy of many, as Warleigh is, makes many enemies. He could meet his death at any time and the king may wish to take Avington for himself if there is no heir. Why not assure our own claim?"

She continued to look directly into those assessing eyes as she took in this information. She could only think that it was her father's pleasure at the thought of attaining Avington that made him so forthcoming.

She realized her father had fallen silent, that he was

watching her. Quickly she said, "Clearly Warleigh can see to himself." In spite of her father's revelation that Warleigh was not innocent in this, she felt a rush of regret. She soothed herself with the thought that her father had implied he would be safe as long as he did not return to Avington. At the same time she was aware of a certainty that for all his acquiescence to her father's will thus far, Simon Warleigh might not be so easily killed.

All unaware her father nodded. "Very good."

She heard the lack of emotion in her own voice as she answered, "Do I not always do as you wish, Father?"

Obviously feeling too much praise had already been handed out this day, he frowned. "And you will continue to do so if you know what is good for you, wench. I can devise an effective method of teaching obedience whenever it might prove necessary as well as taking back those pretty frocks and jewels should I feel you are not suitably grateful."

She looked at the floor, not wanting him to see the immediate rise of anger and anxiety in her gaze. Neither would she tell him that the fine clothing and jewels meant nothing to her and never would.

Someday she would be free of him and the steel bands of his control. She would have her own life, would be free to love. In order to meet that end she must first have a child. And to do that she must appear to fall in with her father's plans.

Her father interrupted her thoughts as he said, "I will have Warleigh informed that he is to attend you." She could hear the satisfaction he felt at being able to tell the other man what he must do.

Though Isabelle knew a momentary rush of sympathy

for Simon Warleigh she did not dwell upon it. He was, as she had said, surely capable of looking after himself.

It was she who must steel herself to accept the coming events. Her husband was a stranger. Her feelings of unease were not lessened when thoughts of the coming night brought a sudden and vivid memory of his powerful warrior's body.

Simon looked up from his roasted meat in surprise as Kelsey's knight stepped before him. "Sirrah?

The knight made no pretence at civility, his eyes dark with hostility. "My lord Kelsey has bade me inform you that you are to attend the lady Isabelle in her tent."

Simon stiffened. He was aware of all the eyes that focused on him. And in that moment he knew that he could not debate this matter here before the men, and certainly not with Kelsey's knight. No woman, even the daughter of his enemy, should be shown so little respect.

Yet Simon need not have worried on that score. The knight did not linger to gain his opinion on the subject. He swung around and strode away without another word.

Slowly Simon stood. He continued to be aware of the eyes that had followed him as he left the fire. He paused, taking a deep breath as he came to the entrance of her tent.

He had no intention of changing his mind in this. How, he wondered, would he convey his position without offering offense to the woman he had taken as his bride this very morn? That the marriage had taken place under duress did not change the fact that he had no wish to shame her.

He took another deep breath, then spoke softly. "It is Simon Warleigh. I beg entrance."

The husky reply was a moment in coming. "You may enter, my lord."

Simon stepped inside and halted. There in the center of small chamber was Isabelle. His wife.

She looked so beautiful in the light of the candles that for a moment he wished his intention was something completely different from what it was. Her ebony hair had been left in a rippling curtain that fell to her hips. When she shifted slightly beneath his regard the light revealed the hint of deep fire that gave it an unexpected warmth. His gaze moved down over the white shift that was formed from a fabric so fine that he was given the most tantalizing glimpses of the creamy flesh that lay beneath.

The sight of her brought every part of him to life. Deliberately he looked away. He did not know how it could be but there was only the barest hint of huskiness to betray his feelings when he said, "I was told that you were expecting me."

She answered softly, her voice telling him nothing of her feelings. "My father bade me to make myself ready."

Though she did not say so he had the sudden realization that she had been informed of her father's wishes with as little care as he. He took a step closer to her, seeing a way out for both of them. "Isabelle, you need not feel that you must go through with this now. After all, we do not even know one another."

She turned away, her slender shoulders seeming to tense. "I am prepared to do as my father has bid me."

Cool, remote Isabelle. Other than the stiffness in her

shoulders there was no sign of reaction in her. It was as if they were speaking of the weather.

"I see." Simon repressed the urge to run a weary hand over his face. What a day it had been. He must find some way to stay out of his marriage bed while still offering his unwanted bride a way to retain her dignity. In spite of her being his enemy's daughter, it greatly mattered to him that he do so. She had done him no ill.

He was not blind to the fatigue in his voice as he said, "Do you have something to drink? I find I have a great thirst."

Without looking at him, she moved to the low table that held the candles and lifted a pitcher and cup. With what seemed more than usual care, she poured the wine and moved toward him.

Simon was hard-pressed to keep from noting the way the light silhouetted her slim and beguiling form as she passed in front of it. He kept his gaze on the cup as she moved closer and held it out. He found himself wiping away the sweat that beaded on his upper lip as the scent of jasmine and the warm scent of woman wafted over him as he reached for the cup with the other hand. His gaze fell to the shadow between the curves of her breasts, which was just visible at the neckline of her gown.

He forced himself to look up, and came into direct contact with those violet eyes. They watched him with an expression that was impossible to read as her tongue flicked out to dampen her lips. The sight of the moisture on that sweet mouth made him want to press his own to it, made his body tighten.

He forced his gaze away, raised the cup to his mouth and took a long drink.

As he did so Isabelle stepped back and Simon felt a modicum of relief. But no more than that.

He took another long drink of the dark-red wine, which reminded him of the warm lights in her black hair. Angry with himself for this unexplained weakness, Simon turned to her and spoke with more force than he would have if he were not fighting such an intense battle within himself. "I can not lie with you, Isabelle."

She stiffened. "What did you say, my lord?"

He took a deep breath. "It is not my intention to consummate the marriage this night."

There was a hint of shock in her tone. "You will not consummate the marriage!"

He frowned. "Nay."

She seemed somewhat dazed as she went on, "Do you not find me pleasing, my lord?"

His body tightened anew. He did indeed find her pleasing, more than he would have imagined possible. But he would not have her know that. "Although your intention to obey your father is clear, I say again that we do not even know one another. We would not have met until this very morn had it not been for an odd stroke of fortune that brought me along the road at the same moment your wagon had lost a wheel." Feeling those wide lavender eyes upon him he found himself telling her far more than he had intended, found himself revealing the truth. "You know that this marriage was forced upon me. Your father is my enemy. He has denounced me falsely to the king. Am I to fall in with his desires as if I have no will of my own? I may be forced to remain under his guard to keep from having my lands—not to mention my head—taken from me. I can not be forced to bed with his daughter."

She swung on him then. "You can not be forced. It

is I who have been wronged in this. You but pay the price of your own madness in plotting against the crown.''

Simon took a step toward her. ''It is true enough I have been found guilty of that. But I committed no such crime. I am responsible for my own stupidity in under-estimating your father. Had I been wiser I would have been far more careful in my efforts against him.''

''What are you saying?''

''That it is your father who was the target of my ill will, not the king. And well he knows it.''

Confusion creased her delicate brow. ''Why would Father lie about such a thing?'

Simon arched a dark brow. ''If John believes me to be his enemy then he is my enemy. Your father thought that John would have my head. He would then be rid of me and he could petition the crown for the right to oversee Avington. Neither he, nor I, ever foresaw the situation as it stands. He does not want me for a son-by-marriage and but seeks to exert his control over me by insisting that I bed you.''

Isabelle stared at him with wide eyes, so many emotions passing through their lavender depths that he could not begin to read them. ''I do not know…''

He pressed on. ''As he has control over you.''

Isabelle started, ''He does not have…''

His gaze met her painful one and he saw that she could not finish the denial. Her lovely face was filled with confusion and she took deep breaths in the struggle to control her emotions. ''Then why would you offer yourself to a man whom you do not know or want? Was it some strange command of your father's that sent you to the river today?''

She blanched. ''Dear heaven, you saw me.''

He took a deep breath, "Aye, I saw you."

She looked down at her hands. "He did not send me."

"Are you telling me that you…" He stopped, recalling how she had looked back at him that first morning when he had seen her on the road. He put a finger beneath her chin, forcing her to face him. "That first day I saw you looking back at me but I never imagined…"

Isabelle raised her head high, that cool mask slipping easily into place. "I will not deny that I did look on you with some favor that day. But you are not to flatter yourself, my lord. I did not know who you were then. I did not realize you would be at the stream but when I saw you and I knew that I might have to…" She shrugged. "I thought to prepare myself to face the ordeal before me."

"Ordeal?"

She held his gaze. "How else could I view it?" It was as if her outburst of emotion had never been.

"How else, indeed?" His lips tightened with annoyance, though this revelation should please him. He did not wish for Kelsey's daughter to desire him. "Yet you would bed with a stranger simply because your father commands it."

Cooly she continued to face him. "Why would I do otherwise? He is my father and it is my duty to be obedient. He would be very…disappointed were I to do other than what he has bid me."

He heard the concern in her voice, concern for the devious and undeserving Kelsey. "Even after what I have just told you of his falsely accusing me before the king?"

Those lavender eyes gave away nothing, "I have only your word for that."

Simon told himself there was no point in further attempting to convince her. He did not care to whom she gave her unquestioning obedience. He had no wish to gain her loyalty, or anything else, for that matter. He was in fact nothing but a fool for having told her that his target had been her father. He knew it would not matter if she did go to her father with this information, as Kelsey already knew the truth. What troubled him was his lack of self-control with Isabelle, especially when she could seem so vulnerable one moment and so cold the next.

Yet in spite of the return of that abominable coldness, he could not forget that momentary lapse as they had spoken of her father. Nor could he forget the fact that she had admitted to looking on him with favor that first day before discovering who he was. For the sake of what might have been if they were two different people, Simon had to offer her the option of not telling her father she had failed her duty. She could take it or not, as she pleased.

"*Your father* need not know we have not obeyed his orders." He knew that his anger with her father, her, and yes, even irritation with himself for giving in to this impulse to help the frustrating wench, was revealed by his tone but he was past caring at the moment. "I will remain here in your tent, but will sleep upon a separate blanket."

Isabelle felt shame wash through her in a sickening wave. She could hardly believe what had just occurred here. He had refused her, had made it clear that as the daughter of his enemy, he would never want her. And she, dull-wit that she was, had gone so far as to offer herself to him, had in fact insisted upon his compliance as if it were not her own maidenhead they discussed until he offered the solution of pretending that he had bedded her.

And worse than that, she had allowed herself to become overwrought in his presence. What about this man could so make her lose control of herself?

How had things gone so dreadfully awry? Surely it was fear of what her father would do if she did not obey him.

The strange feelings that had risen inside her as she had handed Simon his cup of wine meant nothing.

After her father had informed her that she was to prepare herself for her wedding night, she had done just that. All the while she had told herself over and over again that her trepidation was unreasonable.

She had told herself that she was married now. Though it might be difficult to give herself to the man who was her husband perhaps it would not take long before she found herself with child. It had been these thoughts that had made it possible for her to behave calmly, to act as if what was about to occur was of no more import than a casual invitation to dine.

In one fell swoop, the proud Simon Warleigh had robbed her of everything she had planned for so long.

Isabelle pushed her sadness to the deepest darkest core of herself. As she always had. She raised her head high. "Do not trouble yourself over me, my lord. You need not remain here when 'tis clearly distasteful to you. Pray go on your way."

He frowned. "I would not have you encounter difficulty with your father over this."

As she spoke she was aware of the fact that her voice betrayed the slightest trace of bitterness though she did try to hide it. "I do not require your charity."

Simon Warleigh looked at her closely, thoughtful. She raised her own brows, holding his gaze without wavering as he said, "I am not offering charity, Isabelle. I would not presume."

What she was to make of that she had no idea, so she concentrated on what she did know. That she did not wish for him to know how devastated she was at his rejection of her. "We understand one another then."

Even as she said it she knew it was not true. She did not understand anything about this man and wished more than anything in her life that he would go and leave her to nurse her wounds in peace.

"Nonetheless, I will stay." He went to her bed, the bed Helwys had turned down for the two of them. He hesitated as he reached down to take one of the furs. "We should blow out the candles. Our shadows may be visible on the wall."

Realizing that he would not be swayed, and that arguing further might inadvertently reveal all that she would keep to herself, she nodded sharply. Isabelle went to the bedside, meaning to blow out the candle, needing the darkness to hide the pain that made her eyes sting with unshed tears. Unfortunately their eyes inadvertently met as her unwanted husband swung around to blow out the candle at the same moment that she bent over it. As those warm brown eyes met her damp ones, he stopped, his gaze becoming puzzled, then uncertain.

Quickly, turning away from Simon, she blew out the candle and dropped down onto the bed. It was no great feat to get inside the bed furs. Or it would not have been if she had not been shaking so badly from the top of her head to the tips of her feet.

Simon seemed to stand there for a long moment. "Isabelle?"

She had to swallow around the lump of sadness in her throat, but was pleased with the evenness of her voice. "Yes?"

His voice was too gentle—kind in a way that was unexpected and surprising. "Are you all right?"

Isabelle felt a rush of yearning take her. If only she could believe in that kindness. She knew that she could not allow herself such weakness. This man was no more trustworthy than any other. Although she had no doubt that her father had indeed lied about him to King John, he had admitted to plotting against her father.

Closing her eyes she prayed that he could not hear how deeply his gentleness affected her. "I am fine. Only weary. Please, go to bed."

Yet Simon Warleigh stood there for another long moment before finally moving away. It was not until his deep and even breathing sometime later told her that he was asleep that she allowed her rigid body to relax.

Though hot tears scalded her cheeks Isabelle made not a sound, crying out her misery in utter silence. She cried as she had not cried since her beloved uncle's death when she was eight. Then she had cried for the loss of the only one who had ever shown her love. She had paid for those tears by being locked in her chambers for days until her father was certain she could control herself. Now she cried for the loss of a dream, her hope of having a child, which was no less painful for all that it had not been a reality.

* * *

Simon rose before Isabelle awakened. Leaving the tent in complete silence, he stepped out into the crisp morning.

Simon did not meet any of the eyes that focused upon him. It was not that he felt the men would know he had not bedded his wife. He simply did not like the notion of them thinking about Isabelle and him.

Or perhaps if he was honest he would have to admit that he did not care for the images their knowing looks might conjure in his own mind. They were the very same images that had plagued him until he'd heard the soft but unmistakable sounds of Isabelle crying.

Those tears had moved him more fully even than the offer of her body. And truth be told that had been temptation enough for any man.

He could not allow himself to forget that Isabelle was Kelsey's daughter. Her crying could have been based on no more than frustration at being told nay for perhaps the first time in her life, in spite of his impression that her sorrow had been genuine.

At that moment Simon unintentionally looked up into the face of the man who had brought about all this chaos. Kelsey's hate-filled but triumphant gaze swept him and Simon met it with deliberate indifference.

For Isabelle's sake he was prepared to keep the secret that he had not bedded her. Yet as he swung away to ready himself for the day's journey, Simon realized that Kelsey's attention on this matter did seem somewhat curious.

Why was he so very adamant that Simon bed his daughter?

As they continued on their way to Dragonwick, Isabelle not once looking in his direction, he kept on hearing the barely audible sound of her misery replaying itself again and again his mind. He was beset by feelings of pity.

Which, looking at her as she rode atop the black mare beside her father, seemed utterly and completely mad. Isabelle Kelsey was the only daughter and heir to one of the most powerful men in England. She was lovely beyond description, obviously doted on with her clothes and jewels.

Was she not?

Simon was aware of a growing sense of uncertainty.

Haps there would be no harm in an offering of friendship. But not until they had reached Dragonwick where Kelsey would have other business to occupy his attention.

For reasons he did not yet understand, Simon was loath to let his temporary father-by-marriage know of any change in his relationship with the woman. Even if it was only friendship.

Chapter Five

"May I enter?"

A surprised Isabelle looked up from the sewing on her lap to see her husband standing there in the open doorway of her chamber. Until this moment he had made no effort to speak to her since the unpleasantness between them, not even when he'd come last eve to sleep on the floor of her tent. Nor had he addressed her since their arrival at Dragonwick late this very afternoon.

And Isabelle had no wish for him to do so. She wished to avoid Simon Warleigh whenever possible.

Isabelle had sent Helwys to tell her father she was too fatigued to attend the midday meal, which they had not taken upon the road, being so close to Dragonwick. Surely even her father would not find it odd and would not guess her true intent.

She stood, feeling a rush of discomfort with the notion of her husband's being in her room. The exchange between them in her tent had affected her far more deeply than she cared to admit. Throughout the journey home it had been all she could do to meet his coolly assessing brown eyes. And not wholly because of her guilt at keeping their failure to consummate the marriage a secret.

She felt unexplainably hurt by Simon's rejection of her, and thus vulnerable. Isabelle told herself that this made no sense. She did not care what he thought of her. It was the fact that there would now be no child that plagued her.

A streak of rebellion, and yes, pride, moved her to speak casually. "My lord, do enter."

Warleigh watched her, those mahogany eyes unreadable, for a moment that seemed to stretch on for far too long. He came forward onto the thick carpet that marked the center portion of the room. She saw the way he studied the tapestries upon the walls, the fine carpet beneath his feet and the lush rose velvet hangings of the bed.

His gaze moved from the bed to her. For unknown reasons Isabelle shivered.

Whatever was the matter with her? With determination she inclined her head with careful civility as he came to a halt before her. "My lord Warleigh?"

He arched a dark brow. "'Tis a formal greeting for a husband. Surely, you may call me Simon, even in these untenable circumstances."

"You have made no effort to speak to me for two days, even last eve when you came to make your bed on the floor of my tent. Why would you expect aught else but formality?"

He shrugged wide shoulders, his mobile mouth twisting wryly, seeming unexpectedly uncertain for one brief moment before that unshakable confidence fell back into place. "I thought, now that we have arrived at Dragonwick, it might behoove us to get to know one another a little."

Isabelle was hard-pressed to contain her chagrin. She did not want to become familiar with this man. He had already upset the delicate balance of her peace so very thoroughly, and seemingly without trying. Beyond that, what more was there to know of him? He was her husband, yet not. He could have been the means to her most cherished hope. Yet he had been the death of it instead.

But suddenly she realized something that this might mean. Did this overture indicate that he had rethought the notion of their coming together?

The memory of how he had looked that first evening in the stream, his body all gold and glistening in the evening sunlight made her tingle afresh as it had in that moment. Immediately Isabelle dragged her thoughts back from that unacceptable path.

Her gaze raking his, she spoke coldly. "You are not thinking that I will now…"

His brown eyes widened. "Nay, not that."

She told herself that it was relief she felt in her belly as she forced herself to go on. "That is well, for I would not have you now."

The tightening of his jaw was all the reaction she could detect as he replied, "I would not expect it. Nor do I wish it."

Though Isabelle was angry with this intractable man the words cut deep. With an act of will she held that long-practiced shield in place. "Then to what do I owe this unexpected overture, my lord Warleigh?"

He smiled thinly. "Simon."

"Simon," she replied without inflection.

Unaware he motioned toward the bench before the fire. "May I sit?"

She inclined her head, resuming her own seat as he

did so, realizing as she looked down that her hands were trembling. Not wishing for Simon to see this, Isabelle busied herself with smoothing the silver embroidery on the sleeve of her lavender velvet kirtle.

Isabelle could feel him watching her, but did not look up as he said, "I know this must be a strange situation for you. As it is for me."

She did not disagree. "Aye, strange enough." She was very pleased when her tone remained even.

The silence that followed was heavy enough to try her equanimity further. When she forced herself to look into Simon Warleigh's disturbingly handsome face, he was frowning. He spoke in a tone of disapproval. "You can not truly be as cool and unmoved by life as you appear? That first night in your tent you…you can not deny that you became quite angry with me for a moment."

Isabelle stiffened, but retained her equilibrium in spite of her irritation with this man for speaking of things she preferred not to speak of. "You may rest assured that it is not my way and will not happen again. You, sir, are not of such great import to me."

He arched dark brows over eyes that bore the slightest trace of chagrin. "Perhaps I am not, yet surely the circumstances we find ourselves in are. It would be naught but normal for you to be overset at the events of the past days. At marrying a complete stranger."

She looked at her hands again. "I never expected my life would be any other way." She glanced up at him, not knowing why she was telling him the truth. "When one has no expectations, one can not be disappointed."

He seemed a bit taken aback by her words. Then his expression, amazingly enough, seemed to grow sympathetic as he spoke softly, "'Tis unfortunate indeed when a lovely young woman has so little hope for her own future. I regret that your feelings were not taken into account by the crown. Were I your father, I would have seen to that, no matter how determined the king might be.''

As she looked into those warm brown eyes, Isabelle felt a wave of doubt about her life, about the necessity of remaining distant from others. The immediate yearning that throbbed in her breast made it suddenly difficult to breathe. What would it be like to put her faith in this strong man, to rely on anyone beside herself for the first time since her uncle died?

Her uncle.

Horror swept through her. She could not allow Simon Warleigh to breach her defenses. He had already shown that he was not to be trusted when he had betrayed The Dragon all those years ago. She had no notion of what he would do with any confidences she might inadvertently reveal. He could reveal anything she might say to her father, even if it were unintentionally.

Quickly and with the coolness born of both desperation and long practice she said, ''Have no pity for me, my lord.'' She was forced to look away as she finished, fearing he would read the lie she was about to tell in her eyes. ''I trust my father's judgment in all things and would not wish to decide such an important matter for myself.''

Glancing up from beneath the cover of her lashes she saw that Warleigh was now scowling, as his disdainful gaze swept her. ''Forgive me for being so foolish, madam. I see that you are indeed your father's daughter.''

She had a sudden urge to erase that disapproval from his face. Yet she held to her self-reliance. She would not fall victim to the strange influence this man seemed to have with her.

Simon stood. "I have come in error. I had thought I would try, at least in some small part, to make amends for I did hear you crying on the night of our marriage and thought…"

A gasp escaped Isabelle as a wave of horror tightened her belly at the mere notion of Simon Warleigh's being privy to her weakness. Desperately she denied it. "Crying? You are mistaken, sir. I do not cry." She was reminded of the time her father locked her in her chambers for three weeks when she had cried after her uncle had died.

Lips tight, Simon quirked a dark brow. "Again I beg your forgiveness, my lady. You will not find me rude, I hope, for leaving you now. I find I have no more stomach for conversation with the daughter of Kelsey, even if she be my wife."

She sucked in a breath through her nose, but forced back the retort that sprang to her tongue. Isabelle could not let him goad her into saying more than she wished to, into showing any more hints of weakness. She would think on nothing save the numbing relief that he was leaving.

He paused at the door without looking back at her. "One last thing." He pointed off vaguely to his right. "I will make a bed on this floor as I did in your tent."

Heart thudding, she stood. "But…"

Still he did not look at her. "Do not worry yourself. My actions are not for your sake. Though I can not fathom why your father would be so interested in my bedding you I would have him think me acquiescent to his wishes. I mean to return to Avington at some point and peace with him will no doubt be a requirement of that end.'' He turned to her then, his eyes hard. ''In spite of your decision not to have me, I trust you will not inform your father of our arrangement. For to do so would entail revealing your own part in keeping the truth from him thus far.''

She bit her lip, not willing to tell him that she would not have told her father at any rate.

It would not trouble her for Simon to believe them at odds. It was in fact just the way she wanted things to rest between them. She was far easier with that notion than anything more unfamiliar to her.

How could she bear his intrusion here, in the one place that had been her own? She had not even considered that they would be expected to share a chamber on a regular basis, though clearly she should have. Her father had made his desire for her to have a child most explicit. He could not know she had deceived him. Simon would not trouble her greatly. He would rise and leave each morn before she did. As he had done on the journey here.

Isabelle nodded sharply in acquiescence.

With an equally sharp nod of reply, Simon Warleigh turned his back on her.

Simon strode across the chamber and through the open door. Grabbing the latch he made to slam it closed behind him. And wrenched the latch right out of the hands of the serving woman who stumbled forward. Even as the door slammed shut she fell into him with wide frightened eyes.

Simon caught her as she sputtered, ''Oh...I... forgive...''

Quickly Simon drew her a distance from the door,

which though heavy might not be proof against sound. ''What were you doing?''

Her hair fell across her eyes and when she reached to swipe at it she stumbled again, grabbing at him. Again he caught her. ''Did Kelsey send you to spy upon us?''

The horror in the maid's gaze told him this was not the case. ''Nay, my lord. I would not betray my lady. I was but...'' Defiance lit her eyes. ''You must not hurt her.''

Here at last in this dismal place he found a sign of goodness. He raised his hand to wipe the hair from the maid's face and she cringed in fear. Taking a deep breath, Simon carefully held her shoulders with both hands. ''There is no need to be afraid of me. I would not strike you.''

She looked up at him with uncertainty. ''Yes, my lord. Forgive me, my lord.''

He scowled. ''For what? How can I fault you for being protective of your mistress? She should count herself fortunate someone cares for her despite her cold nature.''

The maid's chin tilted. ''My lady is not cold.''

Simon eyed her. ''Your loyal defense of your mistress is admirable, but seems somewhat misplaced.''

The maid opened her mouth, then closed it again without debating him. But her gaze was far from happy.

Shaking his head Simon stepped back and with a sharp nod moved on. The maid was wise to keep her own counsel if she thought to defend her lady.

Marriage to the contrary and cold Isabelle was proving as difficult as he had feared. He thought of the way she had looked at him when she imagined that he might have come to her because he wished to bed her. Those beautiful eyes could not have been more horrified. Damn her.

He was wasting his time and hers in attempting to talk with Isabelle—in being here at all. Frustration made each hour at Dragonwick seem a week.

All he wished to do was go home, to take hold of Avington and look after it the way his father and brother would have him do. They had been so much alike in body and mind. Never would they have risked Avington by becoming embroiled in such a predicament as he was now in.

He must be patient, as they would have been. He had been hasty and careless in his determination to seek vengeance against Kelsey. He would go slowly, wisely, even though he was more resolved than ever to see Kelsey repaid for his ills against others. This thought kept him from stalking out of the keep, calling his men and riding out of this prison. For there was no doubt in his mind that did he wish to leave none of them could hold him here.

Yet his frustration rode high and he knew he must do something or explode. He went down to the great hall, which was dim on this fall afternoon with only its one enormous hearth and the high arrow slits along the outside wall to illuminate it. Simon found Wylie and Sir Edmund where he had left them, at one of the well-scrubbed trestle tables when he had so foolishly gone to speak to Isabelle after seeing her father leave the keep. The large chamber was not well populated at this time of day and those who were present seemed to be keeping their distance from the newcomers.

Running an assessing glance over them, Simon realized they would likely be no different had the strangers not been present. Though their clothing was clean and in decent repair there seemed no joy in Kelsey's folk and they went about their duties with undue gravity. Recalling the backhand Kelsey's squire had received for not being able to control the unruly stallion, Simon could imagine why.

Gruffly Simon commanded his men to come along with him and to bring their weapons. They obeyed immediately, though he could see the uncertainty on their faces.

Simon went to the enormous oak door, then down the wide stone steps that led to the courtyard. He then strode off to the left of the main gate. He knew exactly where he was bound. Going right would have taken him to the stables. One of the things that so irritated him was his vivid recollection of each and every corner of this keep. He and Christian and Jarrod had left no crevice unexplored in their boyish exuberance, in their pride and wonder at their positions as squires to The Dragon.

Simon had been eleven when he arrived at Dragonwick and nervous at leaving home, though he had tried to hide it. He found a second home here as well as a foster father who was worthy and willing to take his father's place as mentor and teacher between regular visits to Avington.

These thoughts brought on a fresh and fearsome rush of frustration and anger. He quickened his pace. Wylie and Sir Edmund followed, though their expressions were perplexed.

Once the practice field came into sight, the two seemed to realize what he was about. They smiled as Simon moved onto the field and drew his sword.

Sir Edmund met him eagerly. It was as if he, too, felt a need to expend some pent-up energy.

Kelsey's men who were on the field stopped what

they were doing to watch them with wary gazes. Simon ignored them, setting his mind on the clash of sword against sword, the flexing of muscle and bone.

Sometime later, Sir Edmund cried off, wiping a hand across his face, which was covered in dirt and sweat. Simon looked about in frustration, his gaze sliding over Wylie quickly. Though he was not fresh he did not wish to fight the squire who was still far from equal to him.

Frowning Simon ran a hand over his tunic, which was heavy with sweat, realizing that his hair and clothing were gritty with the dirt that clung to that dampness. But he was not yet ready to quit. The last few days had afforded him far too much in the way of frustrations and naught by way of relieving them.

"Will no one give me contest?"

He smiled with relief when one of Kelsey's men, obviously a soldier by his garb, stepped forth.

Sir Edmund frowned and reached out to put a hand on his arm. He spoke so softly that only Simon and Wylie, who hovered close by, could hear, "Do not fight him, my lord. Not surrounded by enemies as we are. 'Twould be too easy a way to see you dead."

He could hear the scorn in Wylie's voice as the boy added his own warning. "Aye, trust him not, my lord."

Simon was suddenly reminded of Kelsey's words to Sir Fredrick when he'd put his hand to his sword hilt on their first night upon the road. Even if Kelsey did mean to move against Simon he was not yet ready to do so. He replied coolly, not wishing to rile the already easily riled Wylie, "He may not find it so easy to do away with me."

The squire's animosity changed to bravado. "Aye, my lord. You will surely show them what we are made of at last."

Simon eyed Kelsey's man, who was a giant in an ill-fitting tunic of rough spun wool, but there was a keen glint to his steely gaze that told Simon of a quick mind. There was also animosity in that gaze.

Simon cared not, for he was in no way surprised. Perhaps it would afford him a better fight. He nodded. "Come forward."

The man smiled and raised his sword. Simon did the same and the clash began.

He felt a renewed rush of energy, knowing he would fight until he was too exhausted to recall that he must bide his time here. He would fight until he was too exhausted to recall that he was married to the coldest, most beautiful and desirable woman he had ever known.

It did not take long for him to be certain that his foe had entered the contest with more than common eagerness. There seemed to be far too much anger and resentment in those gray eyes, which burned into Simon's each time they grappled closely.

Simon had fought many men in his life and this fellow's purpose went beyond what he would expect in one who was acting out of loyal service to his overlord. Something, some inner sense of knowing, told Simon there was something personal in this attack, though it did not appear as if it were meant to kill, but to punish.

He knew not when the crowd began to gather, but Simon gradually became aware that he and his adversary had attracted the notice of the castle folk. It was clear that their support lay with his opponent, for each time the large man landed a particularly brutal blow a sigh of relief seemed to ripple through them.

This only served to make Simon more determined to best him. Yet the man met each thrust of his sword, offering a counterattack for each one Simon launched.

When Simon finally faltered against the giant, he heard a loud gasp. Unable to seek out the source of that seemingly horrified sound, he attempted to raise his sword to, at least partially, block the descending blow.

He was amazed when his blade met air rather than blade. His opponent's gaze widened as one of his legs seemed to give out and he fell onto his back, his sword twisted beneath him. Simon quickly found his own stance once more as he approached the fallen knight. He knew it had been more luck that the other man tripped than skill that had aided his own cause.

He was ready to have it done. Leaning over the other man with his sword, he said, "Do you yield?"

The gray eyes seared his, and the harsh whisper that emerged caught him completely off guard. "Why did you betray The Dragon?"

Shock made Simon reply in an equally harsh whisper. "Dear God, sirrah, would that I had not. I have regretted it each day of my life and will until the last breath leaves my body." He held the man's gaze. "I commend you for your love for him, though I must admit I am surprised to find one still loyal to him here and now."

The man watched Simon with equal intensity. "Haps there is a reason that is not readily seen."

Simon raised his brows. "Haps there is more to the tale of my betrayal of my lord than is readily seen."

A new expression emerged in those eyes, a measuring that Simon did not falter from. "Aye, perhaps."

Simon reached out a hand.

After another long hesitation the other man took it. Simon pulled him up.

As he did so he looked over his shoulder and directly into the lavender eyes of his wife. Simon, still charged with the energy of combat, met that gaze with challenge.

Isabelle raised her head high, raking him with a now unreadable gaze and turned away. It amazed him in no small amount that she would be here watching him, lest it be with gleeful hope that he would be felled. Yet there had been no glee in those lovely eyes.

Even as she stalked from the field he had a sudden memory of that horrified gasp. It could not have been Isabelle. She would likely be very relieved to see him dead.

Simon was distracted from the sight of her slender backside by his opponent's voice, which was now loud enough for all present to hear. "You have fought hard and acquitted yourself well, my lord. Let us now find a cup to quench our thirst."

Simon was surprised at the sudden change of topic as well as the invitation. Even if this man no longer considered him an enemy, his master did. Simon recalled the fellow's remark concerning his presence here at Dragonwick, that the reason for it might not be easily seen. Yet he knew 'twould be best if he did not remark on it. If the man's loyalty did not lie with Kelsey, he would know there could be nothing but danger for him in admitting as much. And in spite of the moment of understanding that had just passed between them, he was unlikely to trust Simon with a confidence such as that.

Simon accepted this unexpected civility in the spirit in which it appeared to be offered. He nodded as he said, "Clearly you know that I am Warleigh. I would have your own name."

The fellow bowed his head slightly. "Jack, my lord."

Simon inclined his head, the name holding no particular meaning for him, as it was not uncommon. He would simply have to wait for the other man to volunteer more. If he did. "Well then, Jack. I find I do have a thirst and accept your offer most readily."

Jack jerked his own silver-streaked head. "Good enough then, my lord." He looked to what remained of the crowd that had obviously dispersed once the fighting had ceased with no one worse for the clash. "Are any of the rest of you to join us?"

Most of the other men stepped back. Only one nodded as he addressed the giant, "I'll join ye, Jack."

Jack grinned. "Very well, Anton, the more for us. I've a great thirst after getting myself throttled."

Simon shook his head, a rueful smile twisting his lips. "Throttled? You acquitted yourself more than fairly."

The fellow nodded modestly, though he did cast Simon another assessing gaze. Simon motioned to Wylie and Sir Edmund who stood nearby. "I hope you do not mind if they join us as well. They have precious little else to do here."

Jack bowed politely. "They may suit themselves. Or indeed you, my lord, as you are their master."

This was indeed true, but Simon was again surprised at this man's unexpected recognition of his authority and position. Especially as it seemed to be given so easily after there had been so much animosity in him at the initiation of their fight.

He found himself frowning thoughtfully as he turned and strode toward the hall. The others followed.

Once they were seated at a trestle table not far from the entrance to the chamber with frothy cups of the brew in their hands, the man named Jack again seemed to study Simon closely. Simon could no longer contain his own curiosity. "Why do you watch me thusly?"

The man looked away shrugging, but seemed to speak carefully, "It is that seeing you, speaking with you this day has made me think of many things." His eyes met Simon's. "I remember you well, my lord Warleigh, though you were but a lad the last time I set eyes upon you."

Simon looked into those steel gray eyes. "Pray forgive me for I do not recall knowing you."

"Aye, I am not surprised that you don't remember me. I was one of—" he lowered his voice "—I was just newly come to The Dragon's keep from my father's farm."

Simon was not blind to the reverence with which he spoke the former lord's name, nor the continued appraisal in those steely eyes. When Simon remained silent, Jack went on with steady care. "I was there that day, as you were, when good lord Wallace met with those who were plotting against King Henry. 'Twas a black day indeed when he allowed those men his ear."

"You loved him."

"Aye. And I now begin to believe the same of you in spite the fact that you and your friends gave testimony against him."

Simon took a deep breath, speaking with complete honesty. "Aye, I loved him, as my own father."

Jack lowered his voice even further. "I would ask you then, after what you have told me this day, if you were forced to speak against him."

Simon could hear the pain in his voice after these thirteen long years that The Dragon had been dead. He heard it and sympathized with it. For the same pain lived in him.

Yet Simon was cautious about admitting anything more to this man, in spite of his appearance of commiseration. It suddenly occurred to him that although Jack might very well be empathetic it was also true that he could be acting on Kelsey's behalf. He might be attempting to encourage Simon to speak some slight against his lord so that it might be used against him.

Simon well recalled King John's admonition to make no trouble for his host. He spoke cautiously, but at the same time he could see no gain in prevaricating on this matter. "It is true that we did not realize what we were doing, but we were not forced to speak. Lord Wallace had taught us that there is honor in the truth and we must not deviate from it." He could not completely hide the pain that colored his voice as he went on. "All we sought to do was tell the truth when asked if we had been present when he met with those who were in league with Richard and if that meeting had been held in secret."

Jack took a deep heavy breath and it was difficult to doubt the sincerity in his voice as he said, "Aye. I know. But you have had to live with knowing that the outcome was the same as if harm had been meant."

Simon could not deny this. It was partially due to their testimony that King Henry himself had sanctioned the raiding of Dragonwick keep in which Wallace and his young daughter had been killed.

Simon drained his cup, then raised it for more wine. Simon resolved to say nothing. He would remain on his guard and always recall that Jack was in the service of his enemy.

The thought of Kelsey brought him back to the subject he was most determined to forget. Isabelle. What had been behind the strange expression in her eyes as he had looked at her across the field? Had he not known better, he would have imagined her to be fearful for him. But that was ridiculous, completely impossible.

Isabelle had made her hatred of him quite clear.

Simon lifted his cup and drank deep.

Chapter Six

In a state of high agitation Isabelle paced the confines of the chamber she had once thought of as a haven. In spite of her intention to put Simon Warleigh from her mind, this day's events seemed to have conspired against her.

Immediately upon the heels of that dratted man's departure Helwys had entered the room. The expression on her well-loved face had been very thoughtful as she said, "He may not be such a bad sort, your lord."

Still angry with Warleigh, Isabelle swung about in confusion. "My father?"

The maid shook her head, holding her folded hands close against her breast. "Your lord husband."

Isabelle felt her eyes widen. "What are you saying?"

"Your husband, my lady. Perhaps there is no need to fret so over the marriage."

Isabelle could not begin to fathom what might have brought on this strange pronouncement. Yet she tried, out of love, to reply evenly, "And pray what has brought you to this mad conclusion?"

Helwys looked at the floor, flushing. "Just now when Lord Warleigh was here with you I was listening outside the door. I must confess as well to listening outside the tent on the wedding night.'' When Isabelle opened her mouth to give a reprimand, the serving woman rushed on to continue, ''I had to be certain you would be safe.''

Isabelle was moved by this care for her. Yet she could not allow this defense of Simon Warleigh to go without challenge. ''If you were listening, Helwys, then you know just how arrogant and intractable the man is.''

''Perhaps he is a bit proud, my lady. But that is very appealing in its way.'' When Isabelle cast her a glare, Helwys had the grace to bow her head but only briefly. ''Lord Warleigh was unpleasant, my lady, only after you had been so with him. And when he found me listening to the two of you in the hallway, I thought he meant to strike me, but he did no such thing. He was kind to me when he realized what I had been doing there, praised me for my care of you.''

Isabelle sighed. ''This is ridiculous.''

''Pray forgive me, my lady, but it is not. And the night you were wed—'' she raised her pert nose ''—he spoke of his own feelings about being held here. But he also spoke of the fact that you two are strangers. I thought it most thoughtful of him to give you time to know him before taking to your bed. It is a sign of kindness, my lady, for it is not an easy matter to share your body with a stranger. I know you were prepared to do as Lord Kelsey had ordered, but it would have been very difficult.'' There was no mistaking her disapproval toward Isabelle's father.

Isabelle could form no reply. Perhaps shock kept her silent. Or a distant wish that the words could be true, even though she knew they were not. Surely it had been less than kind to bring up the fact that he had heard her crying.

Helwys went on softly. "Mayhap my prayers have been answered at last and in spite of the marriage being a forced one it was the best thing for you, my lady. Mayhap you will come to see that there is more to relationships than control and power."

Never were such words to be spoken aloud. She raised her trembling hands. "Nay, Helwys, I will hear no more on it." To allow such a thought to enter her mind would be to set herself up to disappointment and loss. Simon Warleigh sought only to further his own ends. He would not be in this situation if he had not plotted against her father no matter how her father might have twisted the truth of that to suit his own purposes.

Her voice emerged in a harsh whisper, "You are not to mention that man's name lest it be absolutely necessary."

"But—"

"Nay, no more. No one is coming to rescue me from my life and I require no one to do so. To pretend otherwise is to live in delusion."

To her relief, the maid subsided, though she did not look happy.

"Please, fetch the burgundy velvet from my chest." As the maid moved to obey, Isabelle continued to do just what she did not wish to do. She continued to think about Simon Warleigh and to wish the impossible was not.

But Isabelle could not allow herself to believe, no matter what the maid had said. The nurse loved her, it was true. She was one of the very few people Isabelle trusted, but she could be misled by a handsome face.

And there was no denying that Simon was handsome.
Isabelle could not deny that it had been difficult for her
to keep from thinking about him and the glory of his
golden body.

Isabelle shook her head. In spite of that and Simon's
seeming kindness to Helwys she could not relent. If her
own father had never shown her any hint of genuine
tenderness why would a stranger?

As if that had not been enough for one day, Helwys
had just finished lacing her into the fresh gown when
the door was opened by one of the kitchen maids. Her
eyes were round with excitement and she spoke with a
lack of ceremony that was quickly explained by her
words, "My lord Warleigh is fighting Jack on the practice field." She scurried away.

Isabelle started after her without thinking.

Word that Simon Warleigh was fighting one of her
father's knights on the field had obviously spread like
the wind through the keep. The man was none other
than Jack, the giant of a man who kept so much to
himself.

Isabelle halted at the edge of the crowd, wondering
what she was doing there. She told herself it was because she was eager to see the arrogant knave bested.
But it had not been eagerness that had coursed through
her as she watched him fighting the giant.

Anxiety rose higher with each fierce clash of swords.
She also felt a strange sort of unexplainable pride as
she realized that Simon Warleigh was meeting those
powerful blows with vigor and prowess.

As she saw Simon falter, she felt a rush of fear that
she could not understand or even acknowledge. She
could no more stop her gasp of fright than halt the
changing of the seasons.

The relief that rose in her upon the large man's fall made her even more confused. She felt like a fool to react thusly when Simon Warleigh had treated her so ill by speaking of things best left unsaid, by behaving as if she had wronged him!

Yet before she could take her leave he looked into her eyes. The expression in that triumphant face made her feel as if he knew her very thoughts. Isabelle could think of nothing save getting away.

Surely it was only unwanted longings awakening inside her at the notion of having someone to depend on that made her so confused. She hurried back to her room, not caring what anyone might make of her obvious agitation.

Her reactions to Warleigh were far too unpredictable for her own well-being. It had been years since anyone had been able to break through her defenses, to make her feel when she did not want to feel. Yet Simon Warleigh had managed to do just that. And she had known him for no more than a few brief days.

Damn Simon Warleigh to the very fires of hell.

What right had he, who knew nothing of her and her life, to come and upset the delicate balance of her existence? Helwys's insistence that Simon Warleigh was a decent man was nothing short of madness.

Unfortunately if her father had returned he would expect her at the meal, especially since she had taken the previous one in her chamber. Because of her preoccupation with that dratted man she had failed to ask one of the servants to tell her the moment her father arrived home. Since she was a child she had made it her business to know when her father was in the keep. She must put in an appearance at the meal, even if it be brief.

She called Helwys to aid her in finishing her grooming, which had been interrupted by the outing to the practice field. The familiar activities did nothing to ease her thoughts. Would Simon speak to her? What would he say?

She shifted restlessly on the stool.

Helwys's voice interrupted her unhappy thoughts. "All will be well, my lady. Lord Warleigh will behave toward you with chivalry. Did you not see the way he was with Jack, congratulating him on his skill?"

Isabelle spoke tightly to her maid, recalling that he had been quite unchivalrous as far as she was concerned. "I have forbade you to mention that man in my presence, lest it be necessary."

Helwys fell silent as she continued preparing her mistress, but her expression was reproving. Isabelle told herself she did not care if the maid was angry with her. She was justified in her dislike of her husband. She could not let herself forget Simon was not what he seemed. He had been one of the men responsible for her beloved uncle's death.

When finally the maid stepped back with a pleased expression, Isabelle knew that she could delay here no longer. The ivory linen underdress was perfectly set off by the short, low-necked tunic of lush burgundy velvet with its border of pearled embroidery. Through her coiled dark braids Helwys had woven matching ivory ribbons. Feeling in no way secure, even with the armor of her beautiful vestments in place, she went down to the hall.

The deep, boisterous laughter she heard on stepping into the hall made her halt and send a surprised glance toward the source. She could not recall when this hall had last been the setting of such gaiety. She was even further surprised to see her husband, who was seated at one of the tables with several other men. One of those men was the very one he had fought so earnestly only a short time ago.

The fact that the men had been drinking was evidenced by their relaxed demeanor and the pitchers littering the table. Casting her gaze about the chamber, Isabelle breathed a sigh of relief when she did not see her father. She realized she was not the only one who was observing this display of joviality quite closely. All here knew her father would never sanction such behavior. He insisted the meal proceed without loud conversation, and certainly no drunkenness.

Anxiety made Isabelle's heart pound as another boisterous laugh sounded from the group of revelers.

She did not know what to do. One part of her wished to warn Simon, for her father could be formidable in his anger. Another part of her felt that Simon Warleigh was surely able to look after himself. Had he not shown this thus far?

Her father was not present. She thought she might return to her own chamber and have Helwys bring her a tray.

Still, she hesitated.

For too long.

As he cast a sweeping arm wide to illustrate some point he was making, Simon's gaze came to rest upon her. His warm brown eyes widened, then slowly moved down over her, before coming back to her face. A languid smile curved his lips even as she noted that his eyes seemed to have darkened, the lids having grown heavy.

There was a strange fluttering in her belly. Without conscious thought she moved her hand down to cover the spot, her breath quickening as she realized that he was looking at her as if…as if he found her desirable.

As she watched Simon smile, his gaze darkened further. He seemed almost to read her very thoughts.

Flushing, Isabelle sucked in a deep breath as her belly fluttered anew.

She must be mad. She had no desire to be leered at by a drunken lout, even if he was her husband. For he was husband in none but name and that was just fine with her.

Isabelle turned and hurried back down the long narrow corridor that led to the stairs. She took the equally narrow stairway to the upper floor. She was able to enter her own chamber without seeing anyone, including Helwys. Closing the door behind her she took a deep calming breath and moved to sit on the edge of her bed.

She must gain control of her untoward reaction to the man. Why it was proving so very difficult she could not fathom. He meant nothing to her.

When the door opened, she did not raise her gaze. Isabelle did not wish for Helwys to see her agitation. "I will hear no more on Warleigh. Please, leave me in peace for a time, Helwys."

"It is not Helwys."

A gasp of surprise escaped her lips as she heard her husband's deep voice.

She gained her feet on suddenly shaking legs. "My lord Warleigh!"

He spoke with unusual care. "Isabelle, I thought we had agreed that you would call me Simon."

His lack of formality was not lost on her, nor was the way his unreadable gaze moved over her, nor was the fact that he had been drinking. She raised her head high. She was determined to make him understand that she did not welcome familiarity from him now, not in this situation.

But there was a decidedly pleased and devilish glint in his eyes as he added, "You and the maid have been discussing me."

She gasped at his insufferable arrogance. "Since you know that, you also know I do not wish to do so."

He sighed with exaggerated regret as he said, "Then it must have been anger I saw in your eyes when you were watching me fight. Although you did say that you would not allow yourself to become angry with me again."

Isabelle flushed from the top of her head to the tips of her toes. Was no unchivalrous remark beyond him?

She said, "I was not angry, only disdainful of your poor fighting skills." When he continued to watch her with obvious disbelief, she wished for nothing more than the strength to strangle the blackguard with her bare hands. But never would she give him the benefit of knowing how thoroughly he plagued her.

"My lord Warleigh," she proclaimed, deliberately using the formal title, "I am not prepared to receive you at this time."

He swept the room with a wide gesture. "Not prepared to receive me? You can not have forgotten that I share this chamber."

She swallowed, "I have not forgotten. You may certainly come back after my maid has prepared your bed." She paused. "That is if you are prepared to go to sleep."

He scowled, then shook his head. "Nay, 'twill not serve. I will come and go as I wish. This is my chamber and you are my wife." He moved toward her slowly, deliberately, his gaze raking her from head to foot. "It is not improper for me to be alone with you." He stopped before her, this time perusing her form far more slowly. "To do anything I wish with you."

She sucked in a deep breath, as a rush of something dark and unknown raced through her. Desperately she fought for control at her reaction to his implication. She told herself that the knave was obviously behaving this way because he was drunk.

Deliberately she stood, running her hand down her skirt. "I would not say that you may do as you wish with me, my lord. Wed though we may be, it is not a real marriage."

"Do I detect a note of disappointment, Isabelle?" His husky tone sent a chill down her spine that had naught to do with being cold.

Again she reminded herself that he was drunk, and was saying things that made no sense. He had made his desire to remain apart from her clear. Once his head had sobered he would be angry with himself and her.

She must hold tightly to her control.

Yet when Simon came closer to her, leaning over her, his breath warm on her cheek, she was forced to call upon all her powers of will to remain unmoved. His words only further served to enervate her as he spoke with soft intimacy. "I would not be above remedying the oversight."

She gasped aloud, stumbling back. "How dare you, you drunken lout."

He studied her. "Drunken lout I may be. But I am your husband, Isabelle, in spite of the fact that I've been granted not one moment of privilege because of it. Not even my freedom."

Desperation made her speak frankly. "But you do not want me. You have said as much."

He put his hands on her shoulders, holding tightly to her. "Aye, I have said that." She forced herself to remain impassive beneath his strong hands, though her breath caught in her chest at his touch. She would not give him the satisfaction of a struggle.

Yet she was shocked into resisting when he pulled her against the hardness of his chest. Her strength was nothing compared to the power of his battle-hardened arms. His mouth found hers.

Isabelle tasted wine, and the coolness of the outdoors and something more elusive she could only think was Simon himself. Then all rational thoughts disappeared as a shaft of indescribable heat coursed down her body.

And just as suddenly as Simon had grabbed her he set her away. Confused and dazed Isabelle looked at him through heavily hooded lids. "Simon." Her voice was far too breathless. "I did not imagine…"

He arched a dark brow. "Nay, but now you will. I am no one's pawn."

Ah, she realized suddenly, dragging the shattered edges of her composure about her. He thought to punish her as he was being punished. This was much easier to deal with than the notion that he might actually be attracted to her—desire her.

That thought chased the last bits of fog from her mind. She drew herself up, meeting his gaze with anger. "Do not again forget that I have done naught against you, my lord Warleigh. If wronged you have been, it was not wrought by me. You will not again approach me with the notion of avenging any wrongs you feel have been done to you."

She watched as what appeared to be a grudging respect dawned in those eyes. But she did not allow it to soften her stance.

Finally he answered. "Very well, Isabelle. I will never again approach you with the notion of revenge."

He said the words. But something, an unreadable something that seemed strangely like an unspoken promise, kept her from feeling relieved by them.

Without another word Simon went to the bed and took the top fur from it. He strode to the far wall, lay it upon the floor and threw himself down upon it. The deepness of his breathing only moments later told her that he was already asleep.

Simon woke to a terrible throbbing in his head.

The wine!

He opened one eye and closed it again, raising his hand to block out the light that sent a shaft of agony down the top of his head. Saint George, it hurt, but not enough. He groaned, wishing his head hurt so much that he did not remember what he had done the previous evening.

The stillness of the room told him Isabelle had risen and left without waking him. He was not sorry. It would be best if his sickness eased somewhat before he faced the recriminations she would surely heap upon him.

What had he been thinking to approach the ice maiden as he had? An image flashed in his mind of the heat in her eyes when he'd set her away after kissing her. But quickly he dismissed it. Surely it was the wine that made him see desire where there was only anger.

It was her maddening defiance and resentment that had driven him past rational behavior. That, and God help him, her beauty. What had the Good Lord, in all

His wisdom, been thinking when he created such a perfect form to couple with so disagreeable a disposition?

Surely she was put on earth as temptation for the weak of mind and will. And Simon was in no way weak of will.

Yet when he had kissed her he had felt his body respond in a way he would never have expected, with instantaneous fire. Again he was beset by a memory of Isabelle's heated response. Was it indeed the wine that made him recall it thusly, or could there have actually been passion in her response?

The conversation with her afterward, which he remembered with equal vividness, did not lead him to trust his memory of that kiss. Isabelle had made it all too clear that she did not wish to be with him. That it would be a form of punishment for her.

Simon sat up in a rush of anger. Never in his life had he taken an unwilling woman. He would not do so now simply because the woman was his wife.

Simon entered the great hall and stopped as the unnatural stillness of the chamber intruded upon his thoughts. He scanned it quickly and saw that all present seemed to be watching Kelsey, who stood beside the high table.

At his feet was Isabelle's maid. Helwys was lying upon the floor, a bowl clutched in her outstretched hand.

Without thinking Simon moved toward them.

As he approached Kelsey growled, "You fool."

Now Simon was close enough to see the expression of horror that contorted Helwys's pleasantly featured face, as she stared at the front of Kelsey's tunic. Immediately Simon realized the reason for this. The thick gruel that had once been contained in the bowl now stained the front of the earl's garment.

The rage on Kelsey's face was obvious. He opened his mouth, but before any more words could issue forth, Isabelle's voice, sharp with reprimand, interrupted. "Helwys, you lack-wit. What have you done? Have I not told you that you must have a care for your clumsiness?"

Simon looked to where Isabelle had risen from her place at the table. Her face was set in that cool and emotionless mask that was beginning to wear upon him. He felt his stomach tighten at her words and unfeeling tone. Surely what had occurred had only been an accident.

Again Kelsey opened his mouth, glaring his own outrage at the maid.

Again Isabelle broke in. "Helwys, you will begin by going to my chamber and removing every garment from my chests. Check each seam, each bit of embroidery, every jewel, no stitch is to escape repair." Isabelle met the maid's wide terrified gaze directly, her tone frigid as December wind. "It is a task which even you can not fail."

The maid scrambled to her feet, ducking her head in fear and subjection, before running from the hall.

As soon as she was gone Isabelle turned to her father. "Forgive me, Father, I must bear the responsibility for this slight to your person. Clearly I have been lax in my instruction of late. As we have discussed on occasion, Helwys is dull-witted and clumsy. I will see that you need never suffer such indignity again."

Her father found his tongue. "She should be beaten."

Isabelle stiffened, looking down at her hands, which were folded before her. "Father, no doubt you are right. But as we both know there are other methods of teaching." She looked up into her sire's face. "I have learned from the most thorough of teachers. In the future she will have a care in all she does."

All of this had taken place in the space of mere moments. Before Kelsey could reply Simon moved forward again, drawing their gazes as he came to a halt beside his wife. "Are you both mad? The nurse must have tripped or stumbled. That is no cause for such cruelty toward her."

Sir Fredrick came from seemingly nowhere and pushed his chest into Simon's, his blue eyes filled with hatred as he said, "How dare you speak to my Lord Kelsey that way? I shall gut you like the—"

Simon pushed him away, his own voice hard with rage, not only at the knight, but all of them. "Come then, sir lackey." Simon put a hand to his sword hilt.

Kelsey's voice stopped the knight in the act of removing his sword. "Fredrick! Have we not discussed this?"

Stepping back the knight turned to him. "As you will, my lord." But that did not stop him from casting a hate-filled glance at Simon. A glance of warning.

Simon cared not what deeds the two might have planned for him. They would find them difficult to carry out. Kelsey swept him with a disdainful gaze. "Have I not told you to mind your own affairs, Warleigh?"

Isabelle spoke up again, seeming somewhat impatient with what had just occurred. "Father, you should be treated with all the respect and care you are due. I ask again for your permission to see to the punishment for my maid."

Simon was sickened by his wife's steadfast desire to punish Helwys herself.

Kelsey reacted quite differently. He smiled thinly. "You have indeed learned much, Isabelle. You may see to the maid and I will rest assured that you will not suffer from unwarranted pity that will only lead to further mishaps.''

Isabelle inclined her head with pleased modesty.

Simon, watching her, thought he saw something odd pass through her lavender eyes as she spoke, but he was so angry that he had little care for what it might mean. He cast a scathing glance over her. ''I will not stand here and bear witness to this for another moment.''

Simon strode across the chamber. Neither of them might have any consideration for the maid, but he did. Though Simon had no notion of what comfort or aid he might give to the poor woman he was determined to interfere in whatever punishment Isabelle might heap upon the ludicrous one already given. It was especially distasteful to him in light of the fact that the maid was so very defensive and admiring of her mistress.

He went directly to Isabelle's chamber.

Simon expected that he would enter a scene of chaos. From the number of trunks in her chamber the variety of garments she owned was surely staggering. What he saw when he opened the door made him pause with shock.

Far from being surrounded by a sea of her lady's finery, she stood, quite unoccupied, in front of the open window, gazing out upon the scene below. What could she be thinking to bring more retribution upon herself?

Perhaps the maid had been too distraught to begin her assigned tasks. Even as he stepped into the room, Helwys began to swing around, speaking in a tone of gratitude, ''Thank you, my lady Isa—'' When she saw who it was she stopped, her eyes going wide. ''My lord Warleigh!''

Simon approached her slowly. There had been no fear

or anxiety in her voice when she had clearly thought it was Isabelle behind her. He had heard only affection and welcome. He was puzzled at this.

Helwys looked down at something in her hand and Simon followed her gaze. She was holding a little bird, which pecked at a bit of bread on her palm.

Immediately she turned and placed the bird on the sill, before swinging back to face him. "Is there aught I can do to be of assistance, my lord?"

He frowned, noting absently that the little bird remained where she had placed it, even as he said, "I... What is going on here between you and Isabelle?"

The maid moved to one of the huge trunks that rested along the wall. "I..." It was obvious that she was searching desperately for words. "Forgive me, my lord. I should have obeyed my lady without delay. Pray forgive me, but I will begin now."

Simon was no fool. He shook his head. For whatever reason the maid and his wife had enacted a hoax.

He spoke sharply, "What are you and Isabelle doing?"

Silence.

Looking at the maid's profile as she delved into one of the trunks, he knew that she would tell him nothing. Taking a deep breath Simon turned and stalked from the room.

Simon was angry with the both of them, his wife for being so maddeningly confusing, and with the maid for refusing to explain any of it. One thing was clear though: Isabelle's actions below had been her way of protecting the maid rather than punishing her.

For reasons he could not begin to understand, this only troubled him more than believing her cruel and unfeeling.

The fact that Isabelle would go to such lengths to protect Helwys from her father meant nothing to him. She was not willing to face her father's cruelty openly, which would be a true display of courage. She had to resort to this devious playacting.

He was more determined than ever to escape from this farce of a marriage.

Chapter Seven

The next week passed in a blur of anger for Simon. He slept on the floor in Isabelle's chamber each night, and spent his days on the practice field with Sir Edmund and Wylie, along with Jack and the few other men who had decided to join them.

He rarely saw Isabelle or her father, the latter being much gone from the keep. Simon could not doubt that ruling his lands by fear and intimidation would require a heavy physical presence.

Only at night, when he lay awake listening to the soft rhythm of his wife's breathing, did his anger abate. But like a talisman of protection Simon would pull it to him once more, for the emotion that strove to replace it was much less welcome and far more dangerous to his well-being.

On the seventh day, after a particularly sleepless night, he rose and went to the great hall before the bedrolls had all been removed to make way for the trestle tables. Sighing, he went out, rubbing the back of his neck as he looked up into the crisp blue sky. The decided chill in the air marked the encroachment of late autumn.

Simon had a sudden and overwhelming urge to get
out into that brisk air. Surely it would wash away some
of the frustration that had been his constant companion
since he'd come to this cloying keep of secrets and si-
lences.

In the stable he found the just risen Wylie coming
back from his morning ablutions. He heard the tightness
in his own voice as he said, "Ready my horse for riding."

A young blond fellow who had been feeding the
horses approached Simon hesitantly. "Pray forgive me,
my lord, but I have been told you are not to be given
your horse."

Wylie, swung about, bristling like a rooster. "How
dare you speak thusly to my lord Warleigh?"

Simon took a deep breath as he felt his own anger
stir inside him. It was only by a great act of will that
he held it in check.

Yet Wylie was ever quick to take offence. Simon
addressed his squire with a calm that pleased him.
"That will be enough. It is beneath you to harry this
man for doing his master's will."

It was true. Kelsey was responsible for all the ills
here. Simon swung around and stalked back to the keep.
The earl would not prevent him from riding. Simon told
himself he must find some reasonable method of ap-
proaching Kelsey in order to convince him that Simon
had no intention of attempting to escape.

He easily found his host in the great hall, where the
morning meal was now being laid. Kelsey frowned with
displeasure as Simon approached him, and Simon did
his best to ignore the expression, though it gave him
the impulse to run the bastard through with his sword.
It was only the knowledge that he would likely lose

Avington to the crown that prevented him. Simon forced himself to speak evenly, "My lord Kelsey."

Unfortunately the other man behaved with his usual lack of civility. "Ah, the proverbial ill wind."

Simon bristled in spite of his good intentions. "You would dare to say such a thing to me, when all here shiver in the wake of your passage?"

The earl frowned. "You have been warned. What happens in this hall is not your affair. You are my prisoner."

Simon's gaze narrowed. "I am your daughter's husband."

The earl raked him with cold gray eyes. "Not by my own will. Haps you will prove yourself worthy of some consideration when you have produced a child."

"*That* is none of your concern."

The earl laughed a harsh sound that had no mirth in it. "All that goes on in this keep is my concern."

"Not in the matter of myself and my wife."

Kelsey shook his head. "You will find, my lord cockerel, that Isabelle's place as your wife will ever be second to her obedience to me."

That this was true did not ease Simon's displeasure. In spite of her occasional secret acts of rebellion, her loyalty did indeed lie with her father. Why, he asked himself, did he care? Isabelle had certainly offered no sign of loyalty to him. "You are quite right, my lord." He heard the bitterness in his voice as he continued, "Isabelle is no ally of mine. I concede that without argument."

The earl spoke softly, his gaze superior. "I must further insist that what you do in my keep is also my affair. And you will behave accordingly."

Simon felt his lips twist. "Though I do not agree and

it has galled me to do so at times, that is exactly what
I have done, my lord.''

"Have you?" Kelsey stood, his superior gaze raking
Simon from head to toe. "My lord Warleigh, I have
heard disturbing tales of your behavior."

Simon scowled in chagrin. Had Isabelle told her father of what had occurred the night he'd been drinking?

As he had been on their wedding night, Kelsey
seemed careless of speaking thusly before those gathered for the morning meal. Simon frowned. "I would
not have—"

The older man cut him off angrily. "I dare say you
would not have been so foolish as to disrupt my hall
with your drunken revelry had I been present. Mark me
well, sir, do not do so again, lest I make your misdeeds
known to King John."

Simon took a deep breath of shock. It was the drinking he was angry about. And after a week had passed,
although clearly he had not known until recently or he
would surely have remarked on it. Simon was more than
slightly taken aback at what offended the man's sensi-
bilities. He, who had betrayed his own brother to gain
an earldom, was appalled at a bit of merrymaking.

The man had insisted Isabelle bed with Simon, but it
would be obvious to him that there was strain between
them. Kelsey simply expected Isabelle to overcome her
aversion to Simon and do as he instructed. Her distaste
of Simon would make it all more acceptable. For reasons he could not quite name, Simon did not wish for
Isabelle's father to know of the passion that had flared
between them.

Carefully keeping his expression bland, Simon faced
Kelsey. He had no problem admitting that he had behaved foolishly in allowing himself to drink too much.

"Forgive my lack of consideration in disrupting the peace of your hall. It will not occur again."

For a moment the older man seemed at a loss for words. He recovered quickly. "I only hope that may be true."

Simon shrugged wryly. "Believe what you will. That matter is done as far as I am concerned, yet there is something else I must insist upon discussing." He faced the other man squarely, for Simon was suddenly done with placating his host. "Your man has informed me that you have forbidden me to ride. I would not cause difficulty for one of your servants, for I have seen how any misdeed is viewed, yet I will go riding."

Kelsey put his hands on his lean hips. "Oh, you will? Do not imagine you may simply declare your intention to do as you will and that I must accept it. Your over-blown confidence will not move me, my lord Warleigh."

Simon lowered his voice but continued to hold those cool gray eyes. "I do not mean for this to be a contest of wills. I have made myself amenable to all that you have demanded thus far and give you my word here and now that I will not try to escape. But I *will* go riding."

"And your word should mean something to me?"

Simon cast an assessing glance over him. "Do not judge me by yourself, my lord."

The earl's lips set in an angry line. "How dare—"

Simon shrugged. "How dare I? You try me greatly with your lack of goodwill, my lord. I could have escaped many times over on the journey here, had that been my intent. I simply wish to go riding."

Kelsey frowned. "Do you imagine I can spare a man to make sure you honor your word?"

Simon shrugged again. "That is your concern. Do

you wish to persist in believing me a liar, it will indeed cost you a man to act as my guard.''

The earl's scowl darkened as he glanced about the chamber. No doubt he was doubly angry at Simon's defiance of his authority before those gathered for the meal, though all were giving them a wide berth. No doubt because of their lord's angry expression, Simon thought.

Kelsey paused then as his gaze came to rest on something, or someone, beyond Simon's left shoulder.

Simon spun around to see Isabelle standing there, looking lovely as ever in a peach velvet kirtle and soft green linen underdress. Although her perfect features were set in the same imperturbable expression that he was quickly becoming accustomed to, he was aware of the fact that she avoided meeting his gaze. Perhaps she had spoken to the maid and knew that he was aware of their game.

Unaccountably pleased at this evidence of disquiet in her, Simon felt an unexpectedly strong rise of triumph.

Intruding upon his satisfaction came his enemy's self-satisfied voice. ''Isabelle will accompany you riding.''

Isabelle heard her father from across the chamber and felt horror sweep over her. She would not—could not—ride with Simon. Not after the way he had kissed her. Not after the way she had responded.

Not after what Helwys had told her of his coming to her chamber to find the maid playing with the little bird she had adopted as a pet, rather than going through the trunks as she had been instructed. That the maid had refused to answer when he had questioned her on their charade did little to soothe Isabelle.

Though he was many things Warleigh was not dull

of wit. He must realize what was going on between them. How he might use that against her she could only imagine, but she was not sorry she had spared Helwys from certain disaster.

Isabelle forced herself to attend her father. She was not at all pleased to see the cold expression that came into his eyes as they passed from Simon's back to her. Nor was she pleased at the open horror on Simon's face, or his immediate response of, "Nay, I—"

She found herself wanting to inform him that it was quite unfair of him to be so emphatic in his rejection of her father's decree.

She said nothing as her father nodded emphatically. "Aye, Isabelle will see to you. She has little else to do." He ran a cool glance over her. "Ready yourself for riding."

She flinched inwardly at his saying she had little else to do. It was her father who declared that she was not to concern herself with the running of the keep. Suddenly she wanted to defy him and his command, and all commands to come, to say that she would never accompany Simon Warleigh anywhere. But she knew it would be for naught. Her father had the power to make her do as he pleased. Too many lessons had been learned to doubt it. She must not allow her father to see she had a preference in this. Letting him know of her reluctance to be with her husband would only give him power over her. She bowed, keeping close guard of her expression. "I will make ready."

Her father said, "Do not cross the river into the town. Stay to the castle lands."

Isabelle nodded. She had only been to the town on rare occasions. Her father preferred for her to stay in the keep or the keep's lands, where he insisted she was safer.

When she risked a quick glance at her husband that horrified expression had changed to one of frustration mixed with forbearance. This she understood no better than anything else about Simon Warleigh.

In her chamber Isabelle wanted to linger over changing into the dark-green tunic and fawn underdress that she wore for riding. She did not allow herself to do so, nor did she allow herself to speculate on Helwys's continued certainty that they should indeed trust Simon Warleigh.

In a relatively short time Isabelle was donning her burgundy velvet cape and heading toward the stables.

Simon was waiting in the bailey with their two saddled horses. She greeted him with a brief inclination of her head. Isabelle then gestured to the stable boy, who stood holding the black mare. "Your hand please, Rob."

He moved to assist her as Simon mounted his own horse without a word or gesture to show that he had noted her reluctance to touch him. Once settled in the saddle she saw that her husband was watching her, an unreadable expression in his brown eyes.

Feeling that a facade of civil unconcern was the best defense against her uncertainty, she smiled toward him, her gaze deliberately trained on his broad brow. Even as she watched he raked the hair straight back from it, before prodding his stallion forward with a cold, "Let us be off."

Isabelle followed, realizing that thus far her husband had given no sign whatsoever as to having any memory of what had occurred between them when he had kissed her in a drunken stupor. Nor did it seem that he cared about what had happened with Helwys. Isabelle was pleased. This outing might prove easier to get through than she had at first supposed, if he continued to be so indifferent and cryptic.

Relief made her sit up straighter. Free of the worry that Simon might remark on what had happened, she convinced herself to enjoy the day, which was indeed fine. The sky overhead was a deep azure and the air smelled of richness of the recent harvest in spite of the fact that it was quite cool upon her bare cheeks.

Simon set a brisk pace and Isabelle urged her mare after him. She enjoyed the rush of the wind. Riding was one of the few pleasures she allowed herself. Dragonwick was lush with rolling hills and verdant forests that she alone seemed to appreciate. Her father, not caring to partake in riding for enjoyment, never accompanied her.

Yet this day, regardless of her wish to relish the ride, she could not do so. She remained fully conscious of the man who rode beside her. Isabelle simply could not allow herself to completely relax. In spite of Simon's seeming disregard of her now, his kiss was not easily forgotten. Just thinking of it drew her willful gaze to Simon's long, lean back and wide shoulders, which she had clung to with such eager abandon.

Simon could not help noting that Isabelle was a very skilled rider. Surreptitiously he watched her, her hood thrown back as she leaned low over the pommel, her slender hand unexpectedly sure on the reins. The journey to Dragonwick had afforded him no opportunity to see her as she was now for they had traveled slowly in her father's entourage.

He noted the look of pleasure on her lovely face and

felt a slight stirring of excitement. He told himself it was simple surprise at learning that she was not indifferent to all things. That there was passion in her. Perhaps it had not been the wine that had made him think she had responded to him.

Searching for something to banish these thoughts from his mind he turned to her and pointed to a patch of forest some distance ahead of them, calling over to her. "Race you to that stand of trees."

Her eyes narrowed. "Challenge accepted."

Before Simon could react the mare shot forward. With a rush of exhilaration, he sent his stallion charging after.

For few moments he and the stallion seemed to be gaining on Isabelle and the mare. But Isabelle, after a quick glance to where he was closing in at her side, simply leaned closer to the saddle and appeared to say something to the mare. Seemingly effortlessly she pulled ahead.

Although Simon gave it all he and his mount had, she reached the shelter of the trees ahead of him. Isabelle had, in fact, dismounted and was rubbing a loving hand over the horse's broad forehead when he came to halt beside her. Seeing the flush of pleasure in her alabaster cheeks, he smiled widely. "Well done, Isabelle."

Simon slipped to the ground beside her. "Never have I seen a woman who could outride you. And precious few men, with the noted exception of my friend Jarrod."

Isabelle's flush deepened and her long black lashes fluttered down to mask the expression in those lavender eyes. "I... You are too generous, my lord."

For the first time since he had met her, Isabelle

seemed like other young women. Yet strangely different
from any other he had known. There was a glow of life
and excitement in her that Simon found deeply and surprisingly appealing.

Simon took a step closer to her, drawn not only by
her incredible beauty, but that spark of life. "Isabelle."
He heard the question, the entreaty in his voice as he
said her name.

She looked up at him, her lilac eyes widening. And
suddenly there was a strange sparkling current in the air
between them. It brought his senses achingly to life.
With it came the memory of the kiss they had shared,
in his mind and his body.

He found himself asking the question that prodded
his mind. "Which is the real you, Isabelle, the soft and,
I am beginning to believe, strangely courageous woman
who could lie to protect her maid, or the cool, aloof
woman you usually present to the rest of us?"

Isabelle shook her head, but her gaze did not leave
his as she whispered, "I assure you, my lord, that I am
in no part soft."

He moved closer, his eyes now on her mouth, which
seemed to tremble even as she watched. "Methinks you
are not so very sure of those words."

Before he even knew that he would do so, Simon had
taken her in his arms. As if in direct defiance of her
own declaration, her lips were indeed soft beneath his.
Her head tilted back as he deepened the kiss. He felt
the quickening of her breathing in the rapid rise and fall
of her breasts against his chest.

Simon raised one hand to slide it over the curve of
her breast, finding it a perfect fit in his palm. She
seemed to press more fully to him as the nipple hardened beneath his hand.

He felt his manhood harden with a longing that had only been banked by his iron will. Simon took his mouth from hers, pressing hot kisses to her temple, felt her tremble in his arms. He spoke in a voice made hoarse by his own desire. "What madness has gripped us? Why do we strive to fight this passion, Isabelle?"

As soon as the words were spoken he wanted to yank them back, for she sucked in a gasping breath, then pushed against him with all her might. Reluctantly he let her go when he saw the panic in her eyes.

She pressed her trembling hands to her cheeks as she took a step backward. "This *is* madness." She took another step back. " I can not... I must be getting back to the keep."

Simon reached toward her. "Isabelle. Speak to me."

She near leapt out of his reach. "Do not."

He sighed. "Forgive me for kissing you. It was a mistake. I had meant to talk of your kindness to your maid, to try to understand why you seem an enigma to me."

She shook her head. "There is nothing to discuss. I was but preventing an injustice. Helwys's fall was no more than an accident. And my father..."

"Is cruel and too proud."

Isabelle's confusion and uncertainty turned to anger. She glared at him. "I will not discuss that with you anymore, nor anything else for you continue to pry where you are not wanted."

Simon stiffened, suddenly outraged in a way he had not expected. "Why would I be wanted in this place that once was filled with joy and life, but now is cold and empty? When The Dragon died all that was good here died with him."

Isabelle seemed taken aback by his words, her reaction coming with a heat that surprised him. "What fault is that of mine? I but accept the lot that has been cast to me."

The pain behind her words softened him instantly. "It does not have to be that way, Isabelle. You need not accept your father's will and treat me as an enemy."

Her gaze held. "I am content with my father's will."

"If you were so contented with your father's guidance, why would you enact the charade with your maid?"

She glared at him. "I have no reason to explain myself to you, but as you have realized I care for her. She has been loyal to me and I would not see her harmed when she meant none."

He shook his head, not sure why he was pressing this matter, but unable to stop himself. "Although you can not even say the word I can see the love for her in your eyes."

She took another step backward. "Leave be, Warleigh. Even if I were dissatisfied with my father's guidance I would not fall in with you. For you are one of those who have taught me that there is no gain in giving your heart."

He shook his head. "That is madness, Isabelle. It is your choice to shut off your feelings. I had nothing to do with what you have chosen and have only been brought into this by my own foolishness in trying to avenge myself on your father."

Her eyes now darkened with sorrow. "You have done me great harm and your lack of understanding in that does you no credit. I lost something that meant a great deal to me because of you."

Simon was so amazed by this that he did not even try to stop her as she climbed onto the mare without aid. He mounted his own stallion and followed though something told him that she would not have queried him had he simply ridden off in the opposite direction.

Isabelle held her face directly into the chill wind, but it did little to cool her hot cheeks. There was no relief from her rage against Simon Warleigh, which burned like a white-hot spear in her chest. It was not because he was wrong in thinking she had chosen her life. It was a sense of suddenly being afraid that he was not wrong.

Over and over she heard him asking which was the real Isabelle. She felt the immediate ache of longing inside herself as he looked into her eyes. Even now she was affected by the unexpectedness of his compliments on her riding. She could no more have stopped herself from returning his kisses than stop the leaves from falling in the autumn. Nor could she stop the passion that had risen up in such an all-encompassing wave. But most horrifying of all was her own fear that she did not know the answer to his question.

Dear heaven, she wondered silently, which was the real her? The one she assured him knew no softness or the one she had hidden behind that mask? Had she worn the mask for too long to truly know?

Had she hidden her fear and hatred of her father so deeply and for so long that she could no longer find them? Or her other more tender emotions?

Isabelle prodded the horse for another burst of speed. It was ridiculous. She did know which was the real Isabelle. She could indeed love, did in fact love Helwys. She was aware of the cold facade she presented. She had worked hard at perfecting it.

But if she was determined to keep anyone else from

ever getting beyond it, what difference did it make? Was pretending to be indifferent the same as being indifferent if no one knew—no one but Helwys, whom she could not be completely free with, either?

This thought was so horrifying that Isabelle was unable to examine it further. She pushed it, along with all the other things that hurt or troubled her, far to the back of her mind.

Protecting herself from vulnerability and pain was what mattered. Simon Warleigh was not going to destroy what she had worked so hard to attain. Safety.

She had already said too much when she'd admitted to lying to her father to protect Helwys. Above all else she must prevent Simon from delving any deeper into her secret world than he already had. Her uncle Wallace had trusted Simon and he had suffered betrayal for that trust. Isabelle could not allow herself to forget that.

Isabelle would continue to live as she had learned to live. She would do as her father told her, while keeping her feelings deep inside. She would even ride with Simon Warleigh, if she was ordered to do so.

Isabelle urged the mare on, hoping the wind would erase the prodding sadness from her aching heart.

Puzzled, Simon stopped in the partially open door. At the far side of the chamber, seemingly oblivious to all but themselves, were his wife and a sobbing Helwys. He did not know what to make of it.

Two days had passed since the ill-fated ride they had taken. In that time Simon had done his utmost to remain too occupied to think about how very maddening a woman he had married. That had proved impossible though he had made ample use of the practice yard.

Isabelle was not easily set aside. The only thing he

had to be grateful for was that he had not bedded the willful, beautiful wench.

The nights were nothing but torment, sleeping there on the floor only a few paces away from her. He was not unaware of the fact that she, too, lay awake long into the night, which was evidenced by her restlessness. The very thought that she might be remembering the desire that had flared between them, as he was, near drove him mad.

Yet when they did chance to meet, she had nothing but cool silence to offer him.

So frustrated was he that Simon had even considered going to Kelsey and offering any guarantee to gain his release. Only the certainty that he would be denied were it anything less than the charter to Avington kept him from it.

As he stood there in the doorway and saw her holding her maid in her arms and comforting her while she cried, he was once again aware of the pull of her. Her aloof and unfeeling manner since they had gone out riding had convinced him her mask of indifference was impenetrable.

Yet here again, when he least expected it, was a hint of that deeper softer side Isabelle seemed determined to deny. This time she was going far beyond lying to protect the maid, far beyond preventing an injustice. She was doing something that seemed a completely extraordinary thing—for her. She was actually giving a comfort so sweet and tender it made him ache for something he could not name.

Her hand was gentle on the nurse's graying head. "I am so very sorry, Helwys. I know how much the little fellow meant to you."

"But the p-p-poor little b-b-bird was no trouble or

harm to anyone. What harm was it to f-f-fly over the lookout tower? Why did they have to s-s-shoot him?''

A bird. Simon recalled the little creature he had seen her feeding the day he had come to comfort her after the mishap in the hall. Obviously it had been killed. He, too, felt a stab of sympathy at her sorrow along with his continued awareness of Isabelle's gentleness.

Again Simon felt a sense of unease, as if this moment were important in some way he did not yet fully realize.

Quickly he shook his head. What a ridiculous notion. He had only come here to fetch a clean tunic after soiling the one he was wearing in yet another bout of swordplay with the giant, Sir Jack. He had simply come upon Isabelle comforting her servant. Nothing more, nothing less. Yet Simon found himself stepping back and returning the way he had come with deliberate care to keep from making a sound that might alert them to his presence.

Simon went to the great hall.

Sir Edmund was standing at the far wall. Simon approached the older man, though he had nothing to say.

Sir Edmund bowed, ''My lord.''

Simon nodded. ''How goes it?''

The knight looked at him closely. ''You seem ill at ease, my lord. Could it perhaps be because I have seen Lord Kelsey about the keep today?''

Simon shrugged. ''I have not spoken with him.'' He was not sorry for his distraction to be misunderstood. At the same time he had to admit that the cumulative effects of all that had happened in recent days was pressing upon his mind.

He spoke with deliberate unconcern. ''What is my squire about?''

Sir Edmund smiled. ''He will be some time in oiling

your saddle, my lord. Long enough to keep him from mischief for a while.''

Simon smiled as well. ''That saddle has never been so well kept as since we came here.''

Sir Edmund nodded again.

A deep voice came from just behind Simon. ''My lord Warleigh, would you care to play a game of chess?''

Simon swung around to see Jack. He, unlike Simon, had donned a clean garment since the morning's sword-play. Simon looked at the man with an outwardly easy smile, though he was no closer to understanding the fellow's obvious interest in himself. Sir Edmund, who was as discreet as Wylie was hotheaded, had made enquiries about Jack amongst the men who populated the keep. He was known for keeping much to himself. None of the other men had mentioned knowing of the intense devotion he still harbored for The Dragon.

This made Simon wonder all the more just what was going on with the fellow. He could understand the devotion. He did not understand why a man so inclined would remain in Kelsey's service for all these years. A man of his prowess could surely find another position.

Simon bowed. ''I would very much like to play chess.''

He was prepared to bide his time in learning why the fellow was so interested in him. If nothing else, the little game gave him something to think on other than the disaster that had become of his life.

Not more than an hour later, Simon was somewhat surprised to look up from his game of chess to see none other than Isabelle standing beside the table.

Simon felt an instantaneous and intense physical awareness at the same time as he was beset by what was now becoming a familiar sense of irritation. For gone was the woman who had so compassionately comforted Helwys, the woman who had taken such pleasure in riding.

In her place was a queen of ice, her head held high, her eyes devoid of any emotion. She addressed him distantly, formally. "My father has instructed me to take you riding again." Only as she said this did he take note of the fact that she was wearing her heavy velvet cloak.

He sat back. "Has he?"

She frowned. "You do not seem pleased."

Simon shrugged, knowing that he was not pleased but not wishing to divulge his feelings to his wife. "I am playing chess." He could feel Jack watching him.

Isabelle inclined that regal head with its burgundy streaked black tresses. "I will leave you to it then."

Her relief was more than obvious and Simon was beset by a sudden urge to bring some measure of discomfort to this woman who had managed to plague him so much. He stood. "Nay, do not go. You have made yourself ready. Jack will not find fault with my attending you. Will you Jack?"

The other man shook his head quickly. "Nay, my lord. We may continue later." He stood, bowed and left them.

Isabelle's displeasure was obvious and she frowned deeply as she stared after the knight. "I did not mean to intrude. My father had made it sound most urgent."

"You did not," Simon informed her. He frowned, "I made no request to ride."

Isabelle, too, frowned. "But my father said…" She flushed deeply and glanced back toward the doorway that led to the upper floor. There was a trace of concern, in her gaze and he knew she was thinking of the sorrowful maid.

Simon found himself speaking gently, even as he wondered why her father would send her to him. "Have no concern for me. I would not have him trouble you. If you have aught else to see to, then by all means do so."

Sighing she looked into his eyes, hers searching. "The matter has been seen to. What little I can do."

The regret in her was palpable and again he felt himself drawn to this mysterious woman. "I am grateful that you would take time to attend me." Again he heard the softness in his own voice and wondered at it even as he noted that Isabelle was now watching him closely. Not willing to meet that gaze, he said, "I will ready our horses. You may await me at the entrance of the keep, if you will. I will be quick about it."

Chapter Eight

It was not until they had ridden out from the keep, Isabelle remaining noticeably silent, that Simon saw the heavy dark clouds gathering in the sky. He was not surprised by the threatening rain. It was autumn. What did surprise him was his failure to note it earlier.

He had, as was becoming usual, been too preoccupied with Isabelle. Simon turned around to face her, pointing up into the sky. "It looks as if it might rain. Perhaps we should delay our ride until the morrow."

She looked at him, then in the direction he indicated. Though she tried to hide it he saw the disappointment in her lavender eyes. "If that is your will."

He found himself asking, "What is your will? I am for risking the drenching if you are. I spent many years in the Holy Land. There the sun is a constant companion. It bakes everything, the buildings, the land, the people. There is a feeling of the ancient, of the eternal. Though it is beautiful I have found in the last months here in England that the rain seems to encourage the new and growing, not only in the land but in its folk."

Curiosity tinged her voice. "What did you there?"

"Fought. First for Richard, which sometimes seems

strange, for it was because of Richard's father's belief that The Dragon had been in league with Richard so much harm was done.'' He shrugged, ''My foster father joined the crusade and Jarrod and Christian were being sent, as well. We were there at Acre...'' His stomach tightened as he recalled that horrible day when so many had been killed. Perhaps disillusionment over that had made the three of them stay on when the king left. She was still watching him. ''We stayed on when Richard left. The Knight's Templar have a constant need of men to help them hold the Holy City.''

Simon looked away. He didn't want to talk anymore. There had been nothing that merited staying away for so long and missing so much of life here.

She seemed to sense his withdrawal and asked no more questions. ''The rain matters naught to me. If you would prefer to ride then I would prefer to ride.''

Strangely Simon was both relieved and disappointed. He reminded himself that she was not truly interested in him. Isabelle was only doing as her father bid.

Simon knew he was mad to allow this to plague him. Telling himself to think only of his relief in being out of the keep for a time, he spoke levelly, ''Then we will ride.''

He set an invigorating pace and for a short while Simon was able to put all other thoughts aside—almost. It was indeed good to be out of the keep, to forget his frustration over languishing here when there was so much to be done at Avington.

But Isabelle's presence could not be ignored indefinitely. Casting her a quick glance where she rode just behind him on his left side, he saw that she seemed to be completely absorbed in her own concerns.

He, on the other hand, found himself once more taken

with thoughts of her. The briskness in the air had brought a flush of rosy color to her pale cheeks. Her hood had fallen back to allow the wind, which was heavy with moisture, to tug at the dark hair at her temples and she held her delicately lovely face straight into it. Forcing himself to look away, Simon rode on, oblivious to all else but his own lack-witted fascination with a woman whose loyalty belonged to her undeserving sire.

When a fat drop of rain fell upon the back of his hand, Simon looked up. The clouds overhead had lowered and thickened, taking on the color of old steel, and the wind gusted through the tops of the trees ahead. He frowned as two drops more fell on his face.

Casting another glance at Isabelle he saw that she, too, had raised her gaze to the sky, even as it lit up with a flash of lightning that was followed by a crash of thunder. Instantaneously the clouds let go their bounty and on a shocking rush of chill wind the drops became a deluge.

Isabelle reached back to pull her hood up over her head. He was quite certain she had no more envisioned such rain as this than he had. Simon knew that the heavy velvet of her cloak would not protect her from becoming drenched within moments.

Overwhelmed by a sense of protectiveness, he wanted to see to her well-being with all haste. He told himself his emotion was perfectly reasonable, as it was his fault they were out riding in this. The shelter of the castle first came into his mind but he dismissed it immediately. It would take some time to return to the keep. It was long enough to become completely soaked.

Casting his eyes about quickly, Simon remembered something he had not thought of since his residence at

Dragonwick as a boy. There was a lodge used by hunt-
ers in the wood. If he recalled correctly, it was very
nearby.

Simon called to her as he turned in what he hoped
was the right direction. "Come. I believe I know where
we might find shelter."

Isabelle rode after him without hesitation.

Simon rode into the trees, finding the trail fairly
quickly. He, Jarrod and Christian had thoroughly ex-
plored every inch of Dragonwick as boys. Yet he still
was surprised how well he remembered the trail.

The lodge was in good condition. He pulled his horse
up and dismounted, turning to Isabelle to find she had
already dismounted as well.

He took the reins of her horse. "I will put the horses
in the shed." He was assuming when he said it that it
was still behind the larger wooden structure of the
lodge. Inside the shed he found some edible hay
amongst the musty pile against the wall. When he returned to the low front door, Isabelle was no longer in
sight. He went inside.

The structure, though clearly unused for some time,
was very much as he recalled it, with a low ceiling,
packed earthen floor and large stone fireplace. The same
heavy oak bed rested against the outside wall. Although
Simon could not recall anyone having slept in it, he
supposed it was there in case a hunter might not wish
to return to the keep at night. Without conscious thought
his eyes swung to where Isabelle was kneeling before
the hearth.

She was attempting to build a fire from the dry wood
that had been laid by for just that purpose. Simon
moved to her side. "I will do it."

It was good to have something to do, something to

think about besides that bed. Something to think about besides the fact that they were alone here.

The fire did not take near enough time to coax into a cheery blaze. When he could no longer pretend to be busy with it, Simon stood and turned to Isabelle where she shivered in the middle of the room.

He spoke hurriedly, "Take off your cloak and we will lay it out to dry."

She did so and Simon pulled the bench from beside the small table, which bore a single dusty glass, nearer to the fire and draped the sodden velvet over it. "Come. Stand closer to the flames where they can warm you."

Isabelle moved forward slowly, holding out her slim fingers. She did not look at him.

Simon noted that she cast a speculative glance toward the bed. He spoke ruefully. "I did not bring you here in order to…"

She looked at him in obvious surprise. "Oh…I did not think you had done so, my lord." She colored as she went on, looking around the dusty and musty-smelling cabin. "My father has expressly forbidden anyone but himself to come here, though it appears not even he has done so for a very long time." She took a deep breath. "It is strange to think of him here. So isolated, so…"

Simon could see that she was disturbed by these realizations. For that one glass, the hard bench, the very air of the place, all bespoke a sense of loneliness that was at odds with the extremely controlled and controlling man Kelsey presented to the world.

Feeling somehow responsible for her discomfort, he spoke softly. "I am sorry for having brought you here."

Her next words shocked him. "I am not. It makes him seem somewhat less…" Again she halted suddenly, those lavender eyes revealing her uncertainty, her vulnerability.

He wondered what indeed she had been about to say. Was it an echo of his own thoughts that there was a side to the earl that he did not allow others to see? He spoke before he could stop himself, "Less what, Isabelle?"

Somehow he knew that if she would talk to him of this, a bridge would be crossed between them. Though why he wished for her to cross that bridge he was not sure.

Isabelle did not wish to look at Simon. She felt exposed and uncertain of her ability to mask her emotions. She knew there was an underlying texture to his question that went far beyond the words.

Some part of her wanted to answer him, to reveal the way she felt about herself, her life, her father. For there was a sense of melancholy to this place that brought visions of her father, a different father than the one she knew, sitting here alone and lonely.

Isabelle resisted this impulse, for it could not be anything but delusion. There was no weakness in her father. He was ruthless and omnipotent as he had proved time after time. He had, this very day, nearly caught her comforting poor Helwys after some cruel knave had put an arrow through her little pet. She had only been grateful that he had seemed too intent on making sure she went riding with Simon to notice. She had assumed Simon had made the request, and though she had wondered what her father could be about when she learned it was not Simon's idea, she knew not to ask.

Even as she told herself this, she wondered how Simon Warleigh, with a smile and a kind tone, nearly succeeded in penetrating her armor when none of her father's small cruelties ever had? What was it about him that moved her?

She suddenly realized how little she knew of this man, of the life he had lived. The things he had said to her of the Holy Land, his pleasure in being back in England made her wonder what drove him. She had seen he did not wish to speak of himself, had honored that. His questions to her now left him open to her own probing. "What is it you want, Simon? Why did you agree to marry me?"

He shrugged. "The truth does not flatter me. But you know that I agreed in order to save my head."

She shook her head, "Nay, beyond that. You were in the Holy Land for many years and could have escaped the king's wrath by returning. It could not have been the rain." She paused as he looked at her in surprise. "Why would you allow yourself to be manipulated into doing something you clearly had no desire to do? It seems…at odds with your demeanor. You could have left if you sought only to save your head, as you put it."

She watched him closely as he shrugged those wide shoulders. "If you know so much of me then you know I have inherited Avington and all the other holdings that come with the title. The king has made it clear that he would confiscate them if I did not wed as he bid me."

Ah, she thought, he was willing to forgo a surfeit of pride as great as his own in order to hold the lands. This she could understand, having seen her father commit the most despicable of acts to gain lands. Yet as Simon went on and she heard the sadness coupled with determination in his voice, she wondered if she might have been too quick in her judgment of his motive. "I would do anything to ensure the future of Avington. My brother Arthur was so like our father. Being twelve years older than me, I never thought of him as anything but strong and invincible, in the same way I did Father. They were ever occupied with the difficulties of running the lands, but they did try to spend time with me, to explain how things worked, or how to use a weapon properly. Both of them were fascinated with the workings of mechanical devices.'' His voice broke. "'Twas such a shock to learn I had inherited Avington, my father and brother both gone.''

"Yet you stayed away for so very long.''

"I had no notion that I was needed here. They were both so busy with the lands. I was… I know they had no notion of leaving me to my own devices. They were simply so much alike and when Christian, Jarrod and I went to the Holy Land I was barely fifteen.'' He took a deep breath. "As a lad I had no real notion that all would not remain as I had left it. In the East, the days seemed to run together, with no real seasons to help to mark the time. One day simply becomes the next. More than twelve years had passed when I received word that my father was ill. The journey home is not accomplished in days but months.'' Again his voice grew husky, "Finding both my father and my brother gone made me realize my life was more than the moment, that I had need to think on how my days—years— would be spent.''

The depth of emotion in his voice could not have been feigned. For reasons she did not understand, it moved her more than she could say. Isabelle took a step toward him. "I am sorry, Simon, for your loss. I had not thought…had not expected you to have such…''

* * *

Simon understood her obvious surprise. He had not known how much he hurt until this very moment. Feeling the ache of loneliness uncoiling like a snake inside him he was utterly exposed as he looked down at her, replying with irony in an attempt to cover his vulnerability. "Isabelle, did you think me immune to sorrow?"

Her lavender eyes held his. She continued to study him as his gaze then moved to her mouth. She whispered, her tone revealing a depth of empathy that her words did not, "Pray forgive me, I did not think…"

Her gentleness only further weakened his defenses, leaving the door inside him open to both his pain and, yes, his desire for her. As she flicked her tongue out to dampen those lips of berry pink, Simon knew he had lost the battle of self-control. "Sometimes it is best not to think." His mouth found hers as he succumbed to the promise of comfort in her lovely eyes.

As a shaft of pure sweet longing spiraled up inside her, Isabelle could not but agree. She slanted her head to better receive him.

Simon pulled Isabelle close against him, enjoying the softness of her. Then as she kissed him back with a heat that surprised him just as it had the first time he kissed her, his reactions made a subtle but definite shift. Passion, as intense and fiery as it was delicate and fragile, awakened in him. Just the feel of her, so very pliant and eager against him, made his body ache with longing to do more than gain comfort.

Seeming to sense his need she reached up her arms, twining them around his neck. At the same time she pressed herself more fully to him. He wanted to touch— to taste—to awaken her desire. The thought of Isabelle eager with a yearning that he had brought on made his breathing quicken, his mouth soften.

Her lips opened and his tongue flicked out to slide over hers. She sucked in a breath, her arms tightening on his neck. When her tongue danced after his, he groaned, feeling an ache of intense need building in his belly.

Simon reached up, resting his hand on her breast and Isabelle's heart stopped. It thudded back to life even as the nipple hardened and she felt a melting warmth gather in her lower belly. When his other hand slipped to the lace of her kirtle she leaned closer to the hardness of his chest to give him better access.

Simon kissed her again, deeply, insistently and Isabelle gave him measure for measure as something inside her seemed to swell and burst to aching life. She put her hand to the back of his neck, threading her fingers through his thick dark hair as she held him to her.

He felt the urgency of her hands and pushed back from Isabelle to ease her dress forward on her slender shoulders. As he did so he watched her face. Her eyes were heavy with desire, unfocused and dark. His gaze dipped lower, across the pulse in her long white neck, down to where her damp shift clung to the curves of her breasts, revealing the deep berry tips. His manhood stirred anew and he dipped his head to tease the nub of one with his tongue.

Isabelle was drowning in sensation, her body aching with each touch. Simon's hot tongue touched the tip of her breast and she moaned, arching into that sweet pleasure.

Passionate, beautiful Isabelle, he was awash in the softness of her body, the heat of her reactions to his caresses, the delicate and womanly scent of her. Simon was trembling himself as he laid her down upon the rug before the warmth of the fire that blazed no hotter than the fire in his blood. He would take her, make her his in reality. His hand slipped down to raise the hem of her gown, sliding over the velvet flesh of her legs, and onward to the moist curls at their joining.

"Oh, Simon, make me your wife in truth." It was this soft cry of encouragement that brought Simon to his senses.

What was he doing here? If he were to do what she wished—what they both wished—there would be no going back. Isabelle would be his wife in truth.

He could not betray his father's memory by giving in to the passion that had left him weak with longing. It had nearly made him forget that he would be putting the well-being of his lands and all who called them home in jeopardy by irrevocably binding himself to Kelsey. For that was what he would be doing with Isabelle's obedience and loyalty so irrevocably given to her father. He could not possibly do this because of his desire for this woman, no matter how deeply that desire ran.

No matter how his blood pounded even now as he looked down into her passion-hooded eyes. No matter how his manhood throbbed at the sight of her so willing and pliant in his arms—at the touch of her soft white hands.

It had only been the grief from speaking of his family. He had told the truth when he said it had never occurred to him that he might never see them again.

He moved to sit up, to turn away from the temptation she offered without even trying.

She blinked, turning to him in confusion. "Simon?" When he made no reply she sat up, holding her gown over her breasts, now shy where a moment ago she had been eager beneath his gaze. Simon refused to acknowledge the regret that rose up inside him as she said, "What is it?"

He shook his head. "We can not. I…"

Isabelle took a deep breath as realization dawned, willing her pounding heart to slow. She had to find some control here, some way to salvage the pride that had deserted her each and every time Simon touched her. Deliberately, giving herself time to calm her mind, she arranged her disheveled clothing. She did it with a casualness that totally belied the fierce ache of regret and shame inside her.

She was amazed at the evenness of her own tone as she finally spoke. "You are right. We can not. It would be madness. We both know how we feel about this marriage."

He did not answer for a long moment, seeming less pleased than she would have expected him to be, considering the fact that it had been he who had ended their embrace. His reply sounded clipped and bitter, "Aye."

In spite of the strain that now tainted the air, she found herself asking him the question that burned in her mind in a matter-of-fact way that continued to surprise her. "What is it that you do want? What do you hope for in this, married to me, but not married?"

He stood up even straighter. "To be free to return to Avington with no further influence from your father on my life. To gain an annulment."

Though the words hit her like a blow she nodded with deliberate aplomb. "Of course. And that would certainly depend upon your not bedding me."

He did not look away from her. "I will do whatever I must to discharge my duty, to honor my father and brother's memories by being the best overlord that I can be. You can not but know how I feel about your father, about his reprehensible acts, not the worst of which was making it appear that I was plotting against the crown.''

She grimaced. She did indeed know her father was capable of great wrong. Had he not betrayed his own brother in just such a way? Yet she did not wish to simply accept Simon's will, either, though she felt a great temptation to do so. The passion he had awakened in her was a compelling master indeed. But Isabelle would answer to no master.

At the same time she felt enough confusion to say, ''You must guard yourself well where my father is concerned, Simon. Do as he wishes.''

He looked at her closely. ''Why would you tell me this? Does this mean that your loyalty has been shaken?''

She took a deep breath. She must not give away too much for she had no reason to trust him either. ''Nay. I… His hatred of you is strong and you are sometimes rash.''

He raised those dark brows high. ''Rest assured I do not fear your father. He would do well to guard himself.''

She shrugged, knowing she could do no more than try. ''Feeling as you do, it would indeed be best if you could end the marriage, but I do not know when or even if the king or my father, would allow you to do that.''

He frowned blackly. ''Haps the day will come when your father will have no say in the matter. I mean to find a way to be free of him.''

Though she did not say so Isabelle could, on one level, understand his feelings. Did she not also long for the day when she would no longer be ruled by her father?

Simon seemed to read her thoughts. He asked, ''And you, Isabelle? What is it that you want?''

Isabelle was so shocked at being asked what she wanted or felt about anything, she found herself admitting her most cherished hope without having intended to do anything of the sort. "I? I would most love to have a child."

Simon's gaze widened. "A child? Of all the things you might have said, that is not what I would have expected."

She looked down, feeling foolish for having admitted this to him. She did not go on to say that her son would honor the memory of her beloved uncle. He would eventually restore Dragonwick to that happy time.

She was glad she had kept this to herself when he cast her with a mocking glance. "Are you trying to tell me something, Isabelle? Is that why you responded to me just now?" The disdain in his voice grated.

Keeping in mind that she might as well allow him to believe this rather than the truth, which was that she had not been able to control her responses, she said, "Perhaps I am, Simon. You are my husband."

He stared at her in amazement. Isabelle felt somewhat pleased at having caught him so completely by surprise.

Her pleasure faded like the cut wildflowers on a hot day, as he said, "You know that having a child would mean that the marriage would become a real one."

She carefully kept her features schooled. "What matter would that have been to me? I must be married to someone and I must lie with that man in order to have a child."

He gave her an assessing glance. "Not necessarily."

She did not take the bait, for the subject was of far too much import to her. She could get a child outside of marriage, aye, but her father would not name him heir to Dragonwick. Her child must be legitimate.

He interrupted her thoughts, "You continue to pretend that there is no love in you and yet you want a child."

She did not look at him, did not answer, but she felt him studying her. He said, "I saw you today, holding the maid. Your tenderness. I know there is love in you."

She raised her chin with disdainful pride to cover the rush of vulnerability she felt at Simon having seen the two of them together. "After what you have just told me of your desire to see our marriage ended I can not imagine why you care. I can not believe you would want love from me."

He frowned at her reaction but quickly interjected, "Nay, even if we wished to remain wed I would not expect, or desire, such an emotion. Coming from you I would only distrust any such displays toward myself. What we could have is a cessation of war. As to why I care," his frown deepened. "I...well, I do not care really other than that I see you do and are denying it." He seemed pleased with this pronouncement.

She raised her head. "You know nothing about me and I would keep things as they are. As far as a cessation of war is concerned, there is no war, Simon. For that, one of us would have to care. What there is, is indifference."

"There is desire."

Isabelle had nothing to say to that and clearly there was nothing more that Simon wished to say, either. The following silence stretched on for what seemed an eternity.

Finally Simon, his voice devoid of emotion, spoke from the other side of the room. "The rain has stopped."

Isabelle realized that the rain was indeed no longer

drumming on the roof as it had been. Risking a quick glance at Simon she saw that his jaw was set, his expression hard. Drat the man for behaving as if he had been the wronged party. It had been he who kissed her, after all.

She took up her still-wet cape and pulled it about her, then moved toward the door. "Most excellent." She wanted to be in his company not one more moment than was absolutely necessary.

Simon did not sleep in Isabelle's chamber that night, nor the next. It was not because he no longer trusted himself to lie so near the woman who had almost made him forget all he held dear. It was simply because too much had been said between them.

It had been madness to remind her of the desire that flared between them. He would not make that mistake again.

As he had told her, he did not care whether she loved or not. It simply maddened him that her pretence of not loving was just another lie in this place full of lies and deceit. That was all.

He knew not what Kelsey would say when he discovered Simon was now sharing a place in the stables with his men. Yet he was certain the earl would learn the truth ere many days had passed. Surely he would not be pleased, having made his desire for a grandchild well-known.

For her part, Isabelle had said nothing on the matter. She had, in fact, said nothing to him since that unbelievable conversation in the hunting lodge.

Simon had thought himself beyond being surprised by anything done by Kelsey or Isabelle. But his wife, who was undoubtedly the most passionate, responsive and alluring woman he had ever met, had done just that. She had, in essence, told him that all the desire she had displayed when he touched her was due to the fact that she wanted a child.

This revelation was difficult to accept as it had been all he could do to control himself as far as she was concerned. Yet he had no real wish for her to want him.

Did he?

He had his plan and she had hers. Surely now that she knew of his wish to gain an annulment she would be as eager as he was for this marriage to end.

Or in spite of her saying that she must be married to have a child she would find some other man to fulfill her need without waiting. Her father was under the impression that they had consummated the marriage. Isabelle could claim the child was his.

For unexplainable reasons this thought was far too disturbing. And not just because he would no longer be able to gain an annulment. Quickly Simon told himself that it was simply because as long as she was his wife, he would not play the cuckold.

Yet Simon found himself watching her even more closely than before. He seemed mesmerized by each movement of her slender white hands as she reached for her cup at table. He was maddeningly enticed by the gentle sway of her hips as she moved through the keep with that unconscious grace that was so much a part of her.

This very day as she brushed him with a slender hip on the stair that led to the upper floor of the keep he knew such a rush of desire he had to bite the inside of his mouth to stifle a groan. Isabelle had appeared completely oblivious to his plight and had gone on her way without so much as casting a cool glance toward him. Damn her eyes.

Had the witch enchanted him? Perhaps, for never in his life had he known such awareness of a woman. He told himself that it was simply her beauty that drew him. Any man would want her thusly. 'Twas the way men were made.

Yet it was not like Simon to become so beset by a woman. Jarrod was the one who quite often found himself in the throws of one passionate distraction or another. Though he got over them quickly enough when the initial rush of passion had cooled, or as happened on rare occasion indeed, the woman was not amenable to his suit.

Simon, although he had been with women, had heretofore been free of any such torment of desire as he was now feeling. In spite of his more levelheaded behavior in the past, Simon realized that surely what was now happening to him could only be termed infatuation.

Even an infatuation such as this would cool. He must simply give it time. Time was something he had far too much of on his hands of late.

It was on the third evening after moving into the stable that Simon looked up from table to see his father-by-marriage enter the hall. The earl cast an assessing glance over the hall in spite of his obvious fatigue. He frowned when it came to rest upon Simon.

Simon had not bestirred himself to join those at the high table, telling himself it was only prudent to avoid Isabelle as long as his fascination with her persisted. She had not put in an appearance. He had told himself that his sense of regret was nothing short of madness and gladly joined Jack and one of the other men for a game of dice when the meal had ended.

After that first brief glance toward the earl he kept his gaze trained on the dice, which Jack rolled before making his next move. But he was aware of the man's approach. Kelsey stopped beside the table, his gaze raking Simon. "Why do you linger here when my daughter awaits you above?"

Feeling his back go rigid, Simon replied as evenly as possible. "I am in the midst of a game."

Kelsey's scowl now deepened. "You need not lie. I have caught you. It has come to my attention that you have taken to sleeping in the stables."

Simon stiffened from head to foot. "I have no need for falsehood. I did not answer because I do not feel obliged to do so." And then something made him ask, "Did Isabelle tell you this?"

The earl scowled even more deeply. "Who told me is of no import to you."

The displeasure in the man told him it had not been Isabelle. Simon quickly suppressed a sense of pleasure. Surely his wife had only curbed her tongue in order to protect her own lovely hide.

Yet Simon said, "As I have informed you, what is between my wife and myself is none of your concern."

"None of my concern." Kelsey sputtered, looking down his narrow nose. "It is your duty to produce a child."

The muscles flexed in Simon's jaw. The thought of getting Isabelle with child was more distracting than this man could know, especially when she seemed as eager for that outcome as her father appeared to be.

Had her own eagerness been based upon nothing more than obedience? He had told her it was an indication that she could love. Haps he had been wrong.

Kelsey's voice prodded him back to the reality. "You

have no right to thwart me, Warleigh, for in doing so
you thwart the king's own command. He bid you marry
my daughter and you have not fulfilled your obligation
as a husband until she is with child.''

Simon raked him with a rage that was brought on by
sheer frustration and disgust. ''And when she is with
child, my lord Kelsey, then will the king believe I have
done my duty to you and to him? I may then return to
Avington?''

Kelsey smiled a cold smile that hid many thoughts.
''Aye, mayhap he would.'' His gaze went to Sir Fredrick, whom Simon had not seen come in. The two exchanged a knowing glance, and Simon knew that as far
as Kelsey was concerned he would never return to
Avington. It was well that Christian would continue to
write letters in order to garner support. He prayed that
John would eventually be forced to release him.

Oblivious to this the earl turned back to Simon. ''Let
that be your encouragement to get her bred.''

As usual the cold tactlessness made Simon's lips
tighten. In spite of his awareness that Isabelle would
not welcome a defense of her honor, Simon found himself slowly standing to face the older man. ''I say again,
and for the last time, this is a matter between Isabelle
and myself. I will not discuss it with you now or ever.
And even the king is unlikely to fault me in this.''

Simon paused then, holding up a hand as Kelsey
opened his mouth to reply, ''And mark me well on one
more thing. Isabelle is my wife, Isabelle Warleigh. You
will remember that, though I have no control over your
treatment of Isabelle as your daughter, never again will
you speak of her so disrespectfully before me, or my
men. It dishonors her as the lady of Avington, and
through her, my household.''

He swung around and strode away, but not before he saw his father-by-marriage's face grow first flushed, then purple with anger. Yet even as he felt a sense of triumph he knew a growing discomfort with not only the earl's insistence on Isabelle's having a child, but her own determination. What were the two of them about?

If they were in league, why had she warned him about her father at the lodge? He had no answers to these questions, but he would.

Chapter Nine

Isabelle had paced the battlements restlessly for the past hour. This had gained her no ease. The relentless stirrings inside her would not be lessened by any amount of activity. She stopped and looked over the darkness beyond the castle walls. The sky overhead hung heavy and brooding with clouds that blocked out the moon and stars.

Over and over again she recalled what Simon had said to her father in the hall. She knew that neither of them was aware that she had overheard their conversation.

It was, in fact, only due to the fact that she had been on her way to get a sleeping posset from the head cook that she had heard aught of what had been said. Although Isabelle realized Simon had not defended her on her own account, because even if only temporarily, she was the lady of Avington, she felt… She was not sure what it was she was feeling.

She did know that she kept remembering the last thing he had said before they left the lodge. That there was desire between them. This left her confused and unsettled as never before in her life.

She was beset by memories of herself and Simon, the things they had done. The fires he had awakened with his touch, his lips, burned brighter and hotter with each invading image. Frustrated beyond measure, Isabelle reached out to grip the edge of the crenelation before her. The rough stone bit into her tender fingers but did not distract her from her unwanted longing.

Simon did not want her, and yet he did. She, utterly conscious of him as she was, could not but note the heat in his glance when he thought she was unaware. She had felt the stiffening of his body as he passed her on the stair the previous day. Inexperienced as she was, Isabelle knew what it meant. The intimacy they had shared at the lodge had removed the veil of innocence she had once known.

The scraping of a heel upon stone interrupted her thoughts and she turned toward the sound. The guard who patrolled this section of wall passed behind her. Though he made a great pretense of staring straight ahead Isabelle felt his attention upon her, knew he was wondering why she would be here alone at this late hour.

Isabelle stiffened from head to toe. She would not be the object of any speculation. Not only did it gall her to think of any of the castle folk wondering about her, she could not have her father noting any unusual behavior.

Simon might find it amusing to bait him. She did not. Nor did she wish to show any hint of weakness, for was that not what her desire was—a weakness?

Yet she knew not how to disguise this relentless longing. There must be something she could do.

Suddenly she bit her lip. There was something, did she but have the courage. Something that would ease this longing while getting her what she wanted most—a child.

Surely it would not be too great a thing to face Simon. She would simply tell him that she would not try to hold him to her, that she would help him to find grounds for annulment in spite of the child. Her father's hope of using the babe to gain Simon's land could not be fulfilled with Simon alive.

The very thought of Simon's touching her again made her heart pound. She took a calming breath, telling herself she must not be caught up in this passion. Simon was available and would do well enough. He had shown her some courtesy in taking her part against her father, which was more honor than anyone else had given her since her uncle's death.

He would be a better father than her father would have chosen for her child. All she need do was make him understand she would not try to hold him. In the event that her father became angry over the annulment and refused to acknowledge the child as his heir, Isabelle would take him and flee Dragonwick, find her mother's sister in Normandy. She would simply say that she was widowed and had left her father, whom the lady had not seemed to like. Surely if that noble lady had come all the way to see her so many years ago she would have pity and take her in. Hope made her heart swell.

Though Isabelle wished for her son to be lord of the lands and owed it to her uncle's memory, she suddenly realized that having someone of her own to love, and leading her own life, was even more important. Perhaps Simon did not truly care for her, but his insistence that she could make her own choices was in fact sound advice.

The sale of her jewels would bring enough to sustain her, Helwys and the babe for a very long time. Though she was quite positive her father did not actually deem them her possessions they were kept in the chest in her room for he would never imagine her capable of leaving with them.

Armed with newfound independence and an astoundingly sensible plan, Isabelle knew she would find a way to convince Simon. She must. It seemed the only way to regain the once reassuring control she'd had over her emotions.

After lying wakeful for most of what remained of the night, she sent Helwys to ask her husband to come to her. She must strike just the correct note with Simon. She would rely upon their mutual desire. He had said he did not wish to consummate the marriage, but he had no more right to decide her life than her father. Though she knew nothing of seduction that was precisely what she must attempt. The way Simon had touched her, kissed her, the way he looked at her with those hot liquid brown eyes, told her he was not immune to her. The fact that thinking of it made her own body tighten did not please her. But soon that ache would be appeased and she would be free of the desire for him.

Even though she did not look about when the chamber door opened, Isabelle knew it was Simon. She could smell the fresh air, the brisk strength that he brought with him.

"Isabelle." The sound of her name on his lips made her tremble and she had to take a deep calming breath before facing him. It would not do to seem too eager.

She stood and turned toward him slowly. "Simon."

A dark brow arched high over narrowed eyes that seemed to study her closely. "You sent for me."

She nodded, ignoring her own discomfort with his manner. "I did." It was understandable that there would be some awkwardness between them after the way they had parted the last time they had spoken.

He continued to watch her with those mahogany eyes.

Now faced with the task of telling him why she had asked for him, Isabelle felt suddenly shy and uncertain. What had seemed perfectly reasonable when she was alone now seemed far less so when faced with her husband's assessing manner and overwhelmingly masculine presence.

Yet Isabelle was no craven. Calling upon all her powers of will she smiled pleasantly and indicated the chair she had just vacated, "Please, sit."

Simon continued to study her, though there was a brief flicker of something unreadable in his gaze as it passed over her deliberately bright smile. Slowly he came forward and took the seat as she took two steps backward.

His gaze met hers again. "You may come out with whatever it is you have called me here to say. You honor neither of us with your false civility and hesitancy."

She nodded, though his directness was somewhat maddening. Subtlety was wasted on the blackguard. "Very well, then. I will out with it. You know and I know that we each of us have our own desires for the future."

He curtly inclined his own head.

She wanted to throttle him for his lack of enthusiasm, yet that would not serve her purpose. Her tone was gracious even as she continued, "I have been thinking much in the days since we last spoke and I have realized there is no harm in each of us getting what we want."

He continued to watch her, waiting.

"Simon...I..." Now that it was time, the words stuck in her throat, refusing to come.

Simon studied the lovely Isabelle as she fought for control, intrigued in spite of himself as she turned and went to the window. She stared out with what appeared to be unseeing eyes. Simon found himself encouraging her to go on. He wondered if this interview was in any way connected to his unanswered questions concerning her involvement in her father's wish for him to produce a child. "What is it you are trying to say, Isabelle?"

She took a deep breath, squaring her shoulders, before coming back to him with another one of those deliberately bright smiles. That smile caused a tiny dimple to appear in her cheek and made his heart flutter in spite of its lack of genuineness. "I simply wish we could find some way to be friends, as you have suggested on several occasions."

Simon gave an inward grimace. He could hear the regret in his voice as he replied, "I do recall that I have told you as much."

Isabelle looked at him closely as she said, "Are you still of that mind?"

He shrugged, deliberately casual as he grew even more suspicious of her motives here. "Why would I not be? It was not me who rejected that notion."

He saw the momentary flash of chagrin in her eyes before she came toward him with slow deliberation. She did not stop until she had moved around him to stand directly behind his chair. When she spoke there was a new huskiness to her tone which surprised him and made him think of things he should not. "I am so very glad to hear that."

He was conscious of the warm soft scent of her and realized how very close she must be. Simon swallowed hard as he felt the fine hairs rise along the base of his neck. He attempted to speak evenly, to remember that he was only letting her play out her game. "Your words are surprising, especially after what occurred in the lodge. I thought that you might be... You have seemed distant." Why he said this he did not know, but he heard the regret in his tone.

He felt the barest brush of her velvet gown against the back of his neck now. Again he swallowed hard.

She whispered. "I was angry, perhaps for a time. But anger is not what I am feeling now, my husband."

He tried to think on what was happening here. His voice was hoarse when he said, "Isabelle?"

She gave a soft breathless laugh that sounded somewhat nervous; or perhaps it was just his own feeling that he was diverting to her. Her softly voiced, "Simon?" did not seem nervous. There was a definite hint of, God help him, seductiveness in her husky tone.

As soon as the thought entered his mind, Simon tossed it away. He could not believe such a thing. Not once in his acquaintance of Isabelle had he ever had any indication she would know of such things. Kelsey's daughter she might be, but he had seen naught but innocence in her. Even her fiery responses to his advances had not disguised that fact.

Even as this thought passed through his mind he felt the cool brush of her fingers on the back of his neck. A jolt of heat as intense as a lightning bolt shot through his body, stopped his breathing, tightened his lower belly.

Simon jumped up, spinning about to face her. "Isabelle, what are you doing?"

For a brief moment there was an expression of uncertainty in those lavender eyes. It was gone in the time it took her to take a quick breath in through her nose.

With what he would have considered undaunting perseverance were she an enemy on the battlefield, Isabelle came around the chair and moved toward him. Those lovely eyes raked him with a heat that shocked him. "I think you know what I am doing."

Simon felt his head swim as the promise in her voice conjured up images such as those that had kept him restless upon his pallet each night. He took her hands in his, and pressed them together as if that would somehow halt the heat that flowed between them. He forced himself to focus on his suspicions. "Has your father told you to say this?"

Her shock could not be feigned. "Why would you ask?"

He made himself go on despite his sudden realization that he was most likely wrong. "Then why do you come to me with this when your father has been so insistent?

She looked up at him, her eyes filled with entreaty. "You do not wish to be wed to me, yet I wish for a child. We need not remain wed. I would not expect it of you. I would help you attain your annulment, say anything you wished me to say. There was no bedding ceremony. You could claim that I had some deformity you were not aware of."

He sprang back from her. "In no way could I fathom fathering a child I would never know. I have learned too well that a father must know a son and a son his father in the loss of my own." His voice was rough with regret and horror as he growled, "Nay, never!"

Isabelle saw the surprise, the confusion and finally horror that passed over her husband's face. Embarrassment swept over her. But it was his harshly voiced denial that stabbed her with shame. After the way Simon had touched her, kissed her that day and the way he looked at her... She had thought if she made it clear she would not try to hold him...that all she wished was...

Clearly she had been sadly mistaken. For he believed that she was somehow in league with her father.

Suddenly the years ahead, the loneliness, the death of her own dreams fell in upon her, bringing a heavy aching to her breast that left her weak.

"Isabelle." It was said in a husky, pitying tone.

She did not want his pity. Desperately Isabelle swung about and ran. Blindly she found the latch on the door, jerking it open and racing down the hall, praying all the while that he would not follow, that he would leave her the tattered shreds that remained of her dignity.

Simon stood very still for a long moment. He knew he should let her go. Let things lie as they were. It was the best for both of them.

He could not. The image of her face, the pain she had been unable to hide, refused to leave him. It touched him even more deeply than the passion she had displayed, for that had been offered in aid of her desire to have a child.

A child he would have no part in rearing. How could she have imagined he would agree to such madness?

Again an image of her, her slender shoulders slumped as she ran from the room flashed into his mind. With a groan of utter frustration Simon went after her.

He caught a glimpse of the skirt of her burgundy gown disappearing at the end of the narrow hallway. He followed, down the stairs and through the keep, passing through the hall without seeing more than a glimpse of Isabelle as she exited the far door, which led to the courtyard.

He ignored the regard of the castle folk, continuing after her. It was only as he saw Isabelle disappear into the stables that he realized whence she must be going.

The hunting lodge. Somehow he knew she would go there.

And one thing he did know about his unpredictable wife was that she would want to be alone right now. When she emerged from the stable a moment later on her mare he knew he was correct in his thinking.

Simon went to the stables and told the wide-eyed stable boy that he wanted his horse immediately. The boy stared at Simon so intently as he began to saddle the horse that his efforts were greatly impaired. With a grimace, Simon took the saddle and completed the task himself.

He was on his way without delay but there was no sign of Isabelle when he left the castle gates. If he was wrong about her destination he would not find her.

But Simon had not been wrong. Her horse was tied outside the lodge. Simon left his stallion beside the mare and moved to open the door without ceremony. Isabelle was not immediately visible in the dim interior. But her quickly indrawn breath of shock drew his gaze to the bed.

She sat up hurriedly, wiping her hands over her face. "What are you doing here?"

Stung by the bitterness of her tone, he took a deep breath, telling himself her anger was not surprising. "I had to talk with you."

She raised her chin high and he felt the rage that emanated from her eyes though he could not see them in the dimness of the room. "There is nothing more to be said."

He took a step closer. "I think there is."

A choking sob escaped her. "Y-you h-have said all." He heard the quaver in her voice and knew she was shivering.

Quickly Simon moved to the hearth.

"Wh-What are you d-doing?" she asked him coldly.

He ignored her tone answering, evenly, "Lighting a fire."

"I do not require—"

He interrupted, "I can see that you are cold so there is no need to deny it."

She said no more and he built a fire with as little effort as he had the first time they had been here. But even that short time gave opportunity for his head to cool further, for him to decide he would face her resentment with calm reason.

When Simon was done, he stood, and she said, "Will you go now?"

He moved closer to her, keeping in mind his resolve to remain calm. "I...pray...forgive me for my vehemence in your chamber. It was not called for. I but meant for you to understand my position."

Isabelle stood, pointing toward the door. "Your purpose has been served. I understand your position."

He held out his hand. "Methinks you do not. I would offer my regret for any hurt I have done you. And my compassion."

She sucked in a quick breath that did not disguise that fact that it was accompanied by another sob. "I ask you, my lord, if there is any bit of compassion in you, to go and leave me with some pride."

"Perhaps you have too much pride."

To his amazement she rushed toward him in one fluid motion that caught him off guard. "How dare you? How dare you accuse me of having too much pride? You who have such a great surfeit of that very thing. You hold your pride before you like a shield."

Before he knew he was going to do so, he reached out to grasp her slight shoulders tightly. His stomach churned with exasperation. Never had any woman held the power to make him lose control of himself. Or, at least, not before this one. "That is a pretty insult coming from you."

She glared up at him, her eyes dark with resentment. "Are you the only one who is free to offer insult, my lord? Do you not see the insults to me?"

He grimaced. "I have behaved badly. But you must imagine how it looked when your father—"

She rolled her eyes, her reaction telling him that this was not the case. "Why would you think such a thing, when I have not revealed that we have not been together?"

Simon shrugged. "He has learned that I am no longer sleeping in your chambers. He again informed me of my duty to produce a child."

She became very still, her eyes now filled with something akin to fear, her skin too white even in this dim light. "Dear heaven, when did he do this? Does he know that we have not been together?"

He frowned. "Late last eve. Nay, I am sure he does not. He said only that I must return to your chambers and that I should not be lingering in the hall when my wife is not yet breeding."

Isabelle put her hands to her cheeks. "Dear God, he did not." She realized this must have preceded the portion of the conversation Isabelle had overheard.

There was no mistaking her genuine horror. "Aye, he did, and I began to wonder about your telling me how much you wanted a child, even a child of mine." He shrugged. "You are very obedient to him." He could hear the tightness in his own voice as he spoke of this.

She covered her face. "Heaven help me, I can find no rest from the desires and suspicions of others."

Again sympathy eased his anger. He let go of her shoulders, gently drawing her hands down from her, his gaze holding her tormented one. "Oh, Isabelle, what have we gotten into here?"

She glared at him, but beneath the outrage he could still see her misery. "Obviously something neither of us wanted." She looked away, tilting her head high. "Now that all is clear to you, I would be grateful if you would leave me in peace."

He stood his ground, willing her to face him and when she did he asked, "Why did you approach me again today when we had already decided this matter?"

Her lids came down to mask those incredible eyes. "You know I want a child. As I said, you would be as good a father as any other and I had thought if I made it clear that I would see that you obtained an annulment…"

He interrupted as his stomach clenched at the thought of her with another, but he forced himself to say, "As you said, any man could produce a child. You do not need me if you intend to give me an annulment anyway."

Isabelle looked away. "In spite of the many irritating qualities you possess you are not without merit as a man. Helwys says that you have treated her well, that you are the same with the other servants and castle folk.''

He was somewhat surprised that she would set so much store in such simple things. She did not realize that most men were not as her father and that Simon had shown no more than human decency.

But she went on, her words and husky tone distracting him from his thoughts. ''Beyond that there are these feelings inside me. These strange things that happen when you touch me. I...'' She halted, flushing as she stared down.

Simon now felt a stirring inside himself. The admission, made so close upon her unflattering statement that he would make as good a father as any other, was far more powerful than it might otherwise have been.

His voice was strangely hoarse as he said, ''I realize it is not easy for you to speak of such things to me. But you need never be shamed by your passion. 'Tis human to feel thusly, to want another in that way, to show your feelings.'' The very words stirred him as he recalled just how open her reactions to his caresses had been.

She made no answer, only bowed her head, the nape of her neck so pale and vulnerable, so kissable. Simon found himself saying her name again and this time he heard the yearning in his own voice. ''Isabelle.''

She looked up at him then, her eyes so very lovely, like damp violets, uncertain, defenseless. ''As I said, I would not have your pity.''

He felt his chest tighten. His gaze moved over her face, which was even more beautiful because of this vulnerability. There was a softness in the previously disdainful angle of her head, and in the gentle slope of her shoulders. This was a woman who might welcome a man, might react to his strength with warmth. Simon's body responded to this thought with a shocking intensity.

Perhaps he had been wrong to be so set on an annulment. Perhaps he and Isabelle could make a life together if they could only get away from this place. Perhaps he was only reasoning this way because he wanted her so desperately. Yet he could summon no will to stop himself.

He heard himself admitting, "I am feeling many things at the moment. I assure you pity is not amongst them."

Isabelle's eyes seemed to darken to purple. She whispered, "I do not know..."

His gaze came to rest on those luscious raspberry lips. "I do." He bent and took them with his own.

Isabelle started, raising her hands to the hard wall of Simon's chest. She meant to stop him. She didn't want him now, not after the way he had rejected her with such cold vehemence.

Did she?

But her wayward fingers reached up to curl around the hard curves of his shoulders. Her mouth, traitor that it was, softened under his and her equally traitorous body pressed itself more fully along his solid length.

Simon felt the softening of her mouth with a feeling of exultation. Isabelle would always respond to him this way—as he did to her.

No more would he attempt to fight a force that was greater than the reasons against it.

His hands slipped down her back, molding the sweet curves of her waist and hips. They paused at her hips, holding her against him and she pressed closer to his body, tilting her head back. Simon dipped his head at this invitation, his mouth tracing the line of her jaw, the fragile length of her white neck.

When he flicked his tongue over the pulse at its base she caught her breath. Isabelle felt the swell of longing inside her and tried desperately to gain control of her breathing. Her head was whirling, her body brought to life with only a few kisses.

But there was no wresting control of these feelings. Those feelings…her body, would have its own way in this. Her hands moved to the front of his tunic, gliding over the heavy velvet that only partially disguised hard muscle and bone, but left her frustrated with a longing to touch his smooth skin.

Simon passed a hand up Isabelle's side, the tips of his fingers brushing over the gentle curve of her breast which was so enticing above the low neckline of that burgundy gown. The gown she had deliberately donned in order to seduce him. The very thought made his blood heat even more.

Isabelle wanted him.

Simon leaned back, looking down at her. She was so beautiful with her eyes heavy with passion, her thick black lashes fringed against her high cheek bones, which were flushed from his kisses.

Isabelle felt Simon's gaze upon her and glanced up at him through her lashes. She flushed with new heat when she saw the passion in his eyes, which seemed to burn with an inner fire.

She leaned close, her hands trembling on his shoulders as she raised her lips, inviting his kiss. His mouth found hers and they kissed again, with a thoroughness that left both of them breathless.

Her lids were heavy as she looked at him, her cheeks flushed with need. "I want…"

Tendrils of need shot through his lower body. He reached down to lift the hem of the garment over his head in one swift motion. He wanted nothing between himself and this woman, this glorious wanton who drove him to new heights of yearning.

He looked into her eyes, holding them with his own as he lifted her in his arms. She did not break that contact as he carried her to the bed. Slowly he let her go, feeling the length of her against him as she slipped to the floor. Still holding her gaze he reached out to slip the velvet gown up and over her head with the same ease of motion that he had his own garment.

Her shift was made of a fabric so fine that it gave away as much of the sweet form beneath it as it disguised in the light of the fire. Sweat beaded on his brow at the very thought of removing it, of seeing those long lovely legs, her…

Then his heart stopped as Isabelle herself lifted up her arms and pulled the garment over her head. His gaze locked on the shift, which fluttered down in a white cloud to pool on the floor.

He took a deep breath, his gaze moving slowly over those long legs, the slender hips, the narrow indent of her waist and, Saint George grant him strength, the gentle but womanly curves of her high, proud breasts.

Again he met her gaze, saw the uncertainty in it. He reached out to her. ''So lovely, Isabelle, so very lovely.''

Heat suffused Isabelle as Simon's gaze scorched her sensitive flesh. It burned in her belly, her breasts, along every inch of her skin. She felt a trembling in her legs that only seemed to increase with the growing dampness betwixt her thighs.

She went into his arms, her lips soft against his hard

male chest. His flesh tingled where her warm breath touched him. His hands found the softness of her slim back, her hips, which seemed made for his hands to hold, the upper curve of her bottom.

Between each eager kiss she placed upon his chest, she whispered his name. "Simon…Simon…Simon…"

He silenced her with his lips even as he lifted her, placing her soft slender form on the bed. He reached up to tug her hair free of the knotted braid at the base of her neck. Then gently, carefully, he worked his fingers through the silken mass causing it to fall forward to her lap.

With trembling fingers he brought a handful to his face to breath in the wildflower scent of it. There was wonder in his voice as he whispered, "I've never seen hair the color of yours. It is like burgundy wine. So beautiful, it takes my breath."

Isabelle shuddered as a shaft of pure sweet longing pierced her lower belly at his words. Weakened by her own desire, she lay back upon the pillows reaching out her arms to him as he bent over her.

But Simon was not yet ready to go into them. He instead dipped his head to her breasts, nuzzling their tender undersides with his lips and cheeks.

Where his mouth and warm breath touched her, she burned, reveling in the feelings that continued to build inside her but yearning for something that lay just beyond her knowledge and experience. Isabelle held her breath. Her head fell backward on her neck with the weight of the hair he had said was beautiful. It was simply too heavy to hold upright with this passion-driven weakness running through her body.

When his lips closed on the tip of her nipple she gasped aloud, her hands going to the back of his head.

She did not know what to do, to hold him or push him away for this wanting inside her seemed too much to bear. But her fingers twined in his thick dark hair, pulling him to her.

Again his name escaped her lips and this time it was a plea. "Simon."

He felt her hands on his back now, urgent and strong. The desperation in her voice told of the intensity of her longing and he knew he could no more wait now than she.

He rose over her, his gaze finding hers again. "Yes, my Isabelle, yes."

Isabelle watched him, hearing the promise in his voice with a sob of stark and reckless need.

Simon placed his hand on the silken length of her thigh and her breathing became even shallower. He swallowed as his manhood throbbed. Not since his first experience with a woman had Simon felt so near to becoming unmanned, of not being able to hold himself back from the brink.

Keeping as tight a hold on himself as his aching body would allow, Simon slid his hand around to the inside of her thigh. Isabelle opened to him with no further urging and once again he was forced to pause, to will his breathing to calm, to try desperately to damp down the fire burning in his belly.

He bit his lower lip, moving carefully to place himself between those silky, warm thighs.

When those soft and eager hands reached out to hold his arms, to encourage him, he knew the struggle was done. He slipped into the warmth of her body with only the briefest of hesitation at the boundary of her womanhood. Yet he paused, his breathing more labored than before as he was determined to cause her no unnecessary pain.

Her soft cry of pleasure told him that he need not worry about hurting her.

And when her body rose up beneath him, he rocked forward, finding a rhythm that matched the sharp intake and release of her breath. The ache in his body built to a fever pitch and Simon was lost, drowning in the sensations that rose and expanded inside him.

Isabelle could not breathe, could not think of anything save the sensations that radiated from the place where their bodies joined. They pulsed and grew until she could feel nothing beyond a need that drove her to she knew not what. But it was clear that her body did know, for her body shifted and rose under Simon's, meeting his thrusts. The sensations grew ever stronger, more compelling, until with a hoarse cry of surprise and unsurpassed joy, a night sky exploded behind her closed eyes, filling her mind, her body, her soul.

When Isabelle stiffened, uttering an inarticulate cry of both surprise and joy, that indescribable spike of need exploded in a fine point of pleasure so intense Simon groaned out loud in ecstasy. His body surged forward meeting hers, pouring into her, his Isabelle, the source of all pleasure.

She lay there beneath him, the stars flashing in her head, her body throbbing so exquisitely that it was difficult to bear. But bear it she did, and even gloried in every rippling streak of light.

At long last, Isabelle opened her eyes and looked up at Simon. There was no reading the expression in those warm brown depths. He seemed...well...different somehow...softer. Or perhaps it was simply the change that she could feel, the vulnerability, inside herself that made him seem so.

Isabelle closed her eyes again and waited. Simon rolled to lie beside her and even then she did not look at him, though she could feel his gaze upon her.

She lifted her arm to shield her face, not wanting him to see her this way. Not understanding what this feeling of having her every emotion bared, her uncertainty, might mean. What they had done, the things he had made her feel, had left her completely open and exposed to this man.

And that she could not accept, especially when she had hope that lying with him would produce just the opposite effect. Simon Warleigh was too much an unknown. He could not be allowed into a position where he might hurt her.

Chapter Ten

Simon became aware of her withdrawal with a jarring sense of disappointment. He told himself his reaction was completely without warrant. He had no one but himself to blame for taking this woman as his wife. Desire had made him mad, the desire that still burned in him even as she pulled away.

Isabelle had made no protestation of affections. She had, in fact, made her feelings clear from the start. That the lovemaking they had shared was the most incredible of his life had no bearing on anything.

Softly he said, "Don't worry, Isabelle. I understand that this doesn't mean anything." His tone firmed, "Yet I would have you know that I will have my child in spite of how things are between the two of us."

He felt her stiffen. She took a deep breath and lowered her arm from where it covered her face. Those beautiful eyes were emotionless, where only moments ago they had been soft with repletion. "And I understand your feelings, but I ask this one thing of you."

He raised a questioning dark brow and she said, "I would ask that you do not speak of the future yet."

He frowned as he realized there was no point in

pressing the matter now. He was not yet free to take his reluctant bride home with him. "If that is your wish." He shrugged. "Am I to take it that it is still your intent to produce a child with me?"

She sat up, looking away. "Yes, of course. I...yes." She faced him with a defiantly raised chin. "That is my desire and there is nothing amiss in that."

He nodded. "I did not say there was." He paused for a long moment. "Well...lest you are already breeding, it will mean that we must..." Simon considered himself something of an experienced man, yet he felt extremely uncomfortable having this unemotional conversation. It was as if their making love again were of no more import than a casual ride about the grounds, when inside him he felt an eagerness that was shocking. He told himself that eagerness was based on his own desire to have a child, an heir, who would love Avington as his father and brother had. As he did.

Her lavender eyes widened. "Do you mean now?"

A jolt of excitement raced through him. Flushing he spoke quickly, "Not necessarily." Despite her enthusiasm Isabelle had been a virgin. He would not use her ill.

She subsided. Was there disappointment in that gaze or was it his own reaction that made him think so? He tried to cover his own need with civility. "Not unless you wish to."

She did not look at him. "I...thank you but I...we would not wish to be gone from the keep for too long."

He grimaced. "Of course." Simon was reluctant for Kelsey to know when and if she became pregnant. He told himself it was because the man had already made too many demands in that area.

Almost as if she had read his mind, Isabelle said, "I

would prefer it if we could keep this to ourselves for the time being.'' He watched her and she went on. ''I...''

Simon held up a hand. ''There is no need to explain. I prefer to keep what we do to ourselves as well.''

Damn Kelsey. Simon realized his having bedded Isabelle meant he would never be completely free of the earl, but he need not have him in his bed. He said, ''I propose we agree to meet here again, in this lodge. It does not appear to have been used by your father for some time and he has been amenable to our going riding together.''

She studied her hands with great care. ''I shall arrange for clean linens and candles.''

He took a breath. ''Very well, then.''

''Yes.'' She flicked him a glance. ''I should like to dress now.''

He bowed his head. ''Of course.'' Simon stood, gathering up his own garments. She avoided looking at him and once he was garbed, he said, ''I shall fetch the horses.''

Isabelle did not reply.

As he went out into the chill fall afternoon, Simon could not help thinking this had been a very odd morning indeed. He had made love to the most beautiful woman he had ever known and had then spoken of it in a manner so matter-of-fact that it offended his senses.

Yet, if that was the way Isabelle wished for things to be, he would not press her. It was not as if he knew whence this marriage was headed. Once he heard word of the nobles' reaction to Christian's father's letters, then they would have to discuss their relationship, their future. But until then he would abide by his word.

Surely if he and Isabelle could get away from here,

from her father, she would begin to warm to him, at least enough to have some semblance of a marriage. Simon shook his head, dismissing an unshakable sense of doubt. There was no need to worry on that until the time came.

Isabelle held her breath until the door closed behind Simon Warleigh. Only then did she expel it in a rush.

Dear heaven above, she thought as she leapt from the bed and took up her clothing with trembling fingers. It had been all she could do to hide her sadness from Simon. He wanted her child, did he? Well, Isabelle had no intention of his having her child. Again she felt a rush of misery. If only he had not made it clear that the babe was his only concern. If only he had said he wanted her.

But he had not, in spite of the fact that they had shared the most astounding moments of her life.

It was, in fact, a complete relief to recall just how things were between them after she had, for those brief moments when their loving was done, felt so exposed. That he had not been moved in the same way as she should not disappoint her. She must think on the fact that Simon was willing to continue to meet her here.

She tried with all her might to believe the level of excitement and anticipation she felt in spite of her regret at his only wanting the child had nothing to do with the force of the passion she had just shared with Simon. Yet she could not deny that she had felt a renewed rush of longing so powerful it shocked her at the thought of being with him again.

Simon himself was so very cool about the whole matter. She must certainly continue to answer his attitude with a similar one.

She threw her cape about her shoulders and with it, her pride. She would take things as they were and live life one moment at a time. If passion could be a part of that, she would also take that, as it came.

There was no more discussion as they mounted and rode toward the castle. It had all been said, but the knowledge that they would be returning soon, and why, hung between them like a spider's web between two branches, connecting the two of them with surprising tenacity.

When she went to her chamber, Helwys informed Isabelle that her father was expecting her. For a moment a rush of anxiety so intense that it made her knees weak rocked her. Could he have found out about her and Simon?

Quickly she quelled it. Her father could not know what she and Simon had just done. He believed, in fact, that they had already consummated their marriage.

Isabelle moved toward his chamber with her head held high. She would give away nothing about what she and Simon were doing, nor her own plan to leave Dragonwick. His determination for her to have a babe with all due haste was solely due to his desire to end Simon's life. As long as they were able to hide a pregnancy—should one occur—until Simon was gone, he was in no danger.

Her father was sitting at his writing table, bent over the long columns in one of his ledgers. He looked up with raised eyebrows as she opened the door. "Isabelle. I sent for you some time ago."

She faced him without wavering, though her heart fluttered with anxiety. "I was riding with Simon Warleigh."

Her father scowled. "Then it could not have been him."

"Of what do you speak, Father?"

He raked her with a preoccupied glance. "I narrowly missed being hit by an arrow this very morn."

She gasped, starting toward him, for in spite of her hatred of him a part of her, the one that had always longed for his love, loved him. "Are you al—"

He raised a hand, "There is no need for sentimentality. As you see I am quite whole." He looked at her more closely. "I had a particularly unpleasant conversation with Warleigh last eve. He was…confrontational." His cold gaze raked her once again. "Why did you not tell me he had moved from your chamber?"

She took a deep breath. "I had not had opportunity to do so, Father."

He frowned thoughtfully. "'Tis true that I have been gone much of late. There is much to do in collecting my portion of the harvests. I would not be shorted."

She knew she should not be shocked that he was more concerned about his harvests than being shot at. "But who could have fired upon you, Father?"

"If 'twas not Warleigh then I know not. You see, he dropped this." He reached to take an object from beneath the ledger. "He was with you the whole of the morning?"

Shock rocked her as she saw the dragon brooch. She had seen it, or its twin, on Simon's cloak. "Yes, Father." She could hear the amazement and confusion in her voice.

He was scowling again. "His men are also accounted for." He shook his head. "It makes no sense for I have seen this brooch upon your husband's cloak. He was very angry after I told him that I expected him to do his duty in getting you with child. He informed me that I had no say in what went on between the two of you."

Isabelle cringed inside but maintained her composure as she answered in the way he expected. "How foolish of him."

He lifted a gray brow. "Precisely. Even if the man is in no way connected to what occurred in the wood this day, which seems impossible, we will be well served to be rid of him once he is of no further use to us."

The first time her father had said this it had troubled her. This time a shaft of ice seemed to pierce her chest. "Father, are you bent on seeing him dead?"

He frowned. "As soon as you are with child, thus assuring my wardship of Avington and all Warleigh's other holdings, he shall meet what I feel to be a most timely end. He was a fool to attempt to plot against me and will lose all because of it."

Simon had told her that her father had been his true target. Isabelle was able to keep any sign of her inner disgust from her voice when she said, "But will not King John be angered after having left Warleigh in your care?"

Her father laughed harshly. "King John will be most pleased to be rid of a problem in the form of one Simon Warleigh. Did Warleigh choose to take up his sword and join the growing number of barons who are against the king, he would certainly influence others to do the same."

"Then why did the king not simply have him hanged at the outset? Why force him into a marriage with me?"

Her father's gaze narrowed. "Why this sudden concern for Warleigh? You do not mean to take my enemy's part?''

She shook her head, but not too quickly, for she knew that would be as telling as to react too slowly. ''Nay, Father, I simply try to think ahead. To prevent any difficulty from falling to you for Warleigh's sake.''

She knew she had struck just the right tone between indifference and irritation when he smiled thinly. ''Very good. But you need have no concern over any complications for me. There are methods of disposing of a man that would seem quite accidental.''

Isabelle's heart stopped as her father went on. ''You will see to your part and get yourself with child so that there will be no question as to my right to oversee the lands.''

Isabelle did not meet his gaze. ''I will do my utmost to fulfill my duty as soon as possible, though, as you say, Warleigh has left my chamber.''

He frowned. ''Surely you can do something to remedy that.''

''I...will do my best.'' She returned his gaze though it took all her will to do so. ''You know how contrary the man is.''

''See that it is done.'' He nodded, looking down at his ledger once more. And that was the end of it.

Isabelle knew she had been dismissed. Without another word, she went to the door and let herself out.

The horror and misery she felt at her father's expectations of her, his devious coldness, remained locked inside her. As they always had.

It was not as easy to dismiss her fear for Simon. She considered warning him again. Yet she knew he would not heed her. He felt himself invincible. She soothed herself with the notion that as long as her father be-

lieved she was not with child Simon would be safe—
lest he acted against her father.

She thought again of the brooch. There was no denying that it was exactly the same as the one he wore.
She would see on the morrow if he still had it. And
what if he did not? It could mean that he had enlisted
someone's aid, someone who was in as much danger as
he if they thought to strike out at her father.

Isabelle could not forget the cold ice in her father's
eyes as he said he was growing tired of the problem of
Simon Warleigh, that he could be disposed of without
complication. She knew he was not speaking idly.

She was determined to discover if he had been involved in the attack. If so, she would convince him that
he must stop before he was found out. Not only she,
but Simon must escape her father. She owed him that
for his willingness to give her what she wanted most—
a child.

So thinking she approached Helwys that very afternoon. "Helwys, I would have you take clean linens and
some other supplies to a lodge that lays in the wood not
far from the castle. You are to tell no one of this. Do
not allow anyone to even see you go there."

The maid looked at her in confusion for a moment
before light dawned in her face. "It is for you and Lord
Warleigh. You mean to seduce him." Isabelle was
shocked at the approval in her tone.

Chagrinned she frowned at the shorter woman. Yet
the years of theirs being the only warm relationship in
Isabelle's life made her answer honestly. "I had meant
to, but it did not prove necessary."

Isabelle was amazed at the smile that lit up Helwys's
face. "I am so very glad, my lady. Now he will find a
way to take you away from this place."

Isabelle stiffened. She could not tell the woman who loved her so dearly that she would not be leaving here with Simon. Nor was she ready to tell her of her own plan for her and Helwys to go to her aunt in Normandy after she had conceived a child.

Not that Isabelle did not trust her maid implicitly. She simply felt it best to keep her plans close to her until she was ready to put them into effect. That way Helwys would not be in a position of behaving normally with two such enormous confidences to hold inside her.

Thus thinking she faced the other woman with what she hoped was a calm expression. "Can I rely upon your discretion in seeing to the cottage? I am more closely watched and must have a care to do nothing that would make my father suspicious."

Helwys nodded quickly. "I will see to it, though I do not understand why you would keep this secret when your father's wish that you produce a child is so well-known."

Isabelle felt her stomach tighten. "Aye, it is. But I have my reasons."

The maid bowed her dear head. "Your wishes are mine, my lady."

Isabelle slept little that night. As soon as she arose a sense of nervous anticipation swept away any hint of tiredness. She did not find Simon in the hall.

She did find him on the practice field with his men.

Isabelle approached him slowly. He looked up from where he was pointing out some specific feature of his sword edge to his squire, his brown eyes meeting hers. There was a sudden and measurable softening in them.

She felt definite tingling along her backbone, a sense of anticipation. Isabelle hesitated, her gaze dropping, as she recalled that this meant nothing really. He did not truly desire her for herself. He but acted on the passion that existed between them and was prepared to have her because of any child that might come of that passion. Isabelle reminded herself of her own resolve to take that passion for what it was. She moved forward even more slowly than before.

When Isabelle could force herself to look at Simon again, she saw that he was motioning his men away with a distracted gesture, not taking his gaze from her. Could it be that he knew why she was there?

He took the last two steps to her. "Isabelle."

She focused on the neckline of his tunic. "Simon."

He spoke softly. "I trust you are well."

Still not meeting his gaze she cast a glance about the field, which was littered with the implements for learning to make war, including arrow butts, quintains and lists. It was far easier to look at anything but him. "I am. And you?"

He laughed softly, wryly. "I find that I am very well indeed this day."

Her gaze skittered to his and away when she saw the warmth in it. She whispered, "Simon, I... Helwys has gone to prepare the lodge."

She could feel him nod. "I see."

She took a deep breath. "Would you care to go riding with me this morn?"

He spoke in what seemed a carefully even tone. "Aye. I would be most pleased to go riding with you."

Another wave of anticipation raced through her body, heating her blood at his reply. At the same time she was beset by a strange sadness at knowing that this really meant nothing to either one of them.

Quickly she reminded herself that she wanted nothing from this man. Though he did not seem cruel and cold like her father she really knew very little of him, other than the passion he could awaken in her so easily.

Her gaze flicked to his shoulder. The brooch was in place. So it had not been Simon.

She quickly brushed aside the wave of pleasure that washed through her, squaring her shoulders as she faced him, speaking as evenly as possible, "After the morning meal then." She and Simon had nothing more than an agreement to accomplish a purpose.

Simon cast a quick but unmistakably perturbed glance over her as he bowed. "I shall be most pleased to attend you...Isabelle." He said her name in a way that brought the events of the previous day to life inside her.

Again Isabelle looked down, shy of his seeing her reactions. With a nod, she moved away, walking in a fog of uncertainty, and yes, anticipation.

It was not until she was upon him that she became aware of her father. "Isabelle?"

She peered up at him surprise. "Father."

He cast a glance from her to Simon. "You do well."

For a moment she could not imagine what he was talking about, though the praise was so surprising that it warmed her. Then remembrance hit. He spoke of her and Simon. "Aye, Father, Simon is going riding with me this morn."

"Very good indeed," he told her briskly. But as he said the words, Isabelle, ever cognizant of her father's moods and reactions could feel a strange tension in him.

She looked down at her hands. "Simon wears his brooch. The one you found could not be his."

The words made his scowl deepen. He leaned close to her. "You seem pleased by this."

She forced herself to meet his gaze. "I would please

you, Father and am only relieved that you need not watch your back within the keep.''

There was nothing discernable in his voice as he went on. "I am well pleased with your loyalty to me, Isabelle, and bid you remember that this does not prove Warleigh's lack of involvement. Be on your guard for any information that might be of interest to me."

She watched him move off toward his waiting horse beside the stable with a sudden and overwhelming sense of sorrow. Why could things not have been different between them? Why was she naught but a pawn to him? Why could he not have loved her as she imagined a father should? But he did not. She had no one but Helwys. And God willing, her mother's sister.

Unconsciously she looked to Simon Warleigh where he now stood once more with his men, his gaze on her father's back as he rode through the gate. Suddenly feeling unaccountably angry with herself, Isabelle turned and hurried into the keep.

They rode to the cottage in near silence, neither of them seeming to know what to say.

Once inside Isabelle saw that Helwys had indeed readied the lodge. The bed was turned down to display fine snowy linens. Fresh candles graced the table beside the bed as did a pitcher and two glasses. Going to it, Isabelle saw that the pitcher contained wine.

She turned to Simon who was in the act of building a fire. "Helwys has left wine. Would you care for some?"

He cast her a glance. "Aye, thank you."

Isabelle was glad for that much to do. It helped to keep her from thinking…

Never was a glass of wine poured more carefully. By

the time she turned back to face him Simon had stood back from the now flickering fire. She held it out to him, carefully keeping her features schooled to unconcern even as she handed him the glass without touching his large hand, the hand that would soon...

Carefully Simon reached around her to set the cup down on the table, his hard chest but inches from her own. His gaze met hers. "Isabelle."

She did not break that gaze. "Yes?"

He raised one gentle finger to trace her cheek. "You ask me not to speak of the future. I ask one thing of you."

"Yes."

"There will be no coldness here between us, not when we are here for this purpose. I have seen you with the maid, offering her comfort, warmth. I know it is in you."

She flushed, stiffening. She looked down at her hands, which were twisted tightly before her and took a deep breath. Was it really so very much to ask? He could only think to enjoy their passion more fully. And was she not determined to do that as well? "I...will try."

He put a gentle hand on hers, and she looked up into those warm brown eyes. There was a trace of irony in his tone. "That will have to serve."

His gaze moved to her mouth and without even thinking, Isabelle felt it soften, felt herself lean into him. Simon closed the space with his lips.

His arms slid about her, pulling her close against his strong form and all at once her awkwardness melted away. Simon did indeed know what to do. His hands moved down her back to her hips, holding her, molding her to his hardness, which grew as she opened her mouth to receive his tongue.

She felt her own core soften and moisten, sending out tendrils of desire through her lower body. She was amazed at her own ready response but too overcome by the force of it to question.

She could only feel the ache in her belly, the pounding in her blood. With a gasp of longing, Isabelle pulled her mouth from his. She grasped the hem of his tunic, this time with no hint of her previous timidity.

Simon put his hands over hers, raining hungry kisses on her face as he pulled it up and off.

He turned back to her, not reaching to her clothing as she had expected but to the coil of her hair. With gentle hands he pulled it free to fall about her to her hips.

Simon smoothed that tangled mass of black burgundy with a trembling hand. He could hear the huskiness in his own voice as he whispered, "This, too, I ask, that you leave your hair unbound for me."

Isabelle could not speak for her throat was suddenly dry from the quickness of her breathing as his passion-darkened eyes held hers. Her reply was to tug impatiently at the laces of her cape. He stopped her, removing it and the gown beneath it with ease and the feel of her hair on her own body was now more sensuous than she would ever have imagined because of the way he saw it.

It was Isabelle who pulled off her shift, tossing it aside. Once bared she moved to come back into his arms but he held her away. "Let me look at you. I shall never tire of looking at you."

That word. *Never.* For a moment it tore through her determination to think of nothing save the now. There would be no *never* for them but that was no cause for mourning.

She overcame her momentary lapse. There was no need for more than this moment, the heat of desire inside her and in this man.

She raised up to press her mouth to his once more, kissing him with an abandon that made her own head spin, her blood sing in her veins. She ran her hands over his chest, tucked her fingers into the top of his hose. Down she tugged and they pulled away, baring him.

Simon felt himself spring free and groaned. He had reveled in and enjoyed Isabelle's passion the previous day. Had it only been a day? It had seemed so much longer when he was waiting for this moment to arrive.

Now he found himself awed, drowning in the eager wildness of his wife's response to him. As her fingers closed over the throbbing length of him, Simon's knees weakened, and he gasped her name aloud, "Isabelle."

He shivered when she laughed softly, her mouth closing over his male nipple. Simon threaded his fingers through her hair, tugging gently until her head fell back. He kissed her. "No, you don't. I have yet to ready you for love."

She did not look away, her lids heavy as she whispered, "I have no further need of preparation, my lord. I would have you now."

He rested his palm over the joining of her thighs. He swallowed hard as his stomach tightened further at finding her so damp. She was indeed ready for him.

But Simon, greedy and determined to have more of Isabelle than this, forced his speeding heart to calm. He looked into her eyes. "Come." He lifted her in his arms and laid her upon those snowy linens. Her body was golden and warm with the firelight playing over it.

She held out her arms and Simon shook his head, dipping his head to her breast. Isabelle cried out with both pleasure and disappointment. She wanted him so very desperately, needed an easing of the ache of longing that was so intense it made her body quiver from head to toe.

When she tugged at him, he raised up, looking into her glazed eyes. "Will you trust me in this one thing, Isabelle?"

As she looked at him she felt something inside her give way, a wall that had never been breached since the day her uncle died. "I will."

He dipped his head once more and suckled at her other breast until she was writhing beneath him, glorying in eagerness for him. When she moved her head from side to side in frustration, he moved lower, felt her stomach quiver under his questing tongue.

Isabelle was aflame, her body aching with a need so great that she knew not what to do. Simon's warm tongue on her belly only served to send another wave of desire shooting through her, making her dig her fingers into the heavy hair at his nape.

She had said that she would trust him, but she burned to have this wanting reach its culmination.

It was not until he moved on, his cheek brushing against her nether curls that she realized what he might be about. Even as she opened her eyes, his tongue found her most secret core. Isabelle cried out, her fingers pushing and holding him at the same time. As he deepened the intimate kiss, her head fell back and she sobbed aloud.

The passion built until Isabelle could do no more than

utter hoarse whispers of wanting as she climbed higher and higher along that path of ecstasy. And then she stiffened as she reached the summit of that fine and indescribable pinpoint of pleasure. She cried out, rising up beneath him, her body opening to him completely.

Only when the ripples of pleasure had ceased did Isabelle open her eyes. She was lying in Simon's arms, his warm gaze upon her face.

He smiled. "You are beautiful."

She studied his face, the handsome lines and angles that so filled her thoughts from the day she had met him. Honesty and the wonder at the experience she had just had made her say, "As are you, my lord."

"Simon."

She swallowed, feeling more uncomfortable than ever at the thought of saying his name, but also knowing it odd to think thusly after the things they had done. "Simon."

Simon felt unaccountably pleased with her and himself. He had wanted to enjoy more of Isabelle's body before ending their interlude. And he had done just that.

He could not but be aware of the pleasure she had taken from his caresses, his kisses. He was also achingly aware of his own unslaked desire.

She leaned back peeking up at him from beneath her heavy lashes. "Are we finished, then?"

He could not help grinning. "Oh, nay, we are not finished. We have not proceeded in the matter of the child." He had bought himself a few more moments with her, for she would not wish to return to the keep until they had performed the act that could produce her babe. He smiled, then bent to nibble the side of her neck.

Was he only putting his own desires onto his wife or

was there relief and pleasure in those lilac eyes? As she tilted her head further back to give him better access to her throat, saying, "We can not forget that," he thought, aye relief and pleasure indeed.

Simon's triumph soon turned to a more pressing emotion as he felt her soft hands on his shoulders. She raked her hands through his hair, sighing with pleasure as he kissed her breasts, which were still swollen, the nipples rigid from his loving. He took one tip into his mouth and felt the tug of longing that raced though his own body.

Isabelle was first surprised and then gladdened by the desire that rose up inside her so soon upon her recent sense of utter fulfillment. She was ever so glad that Simon was not yet ready to go back to the castle. Though she told herself that she should be so, as her purpose was to produce a child, it was hard to recall such things with her blood beginning to pulse in that now familiar way.

The pressure of Simon's mouth on her breast increased and with it the pressure of desire in her lower belly.

Simon felt the changes in her body, felt the passion that made her breath quicken afresh with a wave of longing so strong he felt his own head spinning. When her soft hands urged him to raise his head he did so, looking into those passion-dark eyes.

Isabelle kissed him, deeply and with all the desire that he had awakened inside her. With that kiss came a fresh ripple of need that made her stomach muscles clench, her limbs quiver.

Simon felt her hands, cool and eager on his flesh, tracing the contours of his chest, then moving lower to his belly. He sucked in a breath, holding his breath as her fingers closed over him.

His pulsing response was immediate and unmistakable. He could take no more and judging from her breathing, Isabelle would not have him delay either. Deliberately he rose up over her, his knee slipping between hers.

She watched him, her eyes never leaving his as he eased into that incredible and welcoming warmth. Again he felt the rush of pleasure in his body and stilled himself, closing his eyes for a moment to shut out the sight of her passion, which only made his own all the more intense, more overwhelming.

Isabelle was awed by the powerful beauty of Simon's face. It was so filled with the tension of need, yet so open at the same time in a way that made her heart contract in her chest.

As he began to move inside her, she felt her own body take up a rhythm that it seemed to know instinctively. She met each thrust with anticipation, the pleasure building with each rise of her body, each fall of his. They were in perfect union, she and Simon, rising and falling over and over again, climbing together toward that unutterable crest of ecstasy.

As he stiffened above her, he opened his eyes and looked at her. In that moment Isabelle reached her own completion, feeling as if she were falling into Simon, for he was pleasure itself and she his willing disciple.

Only when the ripples of desire had eased did Isabelle's reaction appall her. As it had the first time they'd been together. Never would she give up her autonomy, her sense of self, for another soul.

She could not do so. Had she not learned by the most difficult road she could conceive of that her heart could not be trusted with any man? If her own father could not be trusted, then no man could.

Isabelle sat up, taking the sheet with her. She did not look at Simon as she said, "I...we should be going back now. That is, if you wish to keep our meetings here from being known, we should not remain so long that we risk being seen here together."

Isabelle knew it was a poor excuse. No one would come, but she simply had to leave, to put some distance between herself and her own mad reactions to this man.

Simon seemed very still on the bed behind her. Finally he replied, "Aye."

Relief filled her as she heard him rise and dress. Only when he reached the door did she stop him. "You will come back again tomorrow?"

He watched her closely, his dark eyes seeming to see far too much. "Is that what you truly want?"

She raised her head. "Of course, we must be certain that I will bear a child." The sooner that deed was accomplished the better, for her response to Simon's lovemaking troubled her greatly.

He looked away. "Of course, the child. I had forgotten for a moment that that was your one reason for being here."

She told herself she was utterly mistaken in feeling that there was an underlying unhappiness in his voice. "What other reason could there be?"

He nodded sharply. "You will get what you want, Isabelle. As I will, for I would see my lands secured if naught else, now that I have commited myself to this..." His lips twisted. "Union." With that he was gone.

Stung by his reminder that it was not her he wanted, Isabelle was grateful that she need make no reply. The tightness in her throat would have given away her dejection. Why she felt thusly she could not say for Warleigh had only reinforced her certainty that no man could be trusted with her feelings.

She gave no more than the briefest thought to her guilt over not providing him with his heir. Once she was gone and their marriage dissolved under whatever grounds he wished, Simon would be relieved to be shed of her.

She was quite convinced that running away was indeed best for both of them. It seemed entirely likely that King John would have little choice in granting Simon his freedom if his bride had abandoned him.

They would both get what they held most dear.

Chapter Eleven

Over a month passed with Isabelle and Simon meeting at the cottage whenever possible.

Her father continued to monitor her actions, clearly interested in success in getting her husband back into her bed. Though, gratefully, he said little on the matter. Since the arrow shot, her father had spent even more time from the keep. He was especially eager to learn who had shot at him when he discovered that though Simon's dragon brooch was indeed in his own possession, the two did match. Perfectly.

Isabelle knew this only added to his impatience to see Simon's life ended. She was even more determined than ever to keep their relationship secret. She feared that if her father thought she might indeed have become pregnant he would have the matter done.

Fortunately keeping their secret was not so very difficult. At the keep not so much as an intimate word passed between herself and Simon Warleigh. When they were at the hunting lodge, well, very few words were necessary there. It was as if they had, by unspoken consent, realized that conversation only caused them difficulty. They spoke with hands and lips and yearning bodies.

With each touch, each kiss, Isabelle grew more and more empty at the thought of their passion's end. For end it must. She would find a life where she was wanted for herself alone. She must remember her own strength was all she could depend upon, even if she longed for him more fully with each day that passed.

One afternoon when the warm flicker of the fire had made her forget that the chill outside their tiny haven confirmed that autumn had become winter, Isabelle lay back upon the pillow with a sigh of repletion. She and Simon had just done things that made her blush as soon as the ripples of passion had passed.

Simon held her close against his side as he always did after they had coupled. And she drew away, as she always did. He never fought her in this nor had he even remarked upon it. Accepting her will, he simply attempted to hold her close the next time.

She could not explain to him that the holding seemed somehow more intimate than the passion. It made her long for things she could not allow herself to dream of, the reliance on a strength that was not her own. For she did indeed in those few short moments before she pulled away feel a sense of safety and protection that was more compelling than anything she had ever known, no matter that it was not his true intent toward her.

These thoughts led her back to the one man who had ever held her heart in high regard. The Dragon.

Suddenly Isabelle had to know, to understand how Simon and his friends could have betrayed him. How they could have given testimony that would assure his downfall.

Simon seemed to sense her withdrawal for he turned to her with a questioning expression.

Isabelle sat up, holding the sheet close over her, yet facing him directly. "Why, Simon, why did you and your friends give testimony against him? Why did you not protect him? He would have done so for you."

He blanched, but did not look away, not even trying to pretend that he did not know what she was referring to no matter that he could not have foreseen that she would ask. His tone was now husky with emotion, "I can only speak for myself in this and say I have wished more times than there are stars in the sky that I had said something other than what I did." He squared his broad shoulders.

"But he might have been able to find a way to absolve himself if you had not..."

Simon nodded. "I know." He looked into the fire and Isabelle could see that he was seeing not the flickering flames but the past.

He began to speak in a voice that was heavy with regret. "He always took the three of us, Christian, Jarrod and me, when he rode out from the keep, though he had no need for three squires. I believe it was simply because he knew how much we enjoyed it, the possibility of some adventure. Even the thought of coming upon a poacher in the wood was a great excitement to us then. That day seemed no different than any other. We thought to do no more than to follow about the lands while The Dragon saw to his usual duties.

"When we rode directly to a small glen at the very edge of Dragonwick I took no particular note of it even though it was somewhat out of the ordinary. Longchamps was there and D'Baercy. The Dragon went aside with them. They spoke for no more than minutes.

The meeting ended with D'Baercy riding off in what looked to be anger. Longchamps stayed only moments longer before following him."

Simon shrugged. "The Dragon came back to us and we went about our business."

He looked at her then. "It was not until later when the king's men came that I even thought to recall the incident again. They seemed overinterested in that meeting and what might have been said." His face was dark with regret. "Christian, Jarrod and I, we all asked The Dragon what we must say if questioned. He told us to tell the truth, that all a man truly had was his honor and he would ask no man to forsake his for him."

He shook his head, staring into the flames once more. "I do not believe he intended to join them in their efforts to aid Richard. The very fact that he took the three of us that day should make that obvious. Anyone who knew him would know he would never endanger the well-being of three green boys by involving them in such a matter."

Simon glanced at her and away. "He said, 'Tell the truth, lads. There can be no harm in it. We have naught to hide.'" He rubbed a hand over his face. "When the king's men asked if The Dragon had met with Longchamps and D'Baercy, who had already been arrested, though we did not yet know that here at Dragonwick, I said yes. I believed I was doing the only thing I could do."

Hearing his pain in the tightness of his voice, she wished she had not asked the question. But she could not bring herself to stop him.

Simon went on. "He was such a decent man, but not perfect you know. He could become angry when things were not done properly or when he felt that one was behaving badly, or if one had told a lie. But all in all he was good, and judged others by his own standard. He would never have suspected his own half brother was behind the efforts to destroy him.'' He took a deep breath. ''We told the truth. The king gave Kelsey sanction to take the keep. The Dragon died.''

He looked at her. ''We were wrong in not protecting him. I must live with that. But it was your father, Isabelle, The Dragon's own brother, who destroyed him. There is no doubt in my mind that he set all in motion.''

Isabelle took a deep breath. The unexpectedness of the statement made her reply with more candor than she meant to. ''Aye, and I have not forgiven him for that.''

He frowned, studying her doubtfully. ''Then why do you play the dutiful daughter, serve his every command?''

Isabelle flinched. ''How could I do any different? My mother died trying to give birth to my brother when I was naught but three. Where would I have gone after my father killed my uncle? To whom? My uncle was dead. I had only my father and he has lessoned me well in his way of seeing the world.'' She deliberately refrained from mentioning her mother's sister, whom she had not thought of as someone to take her in until most recent days.

Simon blanched, reaching toward her. ''I…forgive me, Isabelle. I should not have spoken so harshly. I begin to see that fate has dealt us both some measure of cruelty. I, as boy, made a terrible mistake by telling the truth. As your father's dependent you have been left with no choice but to learn to obey.''

Her throat closed up as she saw the empathy on his handsome face, heard the sadness in his voice. It seemed to release the dam of indifference inside her and she heard her own voice as if from a distance as pain flowed out from her very core. "Aye, no one could conceive, lest they had survived it, what being a child in this place of coldness and calculation has been like."

Isabelle rose, taking the sheet with her. She went to the foot of the bed, smoothing her hand over the surface of the wood. "My father can be..."

There was an odd edge to Simon's tone. "What is it? Does he beat you?"

A wry smile curved her lips though she felt no mirth, only the accustomed ache of loneliness. She did not want to talk of this, not to him, not to anyone.

Simon moved closer to her. Isabelle felt his gentle finger on her chin, urging her to face him. She could not resist. The warmth in his eyes made her heart pound. He spoke softly, though there was still a definite edge in his voice, "Does he, Isabelle?"

She found herself answering that concern, though she would never have imagined herself doing so. "Nay, he does not beat me. He has never had to do so for his method of teaching is far more effective."

He watched her, his gaze now confused. "Tell me." His hand fell away yet she could not turn away from him.

Isabelle took a deep breath, those eyes holding hers and the words came, not pouring from her as a stream but slowly as a very small leak in a very large dam. "When I was eight there was a puppy. I played with him about the keep, taught him to fetch a stick and come when I called the name I had given him, Little Dragon. Though I never spoke it aloud when anyone else was present, for my father would not have approved."

His lips tightened at the name but he said nothing as

she paused for a moment, choking when she felt her throat constrict with the sadness of remembering. But she found herself going on. It was as if the words would not be stopped. "No dogs were kept as pets you see. Little Dragon was one of a litter that had been born to one of the castle hounds. Then, as now, they were kept in the stables so as not to disrupt the hall, or soil it."

"One day when I had been in the stables playing with him I became dirty." She glanced at him and away. She was uncomfortable with the unreadable expression in his dark eyes. "My father had told me from the time I could listen that my appearance must always be equal to my position, to his position as earl of Dragonwick. When he saw me, he..." A tear slid down her cheek and she wiped it away quickly, going on in a stronger voice. "He killed Little Dragon. He informed me it was my duty to accept responsibility for this and learn from it, that I was never to let anything or anyone interfere in the performance of my duty. What was I to do, but heed him? He held the power of life or death in his two hands."

Now that cool, distant expression was back in her lavender eyes. "Is that what you wished to know, my lord?"

But he had seen that tear, no matter that she had tried to hide it.

He longed to take her into his arms but knew she would not welcome this. He had known Isabelle cared naught for intimacy when he had made her his wife in truth. He must accept her as she was. Yet he heard the regret in his voice as he said, "I know not what can be said of such a thing."

She shrugged. "There is no need to say anything at all. It was all a very long time ago. My father accomplished his purpose by what he did that day. He made me see that I must not allow myself to love anything that can be taken away. Which is, in essence, everything."

Simon stood watching her, this strange, proud, beautiful woman, finally understanding some of what lay behind that remote manner. At the same time he realized how deeply ran her inability to trust others. Perhaps it was too deeply ingrained for her to ever overcome it.

As a wave of sadness washed over him, Simon told himself it was brought on by nothing more than sympathy. He desired this woman, aye, had shared a passion with her that was astounding. Passion seemed the one area where she could give in to her feelings. It was very little to base a marriage on, yet that was what he must try to do now that there was no longer a chance at annulment.

Simon felt a sudden sense of loss he could not explain.

Yet he forced himself to concentrate on Isabelle, to speak with compassion in spite of the fact that she would not welcome it. "I am so very sorry, Isabelle. Children should be loved and protected from such pain."

She stiffened. "Do you think so? Should they be protected so that life can teach them such things? Perhaps my father did me a kindness by showing me I must rely on myself and no other. Nothing in my life has shown me that he was wrong."

He stepped back. "Perhaps he did do you a kindness at that." As he had thought, his sympathy had found no welcome. The shield around her heart would not be breached.

Except by that child she was so determined to have.

Something, some inner certainty told him the child would be the beneficiary of all the love Isabelle had inside her, the love that she only seemed to be able to show those who were in no position to hurt her. Such as the maid, Helwys.

Again he felt an unexplainable moment of regret.

He told himself it was brought on by the thought of the babe. The babe, if one did indeed come to them, might not be a son as Isabelle hoped, but a girl child. A girl child, a little one who would look like Isabelle, but who would love him and he would be able to love in return. The thought brought a warm glow to his heart. It did not quite disguise the strange emptiness he also felt, for their child would grow up in household where there was no love between mother and father.

Simon bent to gather up his clothing, not wishing to think about how disturbed he was by his thoughts. He did not look at Isabelle. "We should return to the keep."

She answered evenly, "Aye." He was aware of her dressing but forced himself to keep his gaze averted, though it was not easy when his fertile mind provided him with far too vivid images of the body he had come to know so well, and to want all the more for that knowing.

Simon did his best to push them away.

He had known how things would be when he had given in to his passion for this woman. If the desire she offered ended in being less than enough, it was his own doing.

As they mounted their horses and headed toward the castle, Simon told himself he was only making more of this because of his frustration with being here beneath Kelsey's thumb. If only he could speak with Christian or Jarrod. They would be able to tell him what was happening amongst the nobles. He was impatient to return to the lush rolling hills of Avington, which were so like the lands about Dragonwick.

He felt a fierce stab of hatred as he thought of Isabelle's father. The man was more despicable than he had even known. The tale Isabelle had told him had made him understand how very difficult it would ever be for her to trust or care for anyone.

He wished she would trust him, allow him to take care of her, to show her, just a little, that not all men were so cruel and unfeeling. Perhaps once he and Isabelle were at Avington things might improve with her. Yet the ache in his chest told him her self-reliance and distrust had been too well learned.

Over the course of that night and even into the next morn, Isabelle was unable to escape a sense of horror at herself. She had said things she had never thought to say to another human being, things that could be used to hurt her if Simon wished to. And thinking on all Simon had revealed to her only served to leave her even more uneasy in a way she could not understand.

Isabelle did not want to feel uneasy. As she sat before her open window, feeling the crisp morning air on her cheeks, she sought desperately the sense of self-reliance that had sustained her.

When a brisk knock sounded upon her door, she called out, "Come." Chagrin raced through her as the thought that it might be Simon came into her mind.

It swung open instantly. Sir Fredrick stood in the opening and for a brief moment Isabelle was aware of nothing but disappointment. Taking a deep breath she focused on the knight, realizing that far from his usual expression of watchful cunning he appeared distressed as she had never before seen him.

She stepped toward him without conscious thought. "What has happened?"

"It is your father, my lady. He is ill."

"Ill?" Just last eve he had been hearty and hale, had in fact been well enough to reiterate his intention that she was to get her husband back into her bed. Her face heated with guilt at knowing that Simon and she were in fact sharing a bed. And just how eagerly she was doing so.

Her guilt turned to shock as Sir Fredrick spoke with barely leashed rage, "He has been poisoned."

"It is not possible."

"Aye, it is possible, with Warleigh living in our midst. I have taken the liberty of placing him under guard."

Isabelle had to turn away to keep him from seeing the intensity of her horrified response. Fredrick was her father's eyes and ears. "Have you called upon the physician? Does *he* say it is poison?"

The knight shook his head. "He has not yet arrived, but he will confirm my suspicion when he does."

Unwilling to make protestations of Simon's innocence before Sir Fredrick, Isabelle moved to the door. She must see for herself. Her father's chamber lay at the far end of the hallway where his window overlooked the castle gates.

The large, surprisingly austere chamber was lit by candlelight alone, the shutters having been left closed. Two of the serving women hovered beside the enormous bed with its heavy brown-gold brocade hangings. One of them was holding a bucket into which her father was emptying the contents of his stomach. The other stood by with a basin and a cloth.

Seeing her father in such a state gave Isabelle such a shock that it held her immobile for a long moment. As her father fell back with a groan of misery, the other woman took the clean cloth and wiped it across his pale, sweat-soaked face.

Seeing his face sent a new sensation shooting through her—sympathy. This man, for all his coldness toward her, was her father and she loved him.

Isabelle turned to face the knight, who had followed her. "How long has he been in this state?"

The man took a shaken breath. "For at least an hour, my lady."

"Why was I not told sooner?"

He drew himself up. "It came upon him quite suddenly, Lady Isabelle. We were to go hunting. My lord rose early and broke his fast on some of the stew that had been left in the kitchens. We set off to the hunt and had to come back as this came upon him." His gaze went to his master. "He has only seemed to worsen by the moment."

"Was my lord Warleigh present when my father ate?

"Are you saying you doubt his guilt?"

Isabelle took another deep calming breath, trying to think beyond her own horror at what could happen to Simon. She knew inside her that it would not have been he, but she had no proof. "I am saying that we can not be sure lest the doctor says it is indeed poison." She glanced toward the bed. "I-it is so much a shock to see my father so ill that it is difficult to reason and we do not wish to be hasty. He has never been sick in my memory." Though she was frightened of her father and leery of his cruelty his powerful presence had been a constant in her life.

The knight scowled at her, his own face pale as he, too, looked toward the bed. In spite of all the aspects of his character that plagued her, his loyalty and care of his master was genuine.

Isabelle spoke with as much force as she dared. "You will not act against Warleigh. He was put in my father's care by the king himself. And he must be released immediately, does the physician find no sign of foul play."

He did not face her, but continued to watch his overlord. "We shall see what the doctor has to say."

Even as she realized that it was the best she could hope for, a soft groan of misery escaped the sick man. Feeling that she must try to do something, Isabelle moved toward the bed. The serving women stepped back to allow her room. "Father?"

He peered up at her, eyes glazed with wretchedness, yet his tone was harsh, "I would not have you here, Isabelle."

Knowing that it was the pain speaking through him she answered gently, "I would care for you, Father."

His blue lips tightened. "I do not wish for you to stay, do not require your aid. The women can look after me. The physician..." He folded inward groaning as an obvious cramp took him. "Go."

Her stomach clenched at his rejection. Numbly Isabelle stood there.

Sir Fredrick moved to toward the bed, glancing back at her to say, "He requires the chamber pot now, my lady."

That this was an indirect request for her to leave immediately was obvious. Isabelle spun around, taking herself away with all possible haste.

Once in her own chamber again with the door closed firmly behind her, she sank down on the seat beside the empty hearth. The hurt of her father's sending her away was still fresh, yet she was already beginning to understand why he had done so. Being one who readily and with alacrity exploited the weaknesses of others, including her, he would not wish to be seen in his present state of weakness.

When Sir Fredrick came to tell the men to release Simon from the stable where he had been held since rising, he went directly to the hall. Simon saw it would be a waste of effort to question the knight with his resentful dark eyes.

When Isabelle was not in the hall, he quickly realized she must be with her father. The strained and pale faces of the servants, the obvious fact that the food on the trestle tables was not being consumed, were evidence that word of the lord's illness had spread through the keep.

Seeing Jack, Simon approached him. The soldier spoke without being asked, "Lord Kelsey has fallen gravely ill."

"That much I know and that Sir Fredrick suspected it was poison and I had been involved. It surprises me not poison was suspected. Kelsey was healthy as any man could be when I saw him last eve." Simon had seen the earl speaking to Isabelle at table, had been aware of the pointed glances cast his own way. It had been easy to imagine the gist of the conversation.

Jack's voice interrupted his thoughts. "The doctor is above now. He has not come from the sickroom since his arrival. It seems he has ruled out poison, though there is no word on what indeed is the problem.''

Simon could not simply sit by and wonder what was going on. He rose and made his way to the upper floor. He knew where the lord's chamber lay, though he had never had cause to venture inside. He knocked upon the door.

It was opened by Sir Fredrick, who frowned as he saw Simon. ''What is it you require, my lord?'' The disdain in his voice was barely cloaked in a strained courtesy.

Simon took a deep breath. ''I would speak with my wife.''

Sir Fredrick shrugged. ''The lady Isabelle is not here, my lord.'' A horrific groan sounded from inside the darkened chamber. ''You are not wanted here.'' He closed the door firmly in Simon's face.

Simon had no real concern for this. His true interest was for Isabelle.

Yet as he moved down the hall to her chamber, he could not help but wonder why she would not be with her father when it seemed he was so gravely ill. In spite of the earl's lack of worthiness she was strangely devoted to him.

At the door of her room he did not hesitate but opened it. He sought his wife.

Isabelle was seated beside the hearth, her back to him. She seemed very still, not looking around at his entrance. On closer examination he saw that she was holding a garment in her lap.

He moved toward her. Simon saw with some confusion that she appeared to be repairing a section of embroidery on the sleeve of a gown. It seemed a strange thing to do with her father in such obvious dire straits.

Perhaps she did not even know that he was ill.

"Isabelle."

She spoke softly without raising her head. "Simon."

He knelt before her. "Isabelle. I do not know why they would not have informed you. Your father seems to be quite ill. The physician is with him."

Still she kept her attention on the sewing in her lap, answering just as quietly, no hint of emotion in her tone. "I have been made aware of my father's condition."

He frowned. "Then what are you doing here?"

At last she looked up and he saw the gleam of unshed tears in those lovely violet eyes. "He sent me away." Her expression was haunted. "They believe you poisoned him. I…you did not? He is…but he is my father."

Simon did not look away. Though he might wish to resort to such methods he would never act so despicably. Now… He did not want to think about why it was so important to him that she believe him. For he knew it was related to his strange desire to protect this woman who did not want his protection. "No."

She closed her eyes. "I knew you had not. In spite of his finding the dragon brooch after he was fired upon in the wood, I knew you had not."

Dragon brooch. There were only two others who owned such a brooch. He gripped her shoulders tightly. "What are you talking about, Isabelle?"

She looked up at him. "My father was nearly hit by an arrow some weeks ago. A brooch the exact replica of the one you wear to fasten your cloak was found at the scene. I told Father that it had not been you. Yours was still in your possession.''

Simon knew who had fired upon Kelsey. It could only be Jarrod. He was only a few hours' ride away at Avington. The incident had occurred weeks ago according to Isabelle. Obviously Jarrod had grown impatient with waiting for word of the noble's intentions concerning Simon. Simon could understand his feelings. Yet he could not fathom why Jarrod would act with such slyness. It was unlike him. And if he was caught...

Damn but he must find a way to get word to his friend that he must desist.

Isabelle spoke, drawing him back to the present. ''I knew you could not have behaved so despicably, spending the hours with me in the lodge, while secretly plotting.'' She shook her head. ''You are incapable of such slyness.''

Simon was still for a long moment as her words sank in. Though she did not seem to be aware of how much she had given away and he would not call her attention to it, lest he rend this fragile thread of trust, Simon was struck by hope. He felt a rise of something wondrous and tender that would not be held in. Though he knew that they had agreed to keep any hint of intimacy away from the keep he reached out and pulled her into his arms.

Isabelle resisted for no more than a moment, melting into him. The gown she'd been mending fell beneath their knees in a silken carpet.

With a trembling hand Simon reached up to cradle her head against his chest. She was so soft, so very appealing in her vulnerability, which was a result of having been rejected by her father. He realized that time after time she must have been denied the opportunity to give of the love that had now hidden itself away in her battered heart.

For he knew that it was hidden away. Isabelle would drag the shattered edges of her self-possession back to her as she always did.

And though he felt a sense of regret, Simon brushed it aside. He wanted nothing from her here. He would offer what comfort he could whilst she would accept it.

Chapter Twelve

Isabelle cared for nothing save her relief that Simon had not been involved in trying to harm her father. Hateful as her sire had been to her, she did not want him murdered.

She sighed with relief as she rested her cheek against the hardness of Simon's chest. In spite of Simon's rock solid strength there was also a softness, a gentleness in him that was far more compelling than any effort to govern or control could ever be. She felt the heat of his breath on the side of her neck with a powerful thrill. The embraces they had shared at the cottage seemed to have done no more than fan her desire for this man. Breathing more quickly herself, she turned toward him, her gaze on his mouth.

He moved closer, his breath now on her own lips.

"My lady."

Isabelle gave a start as a woman's voice dissolved the intimacy that had sprung up between them. She jerked away from Simon, turning around to see Helwys in the doorway.

The maid's approving gaze moved from her to Simon.

Isabelle rose quickly. "What is it?" Though Helwys knew that the two of them were meeting the sheer need she felt for Simon was something she wanted no one to be aware of, not even the serving woman. She would not be left vulnerable to pity when Simon was gone.

In spite of his kindness here, she knew it was just that, kindness.

Helwys's reply swept all thoughts of herself and Simon from her mind. "'Tis the housekeeper, my lady. And the head cook. Both have fallen ill, as well as several others and it seems that the effects are the same as those which afflict your father."

Simon moved to stand beside Isabelle as he asked Helwys, "Has the physician been told of this?"

"Has the physician arrived then?" Isabelle questioned him.

He nodded. "I had meant to tell you that he has declared there are no signs of poison, though it seems he has not yet determined the cause of illness." He looked to Helwys. "Has he examined these women?"

Isabelle was aware of the fact that cool competence had replaced his tenderness. She was surprised to find herself somewhat comforted by his strength for though she was relieved to learn that her father had not been poisoned, the rest was troubling news indeed.

"Nay, my lord, he is still with Lord Kelsey."

Simon nodded, and said, "That is understandable. Yet he must be informed that he is to see to the other two as well. He may even gain some clue as to your lord's ailment by doing so."

Helwys dipped a curtsey. "Yes, my lord, but Sir Fredrick will allow no one to enter his chamber."

Simon scowled. The man is a knight in his service. "He has no such authority lest it be given him."

Isabelle realized in that moment she was daughter of this household even though she had never been responsible for any of the duties which usually accompanied that position. In spite of her father's attitude toward her and his command that she stay away from the sickroom she must do what was best for all here. Pride was one thing he had always encouraged in her and she would draw upon it now.

She raised her head high. "I shall deal with Sir Fredrick. Simon is quite right to believe the doctor must examine the others who are ill. The ailment must indeed be connected. Though I have no notion of how, the doctor surely will."

Even as Isabelle moved toward the door, she heard Simon say, "And Helwys, you must discover how many have fallen ill, then inform your mistress of their numbers."

Helwys dipped a curtsey, "Yes, my lord."

Isabelle said nothing of his taking command, for she was not prepared to either encourage or deny him. But when she left the room she felt confident that Simon would see to matters while she confronted Sir Fredrick.

She soon discovered she had been quite right to imagine that Sir Fredrick would not wish to allow the doctor to leave her father's side.

He looked at her as if she had indeed gone mad. "My lady, you can not mean to leave your father to suffer whilst the doctor sees to the servants." Her father moaned from the depths of the bed as if to emphasize this point.

Despite a flush of sympathy, Isabelle stood firm. "Seeing to the women may help the doctor to learn what is amiss with my father. You are, no doubt, in favor of that."

The knight looked at her with grudging agreement. "Aye, Lady Isabelle, haps you have the right of it."

She did not bother to inform him that it had been Simon who had thought of it. She simply nodded. "I am going to see what can be done for the others." She looked to the doctor where he stood with a bowl of fresh blood beside the bed. "Once he has finished bleeding my father send him right down."

She did not linger to see that Sir Fredrick carried out her order. He would, if only for her father's sake.

Isabelle was not prepared for the sight of the two women who, in essence, oversaw the daily running of the entire keep. Someone had had the forethought to make them each a bed in one of the storage chambers off the hall. It would have been a sight to turn all from any thought of eating to have them in the hall where the majority of the castle folk not only took their meals but slept each night.

Isabelle felt her heart turn over at their misery. The women lay doubled up upon their pallets. The physical evidences of their suffering had left a foul odor in the chamber. Next to each pallet was a bowl with a cloth.

The serving girl who stood between them, turning from one to the other as if she were not sure what to do next looked to Isabelle for guidance. Isabelle stood immobile for a long moment, as uncertain as the servant. Never before had she had occasion to be in charge of any portion of the running of the keep. Her father discouraged her from attending to anything beyond her appearance.

And suddenly as she stood there, feeling that pleading gaze upon her, Isabelle felt a sweeping sense of duty that was far from distressing as she might have thought. She was the lady of this keep.

With her father ill, as well the two head women, there was no one but her to decide what must be done. There was no one other than Simon, at any rate. Though he seemed not only competent, but willing to take some responsibility, he was unlikely to be of any use here in the sickroom.

Isabelle raised her head. "Who is attending the other sick? Where are they?"

The girl spoke in a tone of fear. "It is several of the soldiers, my lady. They are in the barracks. Ona and another one of the women are tending them."

Isabelle nodded. Ona was one of the most senior women under the head woman and the best choice for this task. Yet her seeing to this duty would mean there was even more need for Isabelle to take charge.

She spoke with a certainty that amazed her. "Take those buckets out and clean them. Also fetch one of the other girls to help you. That way one of you will always be in attendance here, while keeping the place in a reasonable state for sick folk."

The serving girl dipped a curtsey and took up the buckets, clearly relieved at having someone decide what must be done. As she moved toward the door, Isabelle added, "The doctor will be down shortly. Make sure he is directed here immediately."

Again she dipped a curtsey. "Yes, my lady."

Isabelle looked after her for a moment. Though the castle folk had never been less than courteous of her she sensed a new level of respect in the woman's tone that brought a swell of self-confidence to her chest.

A soft moan issued from one of the beds. Isabelle moved to the pallet of the head woman with a determined step.

It was sometime later that she emerged from the

chamber. The doctor had indeed felt seeing the two women had helped him to ascertain the cause of their illness. From questioning them he had learned that both they and her father seemed to have eaten of the same food that morning. He was sure it had gone foul in some way, rather than being poisoned as the two dogs that had been given the same stew were quite well. He had gone to discover if the soldiers who had fallen ill had consumed the same food, though he seemed sure he would be told they had.

Isabelle could only pray no others would be afflicted.

Simon was waiting for her in the hall. His concerned gaze moved her in a way that she could not quite fathom and she found herself avoiding it as she said, "The doctor says he believes they have eaten tainted food and should be well in a few days."

Now that she was no longer occupied Isabelle was fully conscious of having betrayed her father's confidence by telling Simon of the attempted assault upon her father. It was of little comfort that Simon had not seemed to know of the attack.

He put a gentle hand on her arm. "Praise God."

She looked at him then. "Can you be so concerned for folk who are not your own?"

He shook his head. "They are yours and I can find a gladness on your behalf if nothing else." He looked at her more closely, "The suffering of others is cause for compassion, at any rate."

She found herself studying him, uncaring what he might think of her close scrutiny. "What manner of man are you then, Simon Warleigh?"

"A very common one, I would think," he replied with a self-deprecating laugh.

Though she had a sudden inclination that this was

not quite true Isabelle stopped herself from saying so. She was not certain of anything at the moment, least of all how he would take such a comment, or what she would mean by it.

Recalling where they were, who they were, she stepped back. "We must make certain no one else has fallen ill."

He frowned, but said only, "Aye, they might be in some remote corner of the castle grounds and too ill to come for aid." He held up a hand as she made to start off. "Pray, stay here where you may be needed. I will see that a search is made."

Isabelle nodded. In spite of the wall she had, of necessity, put up between them, she realized again what a relief it was to have Simon's aid.

Simon sensed that the intimacy that had sprung up between himself and Isabelle in her chamber only a short while ago was gone. Though why he did not know.

Perhaps she was sorry she had told him of the attack on her father. He was not. He knew he must find some way to get a message to Jarrod, so he could make sure it did not happen again, though he knew not how. Kelsey's illness had bought Simon some time as there could be no attempts on his life while he was ill in bed.

All he could do was wait, as he had waited since coming here. But he could make himself useful for the first time in many weeks. Isabelle needed him now and he was prepared to come to her aid.

Kelsey's men were not eager to follow his direction. But with their master ill and Sir Fredrick at his bedside, they did obey when he told them what must be done as he would have his own castle folk at Avington.

During those days Simon barely saw Isabelle throughout the day. He did note that she had begun to wear gowns such as he had never seen on her before. They were each of fine wool, it was true, but was far from her usual costume. There were no trims or embroidery as he had always seen in her in the past, yet there was a new easiness in the way she carried her slender form that made the garments elegant for all their lack of embellishment.

She seemed far too busy with whatever tasks she was performing in the kitchens and other deep regions of the keep to emerge for anything other than to direct the household women in their duties.

The most notable thing about her, though, was not her mode of dress, nor her unusual activity. It was the light of determination and accomplishment that fair burned in her, even at a distance.

Never would he have expected Isabelle to react thusly to this upheaval. It was a new side to her that made him think that perhaps she would eventually come to be a good and responsible mistress to Avington and its folk. That was, if she could ever come to care about them enough to make the effort as she was here.

Yet even as he thought this Simon knew that it was something best left in the back of his mind.

He began leaving the hall early each day and not returning until hunger drove him to do so. When he did he would take his accustomed place with Jack, his own two men and a few others. None of them had fallen ill as true to the doctor's suspicions it was only those who had eaten of the same food as Kelsey who had been afflicted.

On the evening of the third day Simon took the steps of the keep with a sigh. He was eager for a cup of cool wine and the savory smells that wafted through the open doorway brought a growl from his stomach.

According to Sir Fredrick, who had only emerged from the sickroom for a short time this very morning, Kelsey's condition had improved a little. The knight had remarked that it seemed strange for Simon to be expending such efforts in the aid of his enemy's folk.

Simon had simply replied that they were not at fault.

But he knew it was for Isabelle's sake that he worked so hard. Isabelle. As always the thought of her brought a sense of anticipation. In spite of his fatigue, his body made him aware that it had been four long days since they had been to the lodge.

Into this state of anticipation came the sounds of discord. Simon's brow furrowed as he lengthened his stride and entered the hall.

At the far end of the chamber a small crowd had gathered. The sound of angrily raised voices came again. One of them Simon recognized immediately.

Wylie.

The boy was once more in the thick of some turmoil. It was the last thing he needed at the moment. Simon had specifically warned him this very morning that he must hold his tongue even more carefully while Kelsey was ill.

He approached the group with both determination and reluctance. Even as he came up to them, his squire cried, "You have dishonored me."

The object of Wylie's rage, Kelsey's own squire raised his own chin to a stubborn angle. "'Twas an accident and all here know it."

It was then that Simon saw his own sword clenched in his squire's hands. Holding the weapon close to his chest Wylie cast an outraged and resentful glance around him. "These folk would uphold whatever you say, even if it be a lie. They care not for the fairness of their words."

An outcry of denial came from those gathered.

Although Simon knew that he must stop this before it went any further, he clenched his teeth tightly to hold back the words of reprimand that sprang to his mind. He did not wish to startle the squire into doing anything more foolish than he already had.

If it was his aim to teach the boy self-control, he must make every effort to display it. And he must not only do so for Wylie's sake. He realized that all present would best be served by calm reason.

Thus Simon's tone was as even as he could make it. "What has happened here, Wylie?"

The boy looked over at him with eager welcome, his grip on the sword relaxing. Simon took that moment to take the weapon from his hand. Wylie released it reluctantly but he did release it before casting another angry glare over Kelsey's squire. "My lord Warleigh, 'tis most well-timed that you have come." He pointed to the squire. "He fell into me deliberately, made me cut myself with the edge of your sword when I was polishing the hilt." Simon now saw the welling wound in Wylie's palm.

It did not appear to be more than a flesh wound and Simon focused on the other boy, who was equally as enraged. "I was only walking by and stumbled on the armor he had left on the floor. I meant no insult or injury, though now I wish I had."

Wylie started toward him, fists clenched tightly, even as Simon ran a quick glance over his own armor which still lay where Wylie must have rested it while he was cleaning it. The squire sputtered as he said, "You lie."

Again he heard unhappy muttering from those gathered.

Simon reached out and put a restraining hand upon his squire's shoulder. He knew he must assess this situation clearly. He continued to watch Kelsey's squire closely. The lad was angry, but it was a clear-eyed anger, which bespoke a sense of injustice. It told him that in spite of Wylie's belief that the accident had been no accident, the squire was telling the truth.

"Wylie," Simon spoke quietly but firmly.

The boy did not even look at him, but continued to glare at the other squire. Simon could feel the eyes of all present, watching him, waiting.

This time he said his squire's name with more force. "Wylie."

The squire swung around at last but there was obviously no lessening of the rage inside him. Simon could see that he hated these folk and the small slights he felt they had all suffered at their hands and had focused his anger for those slights on this incident. Simon realized that Wylie was a boiling pot, that he was not safe to remain here for another day. Once he had threatened others with a weapon in the hall, as he had just now, the castle folk would be watching him, possibly even baiting him to see if he would behave so rashly again.

Because of this, it was not difficult to imagine that the lad could indeed be capable of actually hurting someone. Or of getting himself hurt.

A confused voice interrupted his disturbed thoughts. "What is going on here?"

Simon looked to Isabelle. "My squire has made a grievous error."

Kelsey's squire cried, "He has threatened me with a sword in our lord's hall, my lady."

Isabelle looked to the weapon, which Simon still held. Simon nodded. "'Tis true, Isabelle."

She noted the gathered castle folk. "But what…?"

Quickly Simon explained the situation. Isabelle frowned. "This can not be allowed to go unpunished."

Simon felt Wylie stiffen, but at least the rash lad was not fool enough to contradict the lady of the keep.

Simon nodded. "I concur and will be happy to deal with the matter if you will permit me."

She watched him for a long moment.

He leaned close so she alone could hear him. "Pray trust me in this, Isabelle. I mean naught but good here."

She continued to look up at him, her lavender eyes uncertain. He did not waver under that close regard and finally she nodded. "I will trust you."

Feeling a wave of pleasure that seemed to go far beyond the moment, Simon bowed to her with careful deference. He then turned to Kelsey's squire. "You have my apology for what has just occurred." He looked to the others. "As do you all. You have my assurance that Wylie will be suitably disciplined for disrupting the peace of your hall this day."

Wylie, who seemed to have been experiencing some degree of shock at what was occurring, finally sputtered, "But my lord…"

Simon took him by the arm and led him, none too gently, from the hall. Yet that was greatly due to the fact that the boy resisted, pointing and muttering his confusion and unhappiness over Simon's taking the other boy's part.

Only when they had reached the stables did Simon release his squire. He spoke coolly, deliberately, "You will gather your belongings and your horse and make you ready for a journey."

"Where are we going, my lord?" A gleam of hope entered his eyes. "Are we going home to Avington?"

Simon shook his head, knowing he was making the right decision in sending the lad home. He did not imagine Kelsey would care. The boy's presence at Dragonwick had not pleased him from the beginning. "We are not going. You are going. I have realized that you would best serve me by returning to Avington."

Wylie's eyes widened in rebellion. "But, my lord, I can not leave you alone with these—"

Simon knew it was love of himself that brought about this response and he was not unmoved by it. Yet for the sake of the squire he could not allow him to disobey an order under any circumstances. Wylie had already displayed far too little control this day. "I have determined that you will return to Avington and you will do so."

Wylie scowled. "My lord, I will not go without you."

Simon drew himself up, his tone hardening, "You will obey me, or leave my service." The boy must be prepared to do as he was told without question, for his own well-being.

The squire stared at him in shock.

Simon could not waver. "In the event that you must ever be called to serve me in battle, your defiance of my instructions, even for a moment, could mean your life or the life of another."

The squire's face filled with horror, "My lord, I would never def—"

Simon halted him. "You would do so by continuing to behave as you have. I have warned you again and again in your behavior here. And you have disregarded my warnings. Which could mean life or death in a situation such as this where we are surrounded by those who are our enemies.''

The squire shook his head. ''I had not thought.''

Simon's lips tightened. ''That much is clear, but if you wish to remain in my service as my squire you must begin to think on all you do.'' He watched the boy carefully. ''As my squire you are as close to me as any man will be. Your behavior is a reflection of my own.''

Wylie took a step toward him. ''I would do better from now on, my lord.''

''Then pray attend your actions, boy. You drew a weapon in the hall of the very man who has the well-being of my lands in his hands. And it is my true opinion that you did so wrongly. I do believe that Kelsey's squire was as shocked by what happened as you. And hear this, even if he were not, you would have been wrong to do this. Avington is my first concern and must, as my squire and loyal man, be yours. I and those who serve me must place the continued good of the many who abide there foremost even over our own anger. We must be men of self-control and think before we act in a way that would put their future in possible jeopardy. It is this manner of being that separates man from boy. In which category will you stand?''

Wylie continued to look up at him, his blue eyes filled with a myriad of emotions that rushed through so quickly that it was impossible to gauge them. Finally the lad took a deep breath. ''Like a child I have let my temperament rule me.''

Simon nodded. ''You have.''

Regret filled Wylie's face. ''I will not do so now.''

''Show me this by obeying what is asked of you.''

Wylie drew himself up to his full height. ''It is my

greatest wish to serve you well, my lord. No more will you have cause to question this."

Watching him Simon felt a trace of returning confidence that he had indeed chosen well in the lad. It seemed that this incident had taught him something.

Then as he stood there a sudden and fortuitous thought came to him. With Wylie returning to Avington this day came an opportunity to send word to Jarrod. It must be done with all haste. With Kelsey ill there was far less chance of their being found out.

Simon followed to where the boy had begun to gather his belongings from where he had been making his bed in the hay. "Wylie, I have something very important I wish for you to do. It will require your remembering every detail of what I tell you." The meeting with Jarrod must be timed perfectly so he was not missed.

Wylie straightened, standing tall and proud. "I will see it done, my lord. You will have no more cause to doubt my ability to serve you."

Simon nodded.

Isabelle was in the hall overseeing the changing of the rushes when Sir Fredrick approached her. His face was dark with anger and his tone was barely civil. "Lady Isabelle, your father had instructed me to speak with you."

She drew herself up. "Oh."

"It has come to his attention that your husband has sent the squire away and you sanctioned his doing so."

She held her head high. "He did so as a punishment."

The knight continued to scowl. "You are to refrain from giving the man permission to do anything."

Isabelle could feel the others watching her. "I am

lady of this keep and you will remember that when speaking to me.''

He sucked in a breath. ''Your father has decreed it.''

''Then he may tell me him himself. You will not forget my position again.''

The man's gaze narrowed but he stalked away without another word. Isabelle knew there would be consequences when her father was well. Yet she felt he must understand that she would not accept such insolence from a retainer when he had made so much of her being mindful of her place.

One thing she did know, though, was she must have care for what she did. Obviously her father was being informed of the goings on in the keep in spite of his illness.

Isabelle was torn. Because he was her father she wished for his recovery. Yet at the same time his absence had created a strange sort of peace that would be disrupted once he emerged from the sickroom, especially the peace between her and Simon.

She and Simon had not been to the lodge, and had not made love, but a different sort of bond seemed to have developed between them. When she learned he had sent the squire away she had felt a momentary sense of unease, but it had changed to admiration as it seemed not only a suitable punishment for the hot-tempered lad, but a logical solution to his outbursts. Simon's obvious fairness in dealing with the situation had also changed the way the castle folk treated him. There was more respect in their voices when obeying his direction.

Her own attitude toward him had definitely undergone a strange metamorphosis, as had his toward her. Since the events of that morning she had found excuses to enter the hall when she knew he would be present.

Twice in passing Simon actually placed a gentle hand on her, once on her shoulder, another time on her arm. Each touch was cause for reflection for it awakened in her that strange yearning that went far beyond desire. Although desire was certainly a part of it.

Mayhap being with Simon, who was more than able to quench her physical ache, would ease that other less familiar longing. But it would be mad to place him in further jeopardy. As long as her father believed that Simon could not have produced a child, he was somewhat safe. Sir Fredrick had been very angry about his sending the squire to Avington and she knew as well as anyone that he spoke for her father. She realized that she had been wrong not to force Simon to heed her warning about her father's intention to kill him.

She must try again.

Isabelle sought him out in the courtyard where he was helping some of the men to unload the top portion of a layer of hay so it would fit beneath the entry to the keep.

Simon turned and came toward her with an expression that she could not read, even as the other men went back to work. He spoke softly as he rubbed a hand over one broad shoulder. "Is there something you need, Isabelle?"

She shook her head quickly, vividly recalling the strength of those wide shoulders under her eager fingers. "Oh, nay. I—I simply wanted to talk to you."

He smiled and that smile sent a thrill of renewed longing through her. "What would you like to talk about?"

Isabelle felt suddenly shy, casting her gaze about. The other men were clearly waiting. "I…I pray forgive me. This is not the time. You have much to do, as do I."

''But name a time that is more convenient to you and I shall be in your service.''

She saw the openness in his face and the banked heat in those mahogany eyes. It called to an answering reaction inside her. She forced herself to think on what was important here. ''I...with my father ill, there would be less impediment to your coming to my chamber to talk.''

He bent over her, studying her closely. ''You wish for me to come to your chamber this evening?''

She looked up at him from beneath her lashes. ''If that is your wish.''

His hot gaze swept over her, making the heat rise in her own body. ''I will attend you.''

He turned back to the men and Isabelle realized that she had let him think the wrong thing.

She told herself she could not explain now. Another part of her was not sure that she wished to do so. The very thought of experiencing the promised passion in his eyes was nearly enough to make her forget everything else.

But only nearly, she assured herself.

Chapter Thirteen

As he stopped at the entrance to Isabelle's chamber, Simon was infinitely aware of the fact that he had sent for Jarrod.

Simon took a deep breath as he stood in front of that door. There was silence within.

Perhaps he had misread his wife's intentions when she had come to him in the courtyard. Perhaps she was not expecting him. Yet the pounding in his blood told him to open that door. He put his hand on the latch.

Again he paused. If Isabelle was asleep he would return to the stable.

If she was not...

He moved the latch. The heavy oak door swung inward without a sound.

His heart stopped then thudded to a start once more as he saw that Isabelle was indeed awake. She stood before the fire, seeming oblivious to her surroundings. The light of the flames outlined every perfect line of her body, revealing those long legs, gently curved hips and narrow waist to his heated gaze.

At that moment she turned her eyes meeting his. There was a strange uncertainty in them.

He moved toward her.

Isabelle came forward at the same moment. "Simon, this time you must listen to me."

He forced himself to concentrate on the worry in her face, to damp down the now aching need that had arisen at the very sight of her like this. "What is it, Isabelle?"

She bit her lip, her gaze dark with torment. At last she said, "It is my father. I should have told you long before this. I just could not…but now I…" She squared her shoulders. "He means to do you ill, Simon."

He quirked a brow. "That much I know."

She shook her head. "Nay, you do not understand. My father has told me that once I am with child he means to…"

He nodded slowly. "I see. You mean that he has actually told you he means to have me killed."

She nodded, then spoke with obvious difficulty. "Yes."

Simon was not entirely surprised. He watched her closely, "Why are you telling me this, Isabelle?"

She took a deep breath. "Sir Fredrick came to me this day and told me that my father is very angry at your having sent your squire to Avington."

"But why now? He has been angry with me before."

She looked away. "I have come to respect you. You have proven a good and decent man during my father's illness. I could not repay you with silence in this matter." She looked back at him. "I will rest easily in the fact that you are the father of my child."

Simon took a long deep breath. This was no declaration of love or care. Yet in some part of him he knew that to Isabelle this was great praise indeed. The child was all that seemed to really matter to her.

He refused to acknowledge the regret that twisted inside him. He would take the fact that she had warned him of her father's intent in the spirit it was intended. She cared, at least in some small way, what happened to him.

He held out his hand. "I thank you for telling me this, Isabelle. I know how hard it was for you to do so."

She did not reach out to take his hand. "I...would you please go now, Simon? It is dangerous for you to stay. If Father had any reason to believe I might be with child..."

Simon heard the catch in her voice. He spoke softly. "Is that what you truly want?"

She looked at him then. "I...yes..." His gaze held hers as she faltered. She turned away again. "I do not know what I want."

He put a finger to her chin, urging her to face him. She did so with obvious reluctance. "Yes, you do, Isabelle. You want the same thing that I want."

Her breathing quickened visibly. "Aye, perhaps I do, but what if we are discovered?"

"Tonight that is a risk I am willing to take." Simon placed his lips on hers.

And then she was in his arms, her body molding itself to the length of his. He deepened their kiss, his mouth crushing hers beneath his own. She lifted her arms and clasped his shoulders tightly, pulling herself up to him.

Simon wrapped his arms around her, drawing her up to him, feeling the softness of her with every part of him. How he had longed for this, dreamed of holding her in each hour of the day.

Then he felt another new wave of feeling wash through him as she turned her head and placed her warm mouth at the pulse at the base of his throat. "Simon, how I want your arms about me."

"Isabelle."

Her name came as a caress that made the fine hairs stand up along her flesh.

Isabelle had prayed that he would come. She knew that this aching, this loneliness could be filled by no other than Simon. She needed him—his body, his touch.

She pushed back to look into his eyes, not saying a word as she reached down to push her hands beneath the hem of his tunic. Slowly she moved them up to splay over his stomach, which convulsed at her gentle touch.

Isabelle felt his reaction, was emboldened to go on. She enjoyed the ripple of hard muscle beneath her fingers as she passed over his upper stomach, moved on to the wall of his chest, brushing over the nubs of his male nipples and coming back to them.

Her pleasure was halted when Simon placed his hands over hers. She looked up into his heated gaze, holding his eyes as she lifted her slightly parted mouth.

He slid his arms around her slender and yielding form and his lips took her offering. She tilted her head back, granting him full access to her lips, her throat, the curve of her breasts above the low neckline of her gown.

Isabelle welcomed the heat of passion that flowed through her. For this one moment she would think of nothing beyond her and Simon, her own reactions to his caresses.

He lifted her in his arms and moved toward the bed. As Simon lay her upon it he kissed her closed lids. "As I lay over there on my pallet I dreamed of having you here."

She opened those wonderful, hypnotic eyes. "I, too, have dreamed of it."

He answered her with his mouth. She met him fully, passionately, the heat of her mouth scorching his.

When Isabelle's eager hands again reached to the hem of his tunic he drew back, this time to aid her. It took no more than a moment to pull it over his head. It fell as her hands reached for him and he gathered her back into his arms to kiss her again, with a thoroughness that left his head spinning.

He then drew back to look into her eyes again as he moved to slowly slip his hand up beneath her gown, to slide it slowly upward. Her legs, smooth and lovely and golden in the candlelight, quivered at his touch. He pushed the gown higher, frustrated when diaphanous fabric hindered his desire to uncover more of her.

Her body quaking with desire, Isabelle raised up upon her knees. Her gaze never leaving Simon's, she lifted her arms up above her head. "Take it off."

Simon lost no time in doing so.

Beneath the gown was a soft gossamer shift. Nothing more. Even in the soft light of the candle, the dusky tips of her breasts were visible. The low neck of the shift revealed the enticing shadow between her breasts, which seemed even fuller, riper than when last they were together.

His palms dampened with the force of his reaction to the sight of the body he had loved with such thorough delight. It was as if no amount of intimacy with the woman could ever dampen his reaction to her beauty. He felt his manhood swell and harden, the fabric of his hose an uncomfortable barrier between him and Isabelle.

Sweet, lovely Isabelle, the source of all desire, all pleasure.

He bent his head to nuzzle the shadow between her breasts. That soft weight was completely intoxicating against his cheek and he turned his head to kiss, and then to flick his tongue over it.

Isabelle's head fell back, her hand going to his nape to hold him to her, her heart pounding as the warmth swelled at the joining of her thighs.

With his nose, Simon pushed the barrier of her shift out his way as his lips traced the sweet and tempting curve, stopping only when he reached the already rigid tip. She gasped as his mouth closed over it, her fingers trembling on his nape. When he drew it more fully into his mouth, suckling her, her hips rose up and she pressed herself against him.

He raised his hand to her other breast, which seemed to swell beneath his fingers. Slowly, deliberately as he continued to suckle the other breast, he circled that hard tip with his thumb.

She pressed herself more fully to him. Her tone was hoarse as she cried, "Simon."

But he wasn't yet ready to give in to her pleading. He wanted to savor her and this moment.

Isabelle was floating in a sea of pleasure, her body on fire, each kiss, each touch awakening her body to further heights of longing. She held his head to her breast even as the plying of his thumb increased the throbbing that was centered at the core of her being.

Simon reached up to pull the fabric down, to bare the rest of that delightful body to his view, but the neckline would not come so low. He hooked a finger in the edge of the opening. Isabelle met his hungry gaze, encouraging him.

Simon needed no more urging than this. A quick tug parted the delicate fabric to below her waist. Reaching up Isabelle put her hand over his and ripped again, parting it to the hem. The remnants fell away from her delicate shoulders as if by sorcery. But Simon cared little for this as his burning gaze ran over her.

As he reached for her Isabelle leaned into him, gloried in the feel of his hands on her sensitive flesh. She put her own mouth to his breast, flicking her tongue out to taste the salty smooth surface.

Simon groaned with need and Isabelle pulled him down with her, down onto the softness of the bed, into the heat of her body. He caught his breath in a sweet agony of desire as he felt her close around him.

Isabelle gasped as Simon came into her, crying out with longing as he began to move in a rhythm that made the sensations build until there was nothing but the ecstasy that exploded in her mind, her body, her soul. And she knew that he, too, was overcome with his passion as he stiffened above her, gasping out his bliss.

She lay beneath him, her eyes closed, reveling in pulses of pleasure that continued to take her as their passion ebbed. But as it passed away she began to realize just how mad they had been to let desire make them take this chance.

As he had each time their joining was done, Simon rolled to his side pulling Isabelle into his arms, and cradling her head against his hard shoulder. He knew she would move away as she always did.

To his surprise that did not happen. Instead Isabelle looked up at him, her expression troubled.

Simon tried to concentrate on that rather than his own disquieting sense of happiness. He traced one finger over the crease on her brow. "What troubles you, Isabelle?"

She bit her lower lip. "Simon, we are mad to take this risk. I know you do not wish to listen to me but I must make you understand that my father is most serious in his intent to do you harm."

He shook his head. "I will be fine."

She raised up, her glorious hair falling around her and Simon felt a new stirring at her beauty. But her words brought him up short. "He is capable of doing anything Simon. I know. To think yourself beyond his reach is to court death with open arms."

Looking into those lavender eyes, Simon, for the first time, realized the depth of her fear. He realized in fact that it had been there all along and he had only been too blind to see it. What he had taken as blind obedience had been utter fear.

He reached out to pull her back against him as he felt a wave of protectiveness coupled with regret. For he knew this fear was not something Isabelle could easily overcome. She would ever have a suspicion of others, would ever be expecting the worst for she had seen just what evil man was capable of doing to another. No matter how much her life changed she would never forget her caution because it was her way of protecting herself. His arms tightened around her. If only she would trust in him.

But he knew that would never be.

Simon waited until Isabelle had fallen asleep, preferring not to wake her but reasoned that if he did so he would say he was returning to the stable for the night. Silently he rose and pulled on his clothing. It was more important than ever for him to meet with Jarrod. He had to find a way to get himself and Isabelle away from here.

Simon was able to exit the keep with surprisingly little difficulty. Sir Edmund's duty to see that the stable lads consumed several cups of ale with him had obviously been successful. All slept soundly through the process of readying his horse. There was only one brief moment of anxiety as the guard who patrolled the section of wall above the postern gate came toward him but he was distracted by a rattling noise and went off in the other direction for long enough for Simon to exit the keep.

Simon felt a stab of guilt as he rode toward the lodge, the moon lighting the now familiar path. Though he knew that there was no real reason for feeling thusly.

He betrayed Isabelle in no way by meeting with Jarrod. It would be different if his intent was to do anything against Kelsey.

Yet the feeling persisted. Perhaps it was because of all that had passed between them this very night. Isabelle had been softer somehow, more open to him than ever before. He thought of how he had left her, asleep in the bed where they had just made love with such tender passion.

Perhaps his guilt was brought on by his having hidden his intention to meet with Jarrod from her. Perhaps if he had told Isabelle where he was going and what he was doing he would feel differently?

Simon shook his head to clear it. He could not tell her. He risked Jarrod's life in the event of her revealing the meeting, even inadvertently. He must concentrate on the task at hand.

Simon arrived at the cottage earlier than the appointed time. He dismounted and tied his horse where he had each time he was here.

When he was with Isabelle.

It was not long before he heard the sounds that heralded the approach of a horse. Simon tensed, knowing that it could be someone from the keep. As Jarrod broke through the trees he smiled in relief and welcome. For the sight of him was very welcome indeed after these weeks of confinement.

Jarrod leapt down, grasping his friend's hand even as he threw an arm about his shoulders to clap him heartily upon the back. "You are here, Simon."

Simon smiled returning the gesture before he stepped back to say, "Aye, else why would I bid you to come?"

He frowned, his black eyes flashing anger. "When one is a prisoner there is a great distance between making plans and carrying them out."

Simon grimaced. "You have me there, but I am not so closely held as that. I could, in fact, have left Dragonwick ere this if it were not for jeopardizing Avington. Have you heard any word from Christian?"

Jarrod shook his head with obvious frustration. "Not one word."

Simon rubbed a hand across his forehead. He could well understand his friend's frustration, but he knew that he must control it, for if he was correct, Jarrod had already made one mad attempt against the earl. Simon spoke carefully. "Jarrod, there is something I must ask you."

The other man seemed to sense something in his voice for he became very still. "Yes."

Simon faced him directly. "Kelsey is saying that he was fired upon when out riding. He did not see the assailant, but he did find a brooch with a dragon upon it that is exactly as mine, and thus yours.'' His gaze went to Jarrod's shoulder where the pin was conspicuously absent.

Jarrod arched disdainful black brows high. ''Did he also tell you that he was upon your land at the time? That he was 'questioning' one of your landholders as to the number of men garrisoned at the keep?''

''Kelsey at Avington! Is the man all right?'' No wonder Jarrod had fired upon him. Simon would have done the same.

Jarrod nodded. ''Aye, only frightened.'' He hit his fist against his palm. ''Kelsey is a coward, sneaking about like a fox in the night. I would not have known of it lest I had been out hunting to pass the time. Your steward is very efficient.''

Simon could hardly think past his horror that the bastard was making free to roam his lands at will, to torment his folk. No wonder he had been gone so much from the keep before his illness. ''Kelsey is not waiting until his plans for my death have been satisfied before making himself familiar with his new acquisition.''

''What are you saying, Simon? It sounds like there is more than speculation as to Kelsey's intent in your voice.''

Simon nodded. ''Aye, I have learned that he plans to have me killed once Isabelle is with child and his guardianship of the lands assured.''

Jarrod shook his head. ''Then it is surely providence that led you to decide not to bed her.''

Simon was silent.

His friend looked at him. ''You have not bedded her!''

Still Simon said nothing and Jarrod began to pace the

floor before him. "Are you mad? What could have possessed you to do such a thing?"

Simon frowned. "I am not prepared to discuss that."

"Has this woman given you cause to think she would turn allegiance over to you?"

Simon shook his head. "Nay. She is, I think, too afraid of her father to do so."

"Then you are doubly a fool. You know full well how ill she will have been taught."

Short weeks ago he would have felt much the same as his friend. Now knowing how very difficult it had been for Isabelle, how she did secretly long to break those bonds of fear, he could not feel thusly. "You know not of what you say, Jarrod, and I would have you mind yourself when speaking of my wife." He could hear the edge in his voice.

Jarrod stopped pacing to stare at him. "Dear God, it can not be."

Simon frowned. "That I would expect some measure of courtesy for my lady wife?"

"That you have fallen in love with her!"

Simon felt as if he had been hit in the chest by a battering ram as the breath left his lungs and his head spun. In love with Isabelle!

God, yes, it was true. He did love her, even though he had done all he could to keep from loving her. He'd even held the signs of loving kindness he'd seen in her suspect when he would not have if it were anyone else. From the start he'd known it would only complicate everything.

Even when he'd made her his wife in truth he'd held himself back from her, told himself it was because she could not give enough of herself to be a proper mistress to his folk, who deserved a woman of warmth and care.

Her recent actions during her father's illness had shown she was far from the selfish dame he'd tried to paint her.

It had not been his folk he had thought to protect. But his heart.

Simon took a long shuddering breath. What was he to do now?

A great sense of loneliness swept over Simon.

"Simon, are you all right?"

He heard Jarrod's voice as if from a long distance away. He looked up at his friend whose face was full of concern. With as much self-possession as he could manage Simon said, "I am fine. Only a bit dazed, I think. I had not imagined…"

He could not continue, could not speak to Jarrod of this hopeless, one-sided love. The realization of it was just too fresh—too painful.

He drew himself up. "I must do something about the situation. I can no longer wait for Christian. Something must have happened."

Jarrod nodded. "Aye, he would not have delayed so long lest there be some reason."

Simon stood. "I must go to King John myself, tell him what has occurred at Avington and lay myself at his mercy, promise him any boon. But I must be free of Kelsey."

It was in fact imperative. As long as Isabelle resided under her father's roof, she would never be able to put aside her fear and it was suddenly most important to Simon that she do so. At least in part. He knew that love was more than he could expect from one who had been forced to hold all of herself inside. But perhaps, if they were away from here, there might be some hope that she would come to have some measure of ease in his company.

Unknowing of his tormented thoughts, Jarrod said, "I will come with you and tell what I know."

Simon shook his head. "I mean you no slight, my friend, but your presence would not aid me and you might only succeed in bringing John's wrath upon your own head in the event that I am unable to convince him of the truth."

Jarrod raised his head high. "I am not afraid of what might happen."

Simon reached out to put a hand on his friend's shoulder. "That has never been questioned in my mind, Jarrod. I simply do not wish to see ill come to you for naught. Were this a battle we fought with men of honor I would have no hesitation in asking you to take my back. Since it is not, I beg you to think on how you would feel if I were to offer to do the same."

His friend sighed. "I would never allow you to act so foolishly on my behalf."

"Aye." Simon looked away. "I shall simply have to do my own convincing."

Jarrod shook his head. "But you tried before and it came to naught."

Simon was all too aware of this fact. Yet he said none of this aloud. "Kelsey is ill. He has been in bed for some days. I will go now while he is unable to put in an appearance. Mayhap if I can gain the king's ear without him there he will listen to what I have to say."

Jarrod shrugged. "Simon, have you given any thought to the fact that even if the king does heed you, you will not be free of Kelsey?"

Simon nodded. "I have thought on little else. But there is now nothing I can do on that."

And he realized how true it was. No matter how he hated Kelsey, or how great an opportunity to avenge himself, The Dragon, and all those who had been harmed by the earl, Simon could never take advantage of it.

In spite of her fear and hatred of her father, Isabelle would never forgive him for doing such a thing. For there was a part of her that loved her father and always would.

"Now that he has set his sights upon Avington, he will never rest in efforts to take it as long as he lives. He will be as ruthless as he was in getting Dragonwick. It is his way."

Simon could not deny that.

Well, it would never happen as long as Simon was alive. Simon had no intention of dying, not for a very long time, long after the earl was rotting in his own grave.

He gave himself a metal shake looking to Jarrod. "I ask only one thing of you, Jarrod."

"Aye."

"Make no more attempts on Kelsey's life. Even if he has the temerity to come upon my lands we must be willing to let that pass, lest he so oversteps himself that he attacks the very keep. If he does that, your presence at Avington will be invaluable. Competent as the steward may be, he would have little notion of the best way to withstand an attack, or even a siege."

Jarrod scowled as he nodded, his hand going to his sword hilt. "Does he attack Avington it shall be my personal pleasure to see him repaid for all his misdeeds."

Simon could not deny that the very thought made his own blood pound. Yet he did not allow himself to dwell on this thought because of the pain he knew such a situation would bring to Isabelle. He looked to the door. "I must away tomorrow night."

"Should you not go now, from here?'

Simon shook his head quickly. "Nay, too much of this night is gone. I would be sooner missed." A part of him knew that that was not the only reason. He had to see Isabelle, perhaps to hold her once more as he had this night. For in spite of his own bravado about outliving his enemy he had no way of knowing what would come from his confrontation with King John.

What a fool he had been. He did indeed love Isabelle. When he'd told her he didn't care if she could love, he'd only been deceiving himself as well as her. He had convinced himself he felt only a great sense of pity for all she had endured. He had desperately cared.

Unfortunately Isabelle would never be able to fully give of herself, to him or the folk of Avington. And for that sorrow there was no cure.

Isabelle crouched down upon Simon's bedroll, which still lay in his stallion's stall. She wrapped her arms about her knees, holding herself, for there was no other comfort for the misery that made her chest ache, her throat tight.

Dear Heaven, Simon was gone.

She had woken to find Simon dressing with a great sense of unease. It had been all she could do to pretend that she was still asleep as she had felt him watching her for a long moment in which the air had seemed charged with some indefinable emotion before he had left the room. It was this as much as anything that made her rise and take up her robe to follow him. Something told her to stay back, not to allow him to know of her presence as she moved after him.

It was not anything overt that caused her discomfort. He had seemed perfectly at ease as he passed through the hall and she knew that it was possible that he was simply going to sleep in the stable as usual.

Yet she knew something was amiss. It was just something in the set of his wide shoulders, in the measure of his steps.

Perhaps, she told herself, as she carefully stepped between the sleeping servants it was because she knew his body more intimately than she did her own. Had she not run eager fingers over every inch of that hard flesh? Was she not familiar with the sometimes subtle, sometimes fierce spasms that gripped his flesh in passion?

Not that she wished to think about any of this, not when she was feeling so uncertain of her own feelings for this man. Not when in the deepest part of herself she was wishing he had spoken some words of a future with her. Not when she feared he might be leaving Dragonwick at this very moment without so much as a goodbye.

He owed her nothing. Though he was gentle and tender and kind she was beginning to realize this was simply Simon's way. It did not mean he cared for her, though she had thought that he meant to hold on to her for any child they might have. Obviously he had changed his mind.

And who would take him to task for having done so? As she had told him herself, her father meant to kill him. It would be mad for Simon to ever think of staying tied to such a family.

The desire he clearly felt for her was not enough to risk that. Isabelle would not have him do so. Though she longed for more than desire Simon had no more to give her. Thus she would do well to remember her own plans for the future and accept things as they were.

Yet she could not stop a feeling of betrayal that he would leave without so much as a parting word. Even though she told herself she did not know that this was what he was doing, the ache of emptiness inside her did not ease, nor did her suspicions.

Isabelle followed him through the hall and out the oak door. Though the moon was not full there was enough light to see Simon walking in the direction of the stables. As in the hall he seemed to be in no great hurry, yet to her his eagerness was clear.

She waited, praying he would not come out. Moments later he emerged with his horse, leading him slowly toward the postern gate. The realization that Simon was indeed leaving cut through her like a rusty sword. It burned in her chest and in her mind. The sensation was so intense that it seemed to consume itself almost instantaneously the way a hot fire will do. It was replaced with a numbness that enabled her to breathe again and to see that the guard at the top of the wall was coming back toward the postern gate. Simon had seen him, too, for he merged into the shadow of the wall, then held still.

Something she could not explain made Isabelle bend and pick up a stone from the ground. Quickly she tossed it against the wall in the opposite direction from where Simon was headed. She saw Simon swivel toward the sound as well as the guard, who moved to investigate. Isabelle stayed carefully out of sight in the shadows and Simon moved on, leading his horse out the gate.

Isabelle had stood staring at the spot where he had been for a long, endless moment, then turned and blindly made her way to the stables, needing only to see if he had perhaps left some small bit of him behind. Something she might keep with her in the dark years ahead.

Now sitting where he had slept she knew that nothing would ease this strange and unexplainable void. It would always be with her, the void that had been filled by the passion of his touch.

Her eyes burned, hot and dry and she lay down, pulling his blanket up over her. In a few moments, she told herself, she would put this behind her and go to her own chamber, go on as she always had, but for a few moments she would let herself be comforted by lying here in the darkness where he had lain.

Isabelle opened her eyes as a soft scraping sounded. It was the fact that she had not truly been asleep that allowed her to hear it for it was very soft.

Rising up, she moved to the door of the stall. In the outer chamber she saw the shadowy shape of a man leading a horse. Joy rose in her and she cried out. "Simon."

She realized as she did so that the word had been spoke far too loudly. Even as Simon halted, another cry rose out of the darkness and a torch flared to life. That voice was joined by another and the stable folk rushed to gather around Simon.

One of them held another glowing torch high and its light found her. "It is Lady Isabelle who has alerted us to his escape."

Another of the men said, "Lord Kelsey must be told."

Across the heads of the men who held the torches Simon's gaze met hers. In those brown orbs was anger and betrayal. "How could you?"

Isabelle shook her head as pain tightened her chest as she mouthed. "Nay, I…"

To her surprise his face was immediately colored by regret but she could not forget what he had thought. Though she understood how it must look, surely he must realize that due to the darkness and their zealousness to take him, no one had checked his mount. They assumed they had caught him leaving, not returning.

And even if that were not the case, dear heaven, how could he imagine such a thing, even for only a moment, after all that had passed between them, after she had aided his leaving only hours ago? Although he was unaware of this, she had done it.

She would indeed do well to keep her thoughts centered on her plans to go to Normandy.

The sound of her father's voice behind her caused her to swing around. "Just where were you going, Warleigh?"

Her father came forward. Though his face was still quite pale and his cheeks gaunt from some loss of weight, his eyes held the same cold superiority they always had.

Even as anxiety at what he would do caused her chest to tighten she, too, wondered where Simon had gone. Although he had not left Dragonwick as she had feared, he had certainly ridden out with great stealth for some purpose.

But what?

He faced her father silently.

Her father motioned to the men. "Take him to the cellar."

Chapter Fourteen

Isabelle was not surprised to be summoned to her father some hours later. "Sit down, Isabelle," he said as he glanced up from the ledger he was going over.

She seated herself in the X-shaped chair with forced calm, for she feared her father might suspect the truth about the previous night. He leaned back in his chair, smiling that cool little smile that told her he was pleased about something. "You have done well, daughter."

Surprised she stared at him, having no notion of why he could be so approving of her. "I…thank you, Father. Do you mean in alerting the castle to Simon's escape?"

He raised those well-shaped gray brows. "Nay, that is your duty. So, you do not know?"

"Know what?"

"Why, that you are with child. Though I am somewhat displeased that you did not keep me abreast of this possibility, I am prepared to be lenient."

Isabelle sucked in a breath of shock. She could not help it. No amount of self-control could have been sufficient to hide her amazement at this pronouncement. "But what…" She shook her head. "How would you know this when I myself do not…"

He smiled again. "The linens, my dear. The laundress has informed me that the time for your flux has come and gone by more than a fortnight."

He was oblivious to Isabelle's reaction. "This could not have come at a more opportune moment. All here know that Warleigh was caught escaping in the night. I have the proof that I found in the wood after I was fired upon." He reached out to pick up the dragon brooch from the table where he had obviously kept it since the day he found it. "If he is killed while attempting to escape again who will question me?"

"But will the king not wonder why he was not informed of this?"

Her father looked at her. "I am sending him a letter to do that very thing. It will be sent before I act. Unfortunately Warleigh will not survive long enough for the king's reply to reach me."

Isabelle's horror was numbing. "But Father..."

He frowned. "Do you presume to question me on this? You do not have any feelings for this man?"

She took a deep breath, realizing that she must get hold of herself if she was to be of any use to Simon. She must find a way to help him escape before her father could put his plan into effect. In spite of his assumption that she had informed her father of his leaving she could not see him murdered. Not even if he would always think of her as an enemy. "Nay, Father. I am simply overcome by the news that I am with child. I had not thought... You must see what a shock it has been to me. I am simply dazed."

Dear Heaven, it was true enough. She had not even considered the possibility that she was with child. Especially in the days of her father's illness when she had for the first time in her life been occupied with something that seemed to matter. But now he had pointed out the fact that she was with child, Isabelle knew it was true.

Her father continued to watch her for a moment. "Perhaps. Just be warned that I will not tolerate any hint of disloyalty."

Resentment stabbed her. He would tolerate no hint of disloyalty? But was that not how he had always behaved toward her? He had treated her as if she were nothing but a means to his own ends for as long as she had memory and would continue to do so.

Isabelle was suddenly and irrevocably determined to leave Dragonwick as soon as she had helped Simon to escape. She must, for it was her only hope of ever making a life of worth for herself and her child.

So thinking, Isabelle spoke evenly. "I pray you, Father, do what you will with Warleigh. I would have it done with all the turmoil his coming has brought." It shocked her, how hard she spoke the words in spite of the fact that they were in aid of throwing her father off the scent. "I have the heir of Dragonwick to concern myself with now."

Her father nodded, seeming approving enough of her announcement though there was still a hint of something dark in his gray eyes. She met them unflinchingly and he nodded. "See that you remember that." His gaze raked her and Isabelle was suddenly conscious that she had garbed herself with little care as she had been doing since her father fell ill. His tone was cold. "Pray do not show yourself in such disarray again. I am surprised you would so forget your place."

Isabelle ran a self-conscious hand over the skirt of her woolen gown. "I...forgive me, Father. I have been much occupied in the running of the keep whilst you and the others were ill.''

He raised those brows high. ''The castle women may see to their own duties now and you to yours. I am well enough and they must be, too. I will not tolerate slothfulness.''

Isabelle bowed her head. ''I will see to my duty.''

''See that you do.'' He looked down at his ledger. ''Go now. I have much to see to since my illness. Aside from ridding myself of Warleigh.''

Isabelle nodded with deliberate unconcern and stood. Her pounding heart bid her run from his evil presence ere it somehow taint the new life inside her, yet she left without undue haste.

Isabelle knew she could not delay even one night. She must attempt to act before her father did.

The castle lay in darkness as Isabelle made her way through the keep and down the narrow stair that led to the chamber beneath the hall. Although she had instructed Helwys to give the two guards who were watching over the prisoner a sleeping potion, she was very cautious.

In the light of the lanterns that burned in the wall sconces she could see that the two men were indeed asleep but there was no sign of Simon. Looking about she saw that the bolt had been engaged on the outside of the small chamber where her father's wines were kept. Quickly she moved to pull it back and opened the door. Inside there was neither light nor sound. Holding her breath she stepped inside, then when there was still no indication of life she whispered, ''Simon?''

From behind, she was suddenly pulled up against a hard chest. At the same time a hand covered her mouth. She knew that hand as well as her own for it had touched her in ways that made her ache inside to think on them, made her ache to know it would never do so again.

Quickly she told herself not to dwell on what could never be as he spoke in a hoarse whisper, "You are alone?"

She nodded and he took his hand away. Immediately she swung around. "You must leave the keep tonight."

She watched him draw himself up and her eyes began to adjust to the dim light that came in through the open door. "It is what I had intended."

Pain laced through her at his admission but she forced herself to keep her voice even. "I see."

He grunted with what sounded like frustration, taking her arm in a tight grip. "You do not see. I am going to court to speak with King John. He must release me from this situation."

"That is what you had always intended." She studied the carpet beneath her feet. "I thought that you had left for good when I saw you go last night. Why did you come back?"

"You saw me?" he replied as she looked back into those shadowed brown eyes of his. "Why did you let me go?"

She made no effort to answer, as she did not know herself. "Where did you go?"

He grimaced. "If you must know, I met with my friend Jarrod. It was he who dropped the brooch your father found." His gaze grew distant. "He and our friend Christian, who also wears the dragon on his shoulder, are like my brothers. I had to warn him against making any more attempts on your father's life, although I understood why he did so when he informed me your father was trespassing upon my lands, harassing one of my holders.''

Isabelle blanched and Simon went on. ''Do you not see? Kelsey is determined to take Avington in whatever way he can. You told me yourself that he has plans to kill me in the event that I am able to get you with child. I may not fear him but I grow tired of playing his game.''

Isabelle bit her lower lip, just barely keeping herself from telling him there was to be a child. For reasons she was not sure of, Isabelle could not bear to tell him. His immediate assumption that she had alerted the keep last night had reminded her of how things stood between them.

He went on. ''I have heard nothing from Christian and can only see to this myself. I will speak to John.''

In spite of everything she could not keep the anxiety for her voice. ''But the king did not heed you before.''

He took a deep breath raking a hand through the hair she so loved to touch. ''Your father was there. I may have some hope of having my story believed if he is not present.''

''Why do you not call upon your friends? Surely they would come to your aid.''

The vehemence with which he replied made her realize he was adamant in this. ''Nay, never. It is one thing to call upon my father's friends. They are powerful men, beyond the king's reach lest they commit some crime against the crown in their own right. Not so Jarrod or Christian, though they come from noble families. Jarrod is a bastard and Christian nothing more than the heir to a barony whilst his father lives. I would not have them jeopardize themselves.''

What he planned seemed very dangerous and she

could do nothing. No matter what came she knew it was very likely that she would never see Simon again, even if she were not planning her own escape from Dragonwick. Either the king would listen and free him, in which case he would be going home to Avington, or else…

Nay. The other possibility was unthinkable.

Simon must survive. Why this was so important to her she did not question. She looked up at him. "You must go now."

He nodded and started away then turned, "Isabelle, I am sorry for what I said, for accusing you of calling out to your father's men."

She shook her head, feeling that mask come over her face to cover her hurt. "There is no need explain. It matters not."

Simon frowned, leaning close to her, his breath warm on her cheek. "Aye, it matters. I can see that it does in spite of your desire to hide it and that you will not allow yourself to forgive me for it. You trust no one and use each infraction as proof that your distrust is just."

She closed her eyes. "I do not…"

A groan from one of the men interrupted her. She took a step backward. "This is a waste of precious time and to discuss it would change nothing."

"That does not mean I will not try," Simon told her even as he moved toward the door.

She made no reply as her chest throbbed with sudden misery. She would never see Simon again.

She followed him out of the tiny room and up the stairs, whispering, "Sir Edmund is awaiting you with two horses at the bottom of the hill outside the gate. The horses are not your own as they would be more quickly missed. Helwys informs me that Jack was happy to aid her in obtaining the horses and he will not tell anyone.''

He said nothing until the two of them were standing on the steps outside the great oaken door of the keep. ''Tell Jack he has my thanks.'' He looked down at her and she found herself drinking in every detail of his face, which suddenly seemed so dear to her.

He took a deep breath. ''And for you, Isabelle...'' He did not finish whatever he had been about to say but took her in his arms, his mouth finding hers in a hard pulse-quickening kiss that she knew would stay in her memory for all time. And like a silly fool she clung to him, her heart aching at the loss of this—of him.

Then releasing her just as abruptly, he was gone.

It was only short hours later as Isabelle was sewing the velvet bag containing her jewels to the inner seam of her cloak that her chamber door slammed open without warning. With deliberate casualness she set the sewing down, having a care to keep the bag out of sight. In the light of the candles he held she could see her father's face and the rage that burned in it. He swept a disdainful glance over her, not moving from the doorway. ''Where is your husband?''

Isabelle felt her already aching heart sink further. Only a few short hours had passed since Simon had left. She had counted, obviously unrealistically, on his having at least until the morning meal. Quickly she lied even as she attempted to disguise the signs of her tears by leaning back in the shadows of the bed hangings. ''In the cellar.''

He strode across the room to bend over her, studying her closely. ''He is not in the cellar. Somehow someone was able to give my men something to make them sleep. Whoever it was has helped Warleigh to escape.''

She heard the horror in her own voice and knew it must be convincing though it was not caused by her concern over the question but terror of what would occur if her father discovered who was responsible. ''Who would dare do such a thing?'' She must guard the truth for the sake of not only herself and the child, but also Helwys and Jack.

Isabelle stood swaying as she realized the tremendous consequences they could have brought upon themselves. She must leave this place with all possible haste.

Her father spoke sharply, ''What is the matter with you, girl?''

She forced herself to meet that probing gaze. ''I am sure it is the babe.''

He grimaced. ''Sickly, are you?'' His expression was disapproving. ''I expected better of you.''

Isabelle raised her chin. ''I am sorry, Father. I am sure my illness will pass quickly.''

''See that it does,'' he instructed, thankfully completely unaware of the true source of her pain. ''I won't have you lolling about.'' As he went on she listened carefully. ''I am sending word to the king this very hour. Warleigh will now be outlawed. We must go to court and petition the crown in the interest of the child. He has complicated all by this devilment but all may not be lost if I can convince the king that the child has rights to the title and lands in spite of his father's crimes. I must convince him that the father's nature will leave no mark upon the child, especially as I am willing to give it the benefit of my tutelage. The child's future must be assured.''

Isabelle knew not what to say to this. No one had proved themselves more perfidious than her father.

Yet what he said next washed all other thoughts from her mind. "Methinks, Isabelle, that due to your fragile health 'twould be best for you to rest in your chamber until our departure for Windsor."

She looked at him. "Are you saying you do not trust me?"

He smiled, "Nay, daughter, only that I would protect you, not only from ill health but from those who might attempt to harm you on Warleigh's behalf. He may prefer to end your marriage by whatever means possible."

Isabelle knew this thought had come into his mind because it was the way he himself thought. But she could spare little attention for that. She suddenly realized that she could not leave Simon to his machinations. She had to do something however little it might be, locked in her chamber as she was.

She must appear to be acquiescent as she always had been. She nodded. "I thank you, father, for your concern for me. I will do as you feel is best."

That did seem to please him for he nodded. "Very good. I shall leave you to your rest then." He stepped back, closing the door and sliding home the bolt he had installed outside it years ago.

Isabelle knew she must act. No matter how angered Simon would be by what she was about to do, she could not sit back and allow him to die, for that was surely what would happen if she did nothing.

As soon as Helwys returned to the chamber, she outlined her plan. The maid was pale and frightened, especially when Isabelle's father clearly felt that something might be amiss or he would not have confined her. Yet she did not argue against their helping Simon.

She assured Isabelle that Jack would again come to their aid. Helwys then offered to obtain the brooch, which Isabelle knew they must have in order for Simon's friend to be convinced that the letter she intended to write came from him, from her father's chamber.

Isabelle was concerned that the maid would be caught taking the brooch. Helwys assured her she would not be. Then it was left to Isabelle to write the letter that would accompany it.

It was brief and unsigned: "Come to Windsor."

She knew Simon would not forgive her for doing this, for disobeying him. But she could not do otherwise.

Eight days passed before Isabelle saw her father again. He came with an expression of triumph. "The fool Warleigh has gone to court to plead his case. On receipt of my letter the king has arrested him."

Isabelle only just managed to keep standing as a wave of dizzying horror took her. As her father went on she met his watchful gaze. "Warleigh's fate is assured. You are to garb yourself for traveling. We go to court to secure the lands on the morrow."

She kept her gaze from wavering. "Yes, Father."

"I see you truly are not disturbed by this news."

"No, Father."

He shrugged. "For a time it did seem that you might have been foolish enough to imagine yourself enamored of the man. You did after all create a child together and I can see that a young woman might find him appealing."

She did not waver for what she said was truth. "I knew it would not last, Father. It would indeed be mad for me to allow myself to care for the man."

"Precisely. Attachment is not a weakness either of us would allow ourselves."

"And I have you to thank you for teaching me to be like you in that, Father." There was no sign of the bitterness she felt in her voice.

He nodded. "I have learned that it was likely one of my own men who helped Warleigh escape. The soldier Jack has since disappeared, as has the brooch Fredrick found in the wood after the attempt on my life."

Isabelle shook her head even as she felt a wave of contempt for her father, for he did not add that he had been trespassing on Simon's own lands when it occurred. She shrugged, "I am sure it is your intent to make him pay for his disloyalty to you."

With a self-satisfied smile he said, "Aye, it is." With that he left, closing the door behind him. Obviously convinced that he need distrust her no longer, he did not secure the bolt.

Isabelle's heart thumped in her chest. Here was her chance. Her father would never question that fact that she was packing. She and Helwys could make ready for their escape openly.

She would leave this very night.

Even as she began to open the chest with her jewels inside, she stopped. Eight days had passed. Simon's friends had not gone to his aid. Or if they had their presence had counted for naught.

Perhaps they had arrived after the king's letter had been sent to her father. Perhaps Simon was even now celebrating his freedom.

Yet could she take that chance? Could she walk away without knowing?

She could not. Isabelle sank down on the end of her bed, telling herself that she would never be able to look into her son's eyes, for she was certain the child was the boy she had always wanted, without guilt.

What she might be able to do for Simon she did not know, but she had to try.

The journey to Windsor took three days. Isabelle did her utmost to avoid talking with her father, feigning a slight illness each time they stopped. It was clear that her father was not pleased, but he made no more than passing comment, as she did not delay their progress in any way.

In truth Isabelle was feeling quite well other than an unaccustomed exhaustion and an occasional light-headedness. She was almost disappointed that she did feel so well, for it would have been good to think on something besides the fact that Simon would be very angry with her if he knew she had sent for his friends. More pressing even than this worry was her fear of what her father would do when he learned that it was her intent to speak on Simon's behalf.

His rage would be devastating and it was very likely that she had abandoned her only opportunity to escape him. For she knew he was not above locking her in her chambers for the rest of her days for the sin of betraying him.

It was with this thought fully in her mind that Isabelle followed her father to the king's audience chamber only hours after their arrival at Windsor.

What she saw when the attendant opened the door to grant them admittance made her stop still. King John sat at a heavy wooden table at the end of the chamber. Before the king were two guards, and between them was Simon.

He spun about as she and her father moved into the

room, his gaze widening as it came to rest on her. Isabelle felt her heart thud in her breast, her gaze moving over him quickly. Though her husband was disheveled and there were obvious signs of exhaustion on his handsome face, he seemed unharmed.

Feeling her father's attention upon her, she quickly lowered her eyes. She did not wish for her father to guess her intent and send her away before she had an opportunity to speak, to hopefully make the king hear the truth.

Even as they went forward she heard King John say, "You have pleaded to face the earl, Warleigh. Here he is."

Simon said, "May I now question my accuser?"

John shook his head. "I will first ask my own questions and we will see if there is then any point in your doing so."

Raising her head, Isabelle saw the frustration on his face. The king continued, "Can you deny that you did in fact leave Dragonwick without his permission after I had bid you remain in his care?"

Simon frowned. "You know I can not for I have admitted as much."

King John nodded, "Can you deny that a brooch that is the exact match of your own was found in the exact place from whence an attempt was made on his life?"

This time Simon said nothing. For though the king had brought Kelsey here as he had asked, it was clear that King John was unprepared to believe anything Simon might say.

Obviously Simon was as aware of this as she for he smiled. "I see now that there is no more point in my defending myself than there ever was." He nodded to her father. "You may have won against me and everyone else you have sought to destroy thus far, Kelsey, but eventually you will pay. That is the way of things.''

Kelsey turned to the king. ''Do you hear him, sire? He threatens me even now.''

Isabelle knew that she could delay no longer. There would be no better chance than this.

She opened her mouth, then closed it as she felt her father's gaze upon her. Sudden terror of what he would do to her when this was done dampened her palms and tightened her chest to the point where it was near impossible to breathe. Yet she took a deep breath and said, ''My liege.'' Her voice was nearly inaudible. She tried again, this time with more success. ''King John, I beg your leave to speak.''

Her father took her arm. ''There is no need, Isabelle. The king will hear us on our own concerns when this matter is done.''

She did not look at him, could not. ''It is this matter I wish to address.''

Her gaze met Simon's. The expression in his eyes was measuring, and yes she could see it, hopeful. Even as she tried to send reassurance, that look changed to warning.

King John leaned back in his chair, drawing her attention back to him as he said, ''Speak.'' She could feel the continued intensity of Simon's gaze. His concern for her did not move her to caution as he obviously hoped but fueled her courage to go on. ''I would tell you, milord, that Simon Warleigh is guilty of the crimes he has admitted but there are extenuating circumstances that you should be made aware of.''

Her father snarled, ''Isabelle!''

At the same time Simon said, ''Isabelle, there is no need for you to do this. Naught can come of it.''

She ignored them both, speaking quickly, "These things did occur but it was in his own self-defense that Simon Warleigh acted. My father did in fact lie to you, King John, when he first accused Simon of plotting against the crown. It was indeed my father who was his target. Father has admitted as much to me. It is also true that my father has since plotted to kill Simon Warleigh in the hope of gaining access to his lands. The attempted attack upon my father occurred when he was trespassing at Avington, tormenting one of Lord Warleigh's own folk in order to obtain information about the fortifications there."

Her father spoke then, in a cold and even voice that held no hint of distress. "This is preposterous, my lord king. I had feared this for some time but my affection for my daughter blinded me to the truth. She has fallen in love with the knave and seeks to do whatever she must to save his life."

King John turned to her. "Is this true? Are you in love with this man?"

Isabelle raised her head high. "Aye. I love him."

Her gaze went to Simon as he cried out, "Isabelle."

She held his gaze, unable to hide the truth that burned inside her. She did indeed love him, had loved him from the moment she saw him that first day upon the road to Windsor. Only her fear of being hurt had kept her from knowing it. Now, though she knew that Simon did not return her feelings, she was prepared to face him with the truth. For she realized it was not him she must face as much as her fear.

Simon did not shy away from her gaze. "You love me?"

The king spoke with sharp impatience. "Take him. I

will not have this meeting digress into nothing more than trite declarations of affection.''

As Simon resisted the grasp of the two guards, Isabelle knew that he would have made no declarations of love. What she had heard in his voice was nothing more than curious amazement. There was no surprise in that, for she had informed him that she was incapable of such feelings on more than one occasion. She watched as he struggled with the guards, shouting, ''I will not go with you.''

King John clapped his hands together and from the curtain behind him came two more guards, their swords drawn.

Isabelle held her breath as Simon became still, then stood straight. He cast her father a look of hatred. ''This is not yet done, Kelsey.'' Then there was time for only one more glance in her direction, a glance that held many emotions she could not begin to name, before he was led out.

With Simon gone, her father leveled her with an icy glare as he addressed the king. ''You see the way things are, my lord. Warleigh has seduced her. I had attempted to make her strong but the girl is weak-minded as all her sex.''

There was an edge of icy hatred that only Isabelle seemed to hear as he said this. Unable to understand it she could only shake her head. ''He has not seduced me. He is good and strong and honest. Those are the reasons I love him.'' She turned to the king. ''But more important than why I love him or even that I do is that I am telling the truth here. Simon is not guilty of the things my father has accused him of.''

To her utter despair King John looked to her father

with a sympathetic expression on his narrow face. "Clearly she is besotted."

Her father moved to stand so close that no one but she could hear his words, "You will pay!" but she saw not only anger in his eyes, but also pleasure. He was enjoying besting her, as he always had enjoyed besting everyone who opposed him.

The fact that she was his daughter meant nothing to him. It never had.

She returned his gaze but hers was filled with pity. How very lonely he must be to be unable to love.

No matter what came next in her future, Isabelle was grateful for one thing Simon had given her. He had shown her how to love. Even if he never returned her feelings she had experienced something her father and those like him, those who were so locked inside themselves, so protective of their hearts and feelings, were incapable of.

No matter what pain might come of her loving where it was not returned she had felt that glow inside her, the feeling that moved her to care for something outside herself and her own misery.

Right now she was moved to do whatever she must to save her husband's life. Without thinking she swung around to face King John. "Take me, keep me as warrant that Simon will do no ill. I would gladly forfeit my freedom to prove that he means you no harm, sire."

The king shook his head. "Very prettily said, my lady Warleigh, but your words are clearly brought on by your desire to see your husband released. I have no reason to believe that retaining your person would in any way deter him."

She clenched her hands tightly at her sides in frustration. "There is nothing to be deterred from. It is my father who—'' She could see that she had been mad to imagine that her leaving would influence the King to release Simon. Nothing would have mattered.

Her father motioned to Sir Fredrick where he lingered nearby as he always did. ''Take her. I would have her shame me no more.''

Even as the knight took her arm in a painful grip, Isabelle wrenched herself free. ''Do not put your hands upon me again.''

She glared her anger and he stepped back as she spun about and moved toward the door. She would afford them no more of her misery. She must be alone to think about what could be done.

Chapter Fifteen

Isabelle was in the chamber she had been given to share with her father for no more than minutes before he strode through the door. He waved a dismissive hand to Helwys. "Leave us."

Helwys looked to Isabelle with an expression of fear, and Isabelle nodded. "Go. I am fine."

Once the door closed behind her, Isabelle swung around to face her father. "My lord."

His gaze was angry and cruelly assessing. "Your disloyalty is, to say the least, shameful."

Even though she did not really believe she had been disloyal, the words stung. He went on. "What could one expect of the offspring of your dame."

Her amazed gaze fixed on him. "Why would you speak so of my mother?"

He smiled coldly. "Why indeed?"

Isabelle was shocked by this continuing odd behavior. "Since you never married after her death, or seemed interested in any woman, I had always believed she was the one person you have ever loved. And now you speak of her with such…" She shook her head. "I can not even begin to fathom such new depths of disdain toward others."

"Disdain," he barked. "It is you who could tell me of disdain. You who have betrayed me for my enemy."

"I have not betrayed you. I but tried to right a wrong. It is you who have done ill to Simon. You know he has never plotted against the king, because you know that you were the target of his anger. And you know why."

His hand connected with her cheek. Isabelle reeled, stepping backward with the force of the blow. The actual pain did not come for a heartbeat after.

Before she could say a word, he continued, "You have no notion of what I do or why. You do not know what effort it has taken to gain and hold my place. A place that I richly deserved as payment for what I have been cheated of."

"I do not understand."

"Nay," he nodded sharply and suddenly Isabelle saw a hint of something desolate and lonely in those eyes she had always thought of as cold. "You do not understand."

Isabelle remembered the day she and Simon had first gone to the lodge. She'd gained the impression that her father was a man of great loneliness then but the reality of his behavior had made her brush it aside.

In spite of the fact that her cheek was still stinging, in spite of the fact that her father had never acted as if he desired her sympathy or compassion, she felt a rush of both. Taking a step toward him, Isabelle said, "What is it, Father? Tell me and I will try to understand."

That hint of desolation had been replaced by distrust and he raked her with another cold glance. "Father? You must first begin by hearing that I am not your father."

She jerked back more violently than when he had struck her. "What are you saying?"

He smiled again, seeming to enjoy her horror and confusion. "I am not your father."

"How can that be possible?"

Bitterness colored his voice, though she knew he was attempting to speak as if this revelation did not matter to him. "Your mother, my good wife, got you by another."

She shook her head violently. "Nay. Though I remember her not I have heard others speak of her with great respect. I will not believe that my mother would betray her marriage vows."

"That much is true. She did keep to the letter of those vows. Yet you are another's get nonetheless."

"I can not see how that could be possible."

"Attend me then," he ordered sharply. "Your mother had given herself to another before she came to me." He stared off into the past that only he could see. "She loved a man she met while staying with friends of her family who lived here in England. He had her maidenhead then left for war. I had met her at the same time and had been in love with her all along, unknowing fool that I was. Finding herself alone and with child she accepted my suit in order to give her bastard a name."

Weakened by the realization that her father was speaking the truth Isabelle sank to her knees on the threadbare carpet. He looked down at her. "She told me none of this at the time, of course. She waited until she was dying after the birth of our own stillborn child only two years later to tell me the truth. She said she could not go without confessing all. She desired," he laughed bitterly, "that I should go to your true father and tell him all."

She felt as if she were drowning in shock and confusion, but a question emerged from her numb lips. "You know who my father is?"

He raised disdainful brows. "I do indeed. I have felt the curse of that knowing in each day of my life."

"Who is he?"

He shrugged. "You may as well know. It can make no difference now. All my efforts to raise you to stand above the errors of your mother have been for naught."

Her voice rose with impatience at his rambling. "Who was he?" She had to know.

"The Dragon."

The words should have shocked her. Yet somehow they did not. Perhaps in some place inside her, in the deepest recesses of her heart she had always known without knowing. Had she not loved him so well and unfailingly in all these years? She had set him above all other men until Simon had come to win her lonely heart. "The Dragon was my father!"

He continued to look on her with disdain. "Aye. My own half brother was your father."

"My mother must have been in love with him."

His voice was brittle. "In love with him. Lust more like, as all the other women who scampered after him."

She did not care to hear the desperation in her own tone as she strove to believe that she had not been born from some shameful act. "But he did not misuse her. I am sure of it."

He shrugged, his tone scathing. "Are you asking me if he loved her? Wallace did not return from war until after you were born and Therese was heavy with our own child. She said as she was dying, and I believed her, that they were never again alone together. I never saw either of them so much as look... That was part of the reason it came as such a shock to me to learn the truth. But afterward when I thought on it, I realized he had loved her all along.'' His cold gaze moved over her. ''He spent that love on you, doted and cuddled and fussed over you as he did Rosalind. And it sickened me.''

''But he meant no betrayal to you in that. He did not know I was his daughter. He was simply being kind. He was a loving man to all he cared for.''

Her father drew himself up. ''Yet that really did not matter. The damage had been done in his loving her— putting his hands upon her. She was used by him, and thus not really and truly mine. All my life I had fallen second to him and must even in the bed of my own wife. My brother married, had a child of his wife that was his alone. I had you, who were his as well.''

Isabelle's eyes suddenly widened in pain and regret. ''Rosalind, the little girl who died the day you took Dragonwick, was my own sister.''

He shrugged again. ''''Twas unavoidable.''

She shook her head. ''I pity you, Father.''

He smiled coldly, and she suddenly knew that cold smile covered his feelings, his fear of loving, of being hurt, even as he said, ''Save your pity for one who might need it.''

A sense of freedom surged through her as she held her head high. No longer would she follow his paltry example. No more would she deny her feelings. She had admitted her love for Simon out of desperation only hours ago. Now she wished that it was to do over again, so she might say the words with all the joy that rose up inside her. There was no shame in admitting the truth of her own feelings to him or anyone else, for loving was not weakness but strength.

She looked at her father with new eyes. "I have hated you for your cruelty and coldness while at the same time hoping with all my heart for just one small act of kindness, one gentle word. Though they never came, I never stopped wishing." She put her hand over her heart. "You say that your brother took all from you. He did not, for I was willing to love you. You and you alone have thrown away or destroyed all that mattered in your life."

For a moment there was once again a hint of deep pain in his gaze before he said, "I do not need your love."

"Then all the more reason to pity you." She turned and moved toward the door.

His voice was hard with command. "Where do you think you are going?"

She did not look around. "To my husband. To see if there is aught that can be done to save him."

"Do not be a fool. Warleigh is as good as dead. You are and will continue to remain under my control."

"Do as you will. No more will I obey out of fear, for the damage to my soul is as much a punishment as any physical one you might devise."

As she opened the door and stepped through it she heard him say, "Go, then. See what welcome you get from Warleigh. He never wanted you."

Isabelle knew this was true and though it hurt, she was not willing to let that stop her from doing what she must. It was the giving of her own love that mattered most even if he did not accept it.

Simon looked up at a scraping sound at the door of his cell. Slowly he stood as the door swung open, his head held high.

The resolve he felt changed to shock mixed with confusion and yes, joy, when he saw Isabelle standing in the narrow opening. He moved toward her. "How did you...?"

She glanced behind her and he noted the presence of his jailer who stood admiring the large stone of the ring he held between his thick fingers.

He shook his head. "You should not have come here. Your father—"

She put her fingers to his mouth to prevent him from going on. "He is not my father."

Simon looked down at her in confusion and she said, "I would not go into detail now but I will tell you this, he has said The Dragon was my true father and I believe him."

"But how?"

She shook her own head. "Not now, Simon, just know that learning the truth has freed me from his domination. No matter what he might do to me in the future I will never again fall victim to his emotional control."

He put his arms about her, loving the feel of her against him even as he felt the rage rise up at knowing he was powerless to protect her.

She pushed back away from him and he saw that her beautiful eyes were troubled. "Simon, there is something I have to confess."

Simon did not care what she had to say. All he could think about was the fact that she had said she loved him. He opened his mouth to tell her so, when raised voices sounded from outside the cell.

Isabelle's terrified gaze met his. "They can not have come to take you...."

Before he could reply the cell door swung open with

a loud bang. In the opening stood two of the king's guards.

Isabelle cried out, "No, you can not mean to—"

One of the men spoke without inflection while the other simply looked on, his face set in an expressionless mask. "Come."

Isabelle ran to stand before them and his belly tightened with pain and regret as she cried, "For the love of God, do not do this."

Neither replied. Simon took a deep breath. He had not expected the king to move so quickly. He had hoped for some reprieve. When a sob escaped Isabelle he moved to take her in his arms, holding her tightly for a moment before setting her away. "You can do nothing, Isabelle. Do not risk yourself for naught."

He stepped forward and the men flanked him as they had when they led him here. Isabelle started after them and he turned to look at her over his shoulder saying, "Do not follow."

But she paid him no heed, her lips setting in a stubborn line as tears slipped down her porcelain cheeks. He felt his own heart ache for her sorrow, but could do nothing to ease it.

Simon felt many eyes follow him as he passed into and through the more occupied sections of the castle. He looked neither right nor left, caring only for the quiet sobbing of the woman he loved.

Had he truly longed for the day when she would be willing to share her emotion? Her pain now nearly drove him to his knees.

To his surprise they led him not to the courtyard where he expected whatever sentence the king had decreed to be carried out. They took him back to the very

chamber in which he had again faced Kelsey. The
chamber where Isabelle had told him she loved him.

The taller of the two guards moved forward and
opened the door. Simon stepped inside. As he did so he
stopped dead for it was a long moment before he realized what he was seeing.

On one side of the dais at the far end of the chamber
stood the Earl of Kelsey. He looked on with an expression that was fixed as stone, giving nothing away.

Both Jarrod and Christian stood to the other side.
Next to them were two older men, both of whom wore
their noble bearing with confidence. Though Simon had
never known these two men well he did have a recollection of having seen them before and his heart
thumped with hope as he realized just who they were.

His gaze went to the king and found that narrow vis-
age looking far from pleased. John motioned him forward with an impatient hand. "Come forward, Warleigh."

King John gestured to the four men. "I believe you
must know Greatham, Maxwell, Dempsey and Fillmore."

Simon did indeed know Greatham and Maxwell and
the other two men. The older men were indeed two of
the most powerful noblemen in all of England and longtime intimates of his father.

Simon looked to his friends as he moved to stand
with them. "Why did they not come before? And how
did you know to bring them now when the hour was so
dire?"

Christian shrugged looking to Jarrod who answered,
"Your wife."

Simon had not forgotten Isabelle.

He swung around to find her standing close behind

him, her hands folded before her in a manner of contrition. Isabelle looked up at him, her lavender eyes filled with anxiety. "That is what I was going to tell you. I know you did not wish for your friends to be involved in this, but I could not see you..."

He wanted to hug her and throttle her at the same time but he wanted even more to see what was going on. He took her hand. "We will discuss this later." He turned to the king. "Am I to take it that you are willing to hear my case at last?"

The king frowned. "Your case has been made." His wary glaze slid over Lord Dempsey, then Lord Fillmore. "These two men, two of my most loyal and powerful nobles have spoken on your behalf." There was no mistaking the irony in his tone, yet clearly the king was moved by the power that the two held.

Christian leaned close and whispered, "My father was ill and could not write the letters, but when Jarrod came with the letter and the dragon brooch we knew there was no more time. He and I rode directly to Fillmore and Dempsey to plead your case. They were happy to come, naming your father as friend."

Lord Dempsey interjected, "I also have some knowledge of your character through my son, Warleigh. He spent some time with you and your friends in the Holy Land some years ago and speaks highly of you still."

Simon did remember the quiet young knight and was grateful for his favorable assessment. He bowed to Lord Dempsey, who nodded in return.

Jarrod whispered so only he and Christian could hear, "Methinks they also feel a desire to keep Kelsey from attaining more power than he has already acquired."

Simon was certain this was indeed a factor in their

desire to aid him. Yet he cared not why they had done so, only that they had.

King John cast Simon an angry glare. "Leave me and my court without delay. My time is far too precious to waste more of it upon you, Warleigh."

Simon bowed. He would not be sorry to take himself from Windsor and never again return.

Kelsey's voice made him look up and he could see the anger his father-by-marriage was attempting to hide as he said, "You mean to let him go on the word of these two when I have given my own word on the matter."

King John turned to him. "You honor is not in question, my lord Kelsey. I believe you quite genuine in your belief that this man was plotting against the crown and I commend you for your loyalty to me. I simply find that you were mistaken."

"But..."

"Have no concern in this matter, my lord," the king proclaimed. "You have lost no value in my eyes and will continue in your position of favor in this court." Though John's words were gracious enough there was a hint of warning in his eyes that could not be ignored.

Simon saw that Kelsey was not happy with this. Yet what could he do? Holding his head high, the earl turned and stalked from the chamber.

Simon watched as Lord Dempsey held up a hand. "I am sorry to delay you, my liege, but Fillmore and I would be grateful for just a bit more of your time. Precious as it is, we have come some distance and there are several other small matters you might aid us with."

The king nodded, though his expression was not pleased as he waved a hand. "The rest of you will go now."

Simon felt only relief as he took Isabelle's icy hand and led her from the chamber, aware of the fact that his two friends followed him. Once out in the hall, he looked into his wife's eyes. Free, dear God, free to take Isabelle home with him, to start a life with her, knowing that she loved him. "Isabelle, I..."

Kelsey's voice interrupted. "Isabelle, you will attend me immediately."

Simon moved to stand between them. "Isabelle will be coming with me."

He heard her murmur a surprised, "But Simon, you need not—"

He stopped her with a look. "You are my wife. Your place is with me." She had said that she loved him but obviously the long years of obeying her father's every command were not easy to break. He pushed aside his regret, telling himself that he must only give her time.

Isabelle said no more but her eyes continued to be troubled.

Kelsey's tone was hard with command. "Isabelle."

She kept her gaze on Simon's, "I go with my husband."

Simon saw that Kelsey's face seemed to crumple with what he would have recognized as pain on any other man. Yet Simon, knowing the earl incapable of such emotion, watched as he spun away.

Simon turned to the others. "Let us away immediately."

Isabelle spoke softly as her strangely watchful gaze met Simon's, "I must get Helwys and some of my things for the journey."

Simon's relief that she did not seem to be swaying in her decision to accompany him was great. He was near giddy with relief as he addressed Jarrod, "We will meet you in the courtyard."

Jarrod nodded, his black eyes triumphant as he stared after the earl's retreating back. "I will get the horses."

Christian smiled tightly. "I will go with Simon and Isabelle in case Kelsey has some surprise in mind to keep Isabelle from leaving with us."

Simon was not afraid of Kelsey or anything he might attempt now, but he did not pause to discuss this point. He could not wait to get on the road to Avington; only then would he feel he had Isabelle out of her father's reach.

He did not release her hand as she led them to her assigned chamber. Simon paused in the open doorway, the unexpected tableau before him holding him immobile. Isabelle and Christian seemed to have been affected in the same way for they too halted in the doorway.

Inside was Helwys as they had expected but Kelsey's man Sir Fredrick and Jack, who had proved himself a true friend to Simon in all of this, were there as well. The two men had obviously been engaged in a heated exchange, which continued as neither seemed aware of the new arrivals.

The knight growled, "You betrayed my lord Kelsey."

Jack stepped back against the wall. Though his gaze did not waver it was clear that this was only bravado as he was armed with nothing but the knife in his belt. "There has been no betrayal in my mind for I have never served your master. I have always served The Dragon."

Simon was released from his frozen state, starting forward as Fredrick cried out, "Knave." At the same time he pulled out his blade without warning, running Jack through.

Simon called out, "Nay," as Jack crumpled to the floor. Sir Fredrick turned to face him even as Simon drew his own sword.

Simon charged Sir Fredrick, who barely had time to bring up his own weapon, when he cried out, "Christian, see what can be done for Jack."

Then there was no more time for words as it took all his concentration to answer Sir Fredrick's furious counterattack. All the rage and resentment that had been building in Kelsey's knight since the beginning was apparent in every thrust.

Simon fought on, trying to keep his own hatred under control for he knew it could rise up and overcome him, make him incautious in the face of the other's desire to see him dead. Loyalty, mad as his loyalty might be, was what drove the knight, making him a fiercesome opponent. Simon met each clash of metal against metal with diligence, knowing that one false move could bring his end.

Finally came the telling moment when Simon thrust upward in a desperate move to keep the blow that was aimed at his heart from connecting, and met flesh. Sir Fredrick's sword clattered on the stone floor as he reached with the other hand to clutch at the gaping wound in his shoulder. Looking at Simon with shock he fell to the floor.

A horrified gasp sounded and Simon looked over to see Kelsey standing in the doorway. He ran to his man's side.

Simon had his own wounded to concern himself with. He hurried to Christian, Isabelle and Helwys, where they knelt beside the fallen Jack. It was Christian who said, "We have bandaged the wound."

"How bad is it?" They moved back to let Simon get closer. Jack's face was lined with pain but he tried to smile. "Have no concern for me, my lord. I will be fine."

Simon clasped a hand over his cold one. "Aye, you shall. If you can travel I will take you to Avington."

A shadow passed over the man's face but he nodded as he said, "I thought never to leave Dragonwick. I..." He sighed. "I will go with you now."

Simon turned to Isabelle and Helwys as he stood. "We go to Avington."

Helwys smiled, looking to her mistress. "At last."

Isabelle heard her maid's words but could summon no answering relief. She was reeling from the events of the past hour. The only emotion she could really fix on was her relief that Simon, and Jack, were alive. She moved to stand beside her husband, feeling his strength surround her like a warm cloak.

Helwys took her other side.

The man she'd always thought of as her father glared up at her as he tore the bottom from Sir Fredrick's tunic and placed it over the knight's wound. "Look what you have done by your deceit and betrayal."

Isabelle felt pain lace through her even though she knew that this was not her doing. She felt her shoulders taken in a gentle but insistent grip. "We must go, Isabelle. Jarrod is waiting."

The earl spoke harshly, his eyes holding a wildness such as she had never seen before. "You take nothing of Dragonwick with you. I will see that not even your dower lands go to you."

Though she had known she was making this choice the words hurt. Distantly she watched as Simon and Christian took Jack up between them and moved toward the door. Blindly she took Helwys's hand, stumbling after them. She kept pace easily for it was slow going as the two men supported most of Jack's weight.

Jarrod was indeed waiting with four horses. He realized what had happened immediately and managed to obtain a small cart within minutes. They loaded Jack into it and he laid back smiling up at them gingerly. "Do not worry. The bleeding has nearly stopped."

Taking this as a good sign indeed they mounted with better humor, Christian taking Helwys up behind him. All the while Isabelle remained uneasy at what she knew she must do before too many miles had fallen behind them.

When they had traveled some distance down the road from the gate, Isabelle stopped. Simon, who had been galloping beside her, brought his own horse to an abrupt halt swinging around. She could see the anxiety in his beloved brown eyes as he said, "What is it, Isabelle?"

She looked to the others who had now stopped as well a short distance ahead of them. She spoke softly. "You do not have to take me with you to Avington."

He sucked in a harsh breath, waving to the others to go on as he slid to the ground and moved to stand looking up at her. "Oh, but I do."

She shook her head unable to speak around the lump in her throat. If only he was doing this because he truly wanted her.

He frowned. "Why are you fighting me?"

She closed her eyes. "I know you are aware of my feelings for you and that you are a good man and must feel you owe me something because I love you." Isabelle knew she was rambling but could not seem to stop herself. "Although I have realized that there is no need to hide my feelings, I do not expect, nor want you to take me out of pity."

The silence that followed made her open her eyes again. The amazement on Simon's face could not have been more apparent. "Out of pity?"

She felt a strange flutter of hope in her breast. "You are not taking me to Avington out of pity?"

He shook his head.

She bit her lip. "But you had made it clear that you did not want to be married to me."

Simon raised his dark brows high. "That was before we made love. You knew how I felt about any child we might create together, that I intended to be a father. The marriage was for life when I took you to my bed."

She looked down, her throat and chest tight. "I do not want you to keep me out of duty. It is not a good enough reason for a marriage, Simon. Nor is the fact that I have learned my father is not truly my father. I have devised a plan to go to Normandy where my mother's sister is from. She came to see me once not long after my mother died and though my father sent her away, I have realized she must be a kind person to have come all that way. I have some hope that she might care for me, and Helwys and…"

He barely noted that pause as he suddenly realized why she had hesitated to come with him. It was not because of Kelsey at all but because she was uncertain of his feelings. Joy rose up inside him as he looked into those beautiful lavender eyes. "Is love enough reason?"

For a long moment she only stared at him. "Aye, love would be enough. Are you saying that you…?"

He reached out his arms. "I am. I love you, have

loved you from the beginning and will continue to love you to the end.''

She came into his arms, throwing her own about his neck as she raised her mouth for his kiss. And kiss her he did, with a thoroughness that made her head spin.

She pulled away to look up into his eyes, ''To think that I thought you would be angry with me for sending for Jarrod and Christian.''

He grimaced, though he did not release her. ''And did I say I was not? You must learn, Isabelle, that though I may become unhappy at something that has happened I will never stop loving you, nor will I treat you cruelly.''

A tear slid down her cheek as she leaned her head against his shoulders. ''Oh Simon, I never knew such love, such joy existed in all the world.''

His heart filled with a tenderness so rich and deep that for a long moment he could not have spoken had he wished to. How he had longed for her to believe in him, in life. There was no holding back in her this time. She was well and truly his.

He kissed her again.

At long last she pulled back, her eyes bright with passion and happiness. ''There is one more thing you must know, my love.''

Simon's arms tightened around her. ''What more could life have to offer me than this?''

She took his hand and placed it on her flat belly, her expression filled with love and meaning.

''Do you mean…?''

She nodded.

Tenderness such as he had never felt or even dreamed of swelled in his chest, making his heart feel as if his chest could not contain it. He fell to his knees pressing his lips to her belly, feeling the hot sting of joyful tears behind his lids as he whispered, "So beautiful, my own perfect Isabelle. My dear."

She held him close against her. "I love you, Simon."

He stood and kissed her again, feeling the passion that had been between them from their first meeting burst to aching life inside him. Isabelle felt it, too, for she said, "How I want you, my love." Simon slid his hands down her back to mold her pliant body to his.

A shout made him look down the road and he realized he had forgotten where they were. It was Jarrod and he called out, "Are you two coming?"

Simon wrapped his arms about his wife. "Aye, but we must stop and make camp very soon."

A hoot of laughter was the only reply as Simon helped Isabelle mount and they made their way down the road to their future. Her father, the man she had thought was her father, had said she took nothing of her dower with her.

He was wrong. Her true father had left her something more valuable than lands. Her dower was love, the love she had felt for him and he for her. The love she now felt for Simon and their child.

*   *   *   *   *

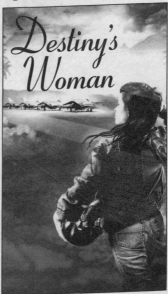
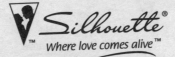

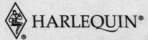

Enjoy the fun and frolic of the Regency
period with a brand-new novel from
New York Times bestselling author

Stephanie Laurens

A Comfortable Wife

Antonia Mannering was a young
woman with plans—and becoming
and old maid was not one of them! So she
proposed a marriage of convenience to her
childhood friend, Lord Philip Ruthven.
Never had she expected that their hearts
would somehow find their way into
the bargain!

"All I need is her name on the cover
to make me buy the book."
—*New York Times* bestselling author
Linda Howard

*Available January 2002
at retail outlets everywhere.*

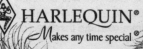

HARLEQUIN®
Makes any time special®

This book is for **Jack Vance,** our finest creator of worlds. It is also dedicated to the memory of **Dr. Carl Sagan,** scientist, author, and teacher, who articulated the noblest dreams of humankind.

ACKNOWLEDGMENTS

The author would like to thank the following people: Kevin Kelly for his account of the evolution of a-life from 80-byte critters in his book *Out of Control*; Jean-Daniel Breque and Monique Labailly for their personal guided tour through the catacombs of Paris; Jeff Orr, cybercowboy *extraordinaire*, for boldly going into cyberspace to retrieve the forty-some pages of this tale kidnapped by the TechnoCore; and my editor, Tom Dupree, for his patience, enthusiasm, and shared good taste for loving *Mystery Science Theater 3000*.

We are not stuff that abides, but patterns that perpetuate themselves.

—Norbert Wiener,
Cybernetics, or Control and Communication in the Animal and the Machine

The universal nature out of the universal substance, as if it were wax, now moulds the figure of a horse, and when it has broken this up, it uses the material for a tree, next for a man, next for something else; and each of these things subsists for a very short time. But it is no hardship for the vessel to be broken up, just as there was none in its being fastened together.

—Marcus Aurelius,
Meditations

But here is the finger of God, a flash of the will that can,
    Existent behind all laws, that made them and, lo, they are!
And I know not if, save in this, such gift be allowed to man,
    That out of three sounds he frame, not a fourth sound, but a star.

—Robert Browning,
Abt Vogler

If what I have said should not be plain enough, as I fear it may not be, I will but [sic] you in the place where I began in this series of thoughts—I mean, I began by seeing how man was formed by circumstances—and what are circumstances? —but touchstones of his heart—? and what are touch stones? —but proovings [sic] of his hearrt [sic]? —and what are the proovings [sic] of his heart but fortifiers or alterers of his nature? and what is his altered nature but his soul? —and what was his soul before it came into the world and had These provings and alterations and perfectionings? —An intelligences [sic]—without Identity—and how is this Identity to be made? Through the medium of the Heart? And how is the heart to become this Medium but in a world of Circumstances?—There now I think what with Poetry and Theology you may thank your Stars that my pen is not very long-winded—

—John Keats,
In a letter to his brother

Acknowledgments

The author would like to thank the following people: Kevin Kelly for his account of the evolution of a-life from 80-byte critters in his book *Out of Control*; Jean-Daniel Breque and Monique Labailly for their personal guided tour through the catacombs of Paris; Jeff Orr, cybercowboy *extraordinaire*, for boldly going into cyberspace to retrieve the forty-some pages of this tale kidnapped by the TechnoCore; and my editor, Tom Dupree, for his patience, enthusiasm, and shared good taste for loving *Mystery Science Theater 3000*.